Lifewalla

Life
walla

INSPIRED BY TRUE EVENTS

NINA JOSHI RAMSEY

Punked Books

A CIP catalogue record for this book is available from the British Library

Paperback ISBN 978-1-908375-28-5

Published in 2015 by Punked Books

An Authortrek imprint

www.authortrek.com/punked-books

Printed in the United Kingdom

First Printing, 2015 www.Lifewalla.com.

PRAISE FOR LIFEWALLA

At a time when our world is beset by natural and man-made disaster, Nina Joshi Ramsey really gets inside the psychology of disasters and the consequences they wreak. It's a very human book and the proceeds are for a good cause. I recommend it.

PROFESSOR JAMIE HACKER HUGHES
PRESIDENT, BRITISH PSYCHOLOGICAL SOCIETY

Lifewalla is a beautiful story that explores the profound psychological impacts [of] disasters...We are proud it tells the story of so many inspirational survivors.

MELANIE HADIDA
BHOPAL MEDICAL APPEAL

Lifewalla is a story that touches your soul
in unimaginable ways.

SADE ADENIRAN
WINNER COMMONWEALTH PRIZE AFRICA

The vividness of the storytelling...felt like watching a film
– which I am sure should be made.

TESSA BELL-BRIGGS,
FILM & STAGE ACTOR

Lifewalla is going to be a big hit!... I'd never read anything like it....What an amazing and original story!

CARRIE HODGKINS
EDITOR IN CHIEF, CONCOURSE MAGAZINE

DEDICATION

For Mum & Dad,
My Rock G
&
Life-affirming
ZAASSYD

ACKNOWLEDGEMENTS

My deep regard for those affected by disasters and trauma all over the world. For enduring the fragility and challenges of life. For their everyday regrouping to summon up strength and resilience. For climbing overwhelming personal mountains, whilst in the midst, allowing lightness and grace for others too. This book is inspired by them.

I acknowledge those who provide empowerment-enabling services at the Sambhavna and Chingari clinics in Bhopal, and appreciate the ongoing support from the Bhopal Medical Appeal (BMA). Fay Weldon, this is indeed a story in its own right. Celia Brayfield, you have always been a supporter. Judith Murray, thank you for the early-stage support.

Praise for the superwomen at WFTV for some timely measures that spoke directly to my conundrums. Max Rambaldi, the cover mods are spot on, and Backpack Studio, the colourising is beautiful! Much appreciation to Bollywood Fever Festival for the platform to raise funds with the print Advance Reader Edition. A special thanks to Kevin Mahoney of Punked Books for supporting this novel fundraiser.

Simon Williamson and Cxandra Paxton, my much appreciated early readers, and Melanie Hadida of BMA, your insights helped me see different perspectives. Thank you Tom Harmsen, for being a gentleman whilst facilitating invaluable feedback. My friends, family and colleagues, past and present, UK and abroad, who generously donated towards the fundraising initiative with the Advance Reader e-Editions, thank you for your support. It has strengthened our connection and helped increase faith in communities.

Those who have been there, especially during rocky times—whether we are related or not, you're family. As much for the laughs as anything else. Big bruv, thanks for believing. This was also a 'pointer-array' moment! And you will smile at the bit from the old days! Shama and Achala, you've both been solid as two rockettes. Shama, thank you for the overall help but in particular for *Baarish*, a song even dearer to me now. And Achala, thank you for much, as well as for patiently listening to a detailed plot breakdown as I worked through it. Thank you Dilip, Yagi, Aditya and Zach for doing more than your parts, including the regular impromptu entertainment! A&Z, 'Bye bye, Babu!'

Mum, you read as much of the book as was ready, always asking for the next chapter and why there were so many swear words—there are fewer now. Dad, you were proud and surprised that a book could help others. It can. This book is in memory of you both and your active contributions to causes throughout your lives.

Graeme, thank you for being a rock. And for being a shoulder, a frank critic and a sounding board. Plus for bantering back and forth, and for laughing at my jokes. I, too, love you just the way I am!

Nina x

We don't create a fantasy world to escape reality.

We create it to stay.

— LYNDA BARRY

1

Secrets in the Corners of
Her Lips

THE BUS WAS rumbling fast towards Jantapur when a hand brushed down the side of Dilkhush's waist and pinched her left buttock. A flush of heat raced through her body. Her throat tightened. She knew who the culprit was. That arse of a donkey had even winked at her after getting on the bus. He needed a good tight slap. But instead, Dilkhush clenched her jaw and tugged her white sari tighter around herself.

Sauntering down the aisle in his leather jacket, the pervert had looked her up and down and bitten his lower lip as if playing a first-class film hero. More like third-class villain. He had manoeuvred himself to stand behind her, bumping into her whenever the bus lurched. Throughout the journey, she had wanted to teach him a lesson, even lift him off the ground by his hair, arms, or legs, and spin him above her head before hurtling him to a distant planet.

She had seen that in a film duel between a demon

and a goddess with multiple arms. But Dilkhush didn't do anything like that. She didn't have multiple arms and was sure no one would side with a wretched widow like her.

If only the villain could see what she was really like inside, that hardened baton he had pushed against her would soon shrivel. She looked around, but there was nowhere to move in that jail of a suffocating bus. Dilkhush chastised herself. This was her karma. In her younger years, hadn't she been hungry for attention, enthralled by villagers' comments about her filmi looks?

'Look at the girl's siren curves.'

'And those high-high cheekbones with Sharmila Tagore lips.'

'Curving up at the ends as if tantalising secrets are hiding there.'

'When she learns to jiggle her breasts and flirt with her green-green eyes even her own father will be in danger.'

Dilkhush remembered replaying such words in her mind again and again, wondering what tantalising secrets lay in the upward-curving corners of her mouth. She used to tinkle her voice and twirl her hair, showing a little skin here and there, relishing in the eyes that followed. But that was then.

Now she was a washed-out widow and didn't want

such attention. Her years of hard labour had taken their toll, but the buttock-pincher didn't seem to have noticed. Another lurch and bump. The bus stopped, and the driver blasted his horn. He shouted for everyone to get off. People pushed past each other, chattering loudly to be heard over the grunts and squawks of pigs and chickens tied up in sacks.

Dilkhush bent down to pick up her cloth bundle. Inside it were all of her possessions: another white sari, two opium pellets, a newspaper cutting, an old peacock feather hair clip, and a faded photo of her family and friends in Jantapur, dressed in their finery. In the picture, her young daughter, Jiyaa, was wearing the feather hair clip. As Dilkhush straightened up with her bundle, she saw the villain.

He had gone ahead, but was twisting backwards to leer at her chest, which had become slightly exposed when she bent down. Something snapped inside her. As if she hadn't gone through enough already, now she had to be wary of such people too. She knew very well these perverted men who preyed on lone women like her. Even the Holy City of Widows had taught her more than only dead-eyed chanting in return for a cup of grains.

Each day, 'Haré Krishna, Haré Rama.' Each night, 'Hari help me, Hari save me,' when the debauched landlord at the widow ashram lifted Dilkhush's sari and rammed himself inside her on his wooden bed. As the bed frame creaked, she cried. Televisions blared in homes and hotels around them. Temple bells pealed, and gods and goddesses continued to be worshipped. Through tears, when Dilkhush reminded the landlord about the holiness of the city, he smirked.

'True, we are in the holy city that sprang with the Ganges from Lord Shiva's hair,' he said. 'But Lord Shiva is the destroyer who enables renewal. His lingum emerges through the yoni and is worshipped by women who pour milk over it. So we are simply worshipping together, are we not? You are a cursed widow seeking resolution, desperate for redemption. What better way than this to destroy the old you and renew?'

Dilkhush wanted her daughter back and for her ache to end. She would have suffered anything for that, but her dark void was never filled in that holy city. She didn't stay to chant for years or wait for her guilt and rage to subside. Instead, she ran away and sought out her brother for refuge. For years, to appease his wife, Dilkhush slept in their cattle pen, instead of polluting their house. Yet even being alive felt like a betrayal and she died inside as she lived.

Now a chance had come for her to right the wrong in her life and this villain was on the bus licking his lips. Who did he think he was? She wished she had the nerve to teach him a lesson herself, or that someone would stand up for her. But the bus had almost emptied. Only an old couple stood between her and the villain. Without pausing to think it through, her mind raced towards an attack.

Do You Know Who I Am?

THE OLD COUPLE slowly got their belongings together. He was in an orange *dhoti*, struggling to pick up a small suitcase. The woman was sliding the handles of a crocheted bag onto her wrinkled wrist. Dry onionskins scattered from the bag and floated down to her feet. Without fully knowing what would happen, Dilkhush stretched an arm towards the villain.

'Eh, you!' she said in a hoarse voice. Her tongue was thick and dry. 'You perverted brute. Have you no shame that you are leering at this poor old mother like that?' It didn't even sound like her own voice.

The few people left on the bus turned around.

'Look at her, you dirty swine. This poor woman is old enough to be your grandmother. And you are bending your filthy mind and body to gawk at her chest! If your mother knew, she would be ashamed for ever having let you dangle on her breasts.' The villain looked confused. Paying him back for his harassment was invigorating. 'If only I wasn't a lone widow and had the courage to slap you myself.'

The old man gripped his dhoti. 'What's this?' he said with a trembling voice as he looked at the villain. 'You dirty, no-good, shameful fellow. Do you have no respect for your elders?'

'No father, I—'

'Don't call me father...*Besharam.*'

'Calm down, old man,' the villain sneered. 'I wasn't looking at your—'

'Not looking?' Dilkhush turned to the old woman. 'Didn't you see him practically wanting to jump inside your blouse, Ma?' She looked at two men standing behind the villain. 'Thank God real men are here to stop such disgraceful behaviour.' Dilkhush saw the men's eyes dart around. For a moment, nothing happened.

Then the old man turned to them as well. 'We are old and poor. We have no money to buy respect, but don't we deserve some decency?'

One of the men's eyes flickered. He shoved the villain towards the nearest seat. 'You perverted young men are all the same. Is your toy too new for you that you can't even shift your filthy eyes away from an old mother?'

The villain put his hands up. 'Listen, brothers, that whore widow is acting all saintly in her white sari, but she is making it all up. I didn't—'

'*Arey*, why should I make it up?' Dilkhush said to the two men, spitting as she spoke. 'What chance does a widow like me have against the world? But he has such a disgusting mind, should I keep quiet about it? Today, it is this poor old mother. God knows who it will be tomorrow.'

The bus driver climbed down from his cabin. 'What's all this?' He grabbed the villain's arm so hard Dilkhush could see the indentations.

The villain struggled to get free and jumped off the bus. 'Do you know who I am?'

'Who?' The driver laughed. 'A minister's undercover *chamché*, riding on the bus with bells on your balls, spying on us?'

The villain glared at Dilkhush. 'I'll see you around, lone widow.' He turned and disappeared into the crowd.

She could almost feel his hot snorts on her face. She should have thought more carefully. She would be alone there. Dilkhush looked around, but the other men had gone. The priest had warned her about managing that snake inside her. It had been stirring and spitting recently, and she didn't seem able to control it. She started to justify her actions in her own mind.

If she enraged someone who ended up killing her, at least she would not have taken her own life. Her torture would end and her soul would still have a chance to reunite with her daughter. In any case, she needed that snake inside her so she could finish her task in Jantapur. She would leave before endangering Jiyaa's soul.

But the priest's warning had been clear. 'You have been stubborn. Ignore my words at your peril. You should have cut off that snake's head already. You would have learned to allay any anger by now.'

The old couple on the bus was still struggling with their bags. Dilkhush leaned forward to console them, but they both flinched. To sticklers like them, she was a milk-curdling widow and wasn't to pass on her curse. The old woman still had fortune on her side, with marital signs intact: a golden *tikka* on her head, a red tilak on her forehead, gold necklaces and bangles, a red sari, and the old man by her side. She hadn't devoured her family.

Dilkhush stood away while the old couple checked their belongings. They took furtive glances at her, as if she were at fault. Selfish wrinklewretches. Hadn't she just saved them from harassment? They didn't know any different and should be grateful to her.

She looked out through the scratched windows. The aroma of fried snacks and bus fumes filled the air. She imagined biting into a crispy pakora but had no money to buy anything. Dilkhush saw the onion skins continue to fall from the old woman's crocheted bag. These could be boiled for flavour. Add a sprinkling of millet and right there was a meal. Was not every town full of hungry beggars that these two ungratefuls needed reminding of that? The snake inside her hissed. She got ready to point out their waste.

Just then, an image of her rebuking priest loomed large in her mind. 'See that snake of yours? I warned you. You keep thinking, "Why me? Why me?" As if your ordeal should allow you to retch out your anger. Everyone's suffering rips them apart. But you don't see that. You only want to languish in your hell. Can't you see that this is your real curse?'

Dilkhush could do nothing but listen. The priest had God's ear.

'That venom will spew inside and outside. It will stop

you reuniting with your daughter. Go back and face those who have wronged you. Do whatever you need to do to get balance. Give and get forgiveness.' The priest's eyes had no sympathy.

He wavered for a moment, and then calmed down. 'You have to understand something.' His voice became almost gentle. Dilkhush looked at him with hope.

'Equilibrium is the main underlying force of the universe,' he said. 'We veer towards it in every way. It is the force that compelled the expansion of the universe. The seeking of equilibrium is a force of nature, bigger than you and me. It is foundational in our Holy Geeta and it is science. We are all driven by it, whether we know it or not, whether we accept it or not. If you die unresolved, with lack of this essential balance, your soul will have to reincarnate. Like gravity, equilibrium happens without you willing it. It is like water finding it's level. And still you don't try to help yourself or your daughter's soul. Where is the mother in you?'

The priest's words stung. But he had not held his dead child to his chest, knowing others could have saved her. Dilkhush scoffed. She had tried to force forgiveness for years. But there was no miracle answer. Where could that snake of rage go except fester inside her? Wasn't rage also a powerful force? She could not betray Jiyaa and Suresh's souls and forgive, simply to overcome her own distress. The priest was the fool.

Even Makodi, the village orphan, understood. She stole opium pellets to soothe Dilkhush's heartache. When there was no opium, Dilkhush cajoled her own pain with illusions. She toiled hard and ploughed the dried-up earth for others. On easier days, she milked goats and ground grains. All the time, she imagined Jiyaa waiting for her, and she hurried home after finishing her labours.

Even in these reveries, she was punished. Her daughter's soul never appeared. What could the priest know about such pain? It was not because of him that Dilkhush was returning to Jantapur. By chance, she had seen a photo of the townspeople in a newspaper.

She was sure it was Kashif in the picture—her husband's best friend, her best friend's husband. He must have returned to Jantapur. Those in charge of the factory at the time of the gas leak were to be there for the big anniversary. But even that was not enough to get Dilkhush there. After all, what would seeing them achieve? The real reason she had got on the bus to Jantapur was a sign she had got from the very same newspaper page.

There was a large photo that showed foreign soldiers with big guns. They had just stormed a remote hiding place and assassinated the man they held responsible for the deaths of their loved ones and their fellow countrymen. Suddenly Dilkhush had realised something. These soldiers were showing her that avenging was sometimes necessary to right an extreme wrong. It meant rage and revenge could be used to get equilibrium. The priest had neglected to tell her that. Forgiveness was all he had repeated. Yet, however much she wanted to do it, revenge was frightening to carry out alone.

Kashif must have seen that same photo in the newspaper. He may even already know about using revenge to get balance. Maybe everyone knew. That hardened and haunted look in his eyes could be for vengeance. She could help him and get resolution for herself too. He had to be back in Jantapur for a reason.

The wrinklewretches shuffled side-to-side down the aisle of the bus. They reminded Dilkhush of Naseema Bi, her former landlady in the town. She had to avoid the old owl, otherwise it would break the owl's heart to know Dilkhush had been alive all these years but hadn't visited. The driver hit the side of the bus. 'Last stop. Out now, everyone.'

The flutter of the old couple's orange clothes disappeared through the doorway. Dilkhush's skin felt clammy. She wiped the top of her lips with her hand and dabbed her cotton blouse into her damp underarms. Memories of the gas leak unfurled from the dark corners of her mind.

As she walked to the front of the bus, the sound of blood pumping into her ears was so loud that all other noise dulled. She pleaded with God for help. She was afraid the despair that had enveloped the town before she left would consume her when she got out into the open air. Instead, when she stepped off the bus, her eyes were dazzled by reflections of the sun in dozens of mirrors, dangling from a rope strung across a stall.

Her ears were filled with horn blasts, high-pitched

mé-mé-ing of goats, and cries of recruiters boasting about unsurpassable jobs. A tea-and-snack seller shouted from his stall: 'Chaaaaaaa. *Garma garam* chaaaaaaaa. Samose, kachori, pakore, biskuut *ke saath* chaaaaaaa. Garma garam chaaaaaa.'

3

Two-faced-agents are All Around

THE STALL WITH the dangling mirrors was almost the same as she remembered. Could that seller she knew still be there? He had rescued Dilkhush when she had first come to Jantapur as a teenage bride. He would help her find Kashif. The sign nailed to the top of the stall made her smile:

BEST MIRRORS HERE.
MAKE LIFE CLEAR.

Underneath was a drawing of a stickman, grinning widely and smoothing down his hair. A second sign was black with red letters:

30 EARS OF INJUSTICE!!!

The drawing was of a stickman clutching his throat.

Above his head was a cloud with the words 'Deadly Gasssssss' painted inside. The number '30' had been painted over many layers built up over time. There was a misspelling on the 'EARS OF INJUSTICE' sign. Dilkhush used to teach street orphans under the banyan tree near their house and remembered scolding them for confusing 'years' and 'ears'. Why did such things even matter?

Some days her husband would finish at the gas factory, wash his face and hands, and come outside the house to see what the orphan rascals were doing.

When they misbehaved, he spoke to them in a low voice. 'You better learn well. She is teaching you out of the goodness of her heart. This luck of yours might not last.' Dilkhush used to wish he didn't remind them of their misfortune. After all, she was only a village girl who had learned reading and writing from her brother. What chance would she have had otherwise?

Still, she used to go to the library in Jantapur for new things to teach the scoundrels. And she also taught them other important lessons she had learned from her father. He had been the head of the Panchayat, and with several other elders, sought to keep their village in some level of harmony. One of his teachings was about bowing without pride, so as to make things happen. Dilkhush made use of that lesson often.

When she first had the idea to teach the street orphans, she needed chalk and slates. She convinced her husband to pay for them by asking how those rogues would ever improve their behaviour. It was his idea that they needed discipline and schooling. Then, at dinner gatherings in their courtyard with friends, Dilkhush made his favourite dishes and flattered him in front of everyone.

'You know how he is so clever and learned all the chemicals and poisons so fast at the gas factory? And he helped all of you learn as well. He is so kind and wants these street orphans to learn to read and write. Then they can get a job at the factory too. He doesn't want them scamming others their whole lives. That is how he is. Always thinking about others.'

Suresh knew her ways, but didn't seem to mind when others praised him. 'Mind you,' he said. 'Not everyone needs to read and write. There are manual labour jobs there as well. Each to their own choice. Just no scamming.' He smiled at Dilkhush.

She hoped that meant he would let her continue teaching the orphans. But after the gas leak, everything changed. There was nothing left for her to laugh about or hope for. Yet now she was back there, she sensed something vibrant about the town, even with the feeling of raw sadness that she thought must hang in the air. She looked at the signs above the stall again. The mirror-seller must have meant, 'YEARS' not 'EARS OF INJUSTICE'. But the way he had sensed her true self and saved her before could mean he was trying to say something else.

Maybe he was showing a count of the deaf 'Ears of Injustice': sewn-up ears of those in charge; deaf elephant ears of their protectors, big for show, flapping and moving hot air around; greedy or scared people with ears stuffed full of money; or people from outside, watching the town, letting ear wax build up around their wick of tolerance, only noticing if the flame got closer to their own skin. Dilkhush remembered a simpler time, when she did not even know there could be such people.

'Chaaaaaaa,' the tea-and-snack seller shouted. 'Garma garam chaaaaaaaa.' He paused for a moment and served someone. 'Samose, kachori, pakore. Chaaaaaaa.'

Dilkhush looked for the mirror-seller, but the stall was empty. She needed to find Kashif. He would not have hidden in Naseema Bi's house. That would put the old owl in danger if he had any revenge plans. The bus driver was smoking a bidi. He had helped her once already with the villain. And his job meant he could have seen people coming in and out of the town.

Dilkhush walked towards him. She saw the old couple from the bus queuing by a food stall. The town was famed for its delicious Jantapuri kachori, mixed with yoghurt, *imli,* roasted peanuts and chopped onions. But the old man had said himself that they were poor. There was plenty of food in their bags, so what need did they have to pay someone else? Idiots. Dilkhush would explain that to the bus driver. They would listen to him. And he would think well of her and help her out.

She told the driver about people being better off cooking their own onionskins with millet flour. 'That old couple doesn't need to buy from a stall. If you explained they would be thankful to you for saving them money.'

The driver followed her gaze, but his eyes didn't

settle on the old couple. Instead, he scanned the bus station and puffed on his bidi. 'All these stalls offer me free food, but I eat at a roadside *dhaba*. The water they use for cooking here - who wants poison water in their food? But people - look at them. They can't control themselves.'

'What would people living here eat then?' Dilkhush blurted out. What poisons was the driver talking about? The factory had blown out gas thirty years ago. 'So it is additional punishment? If you live here, you have to be poisoned and then starve as well. Or go to outside dhabas for food? That costs more money.'

'Suit yourself.' The driver puffed on his bidi. 'Go enjoy their food then.'

Dilkhush couldn't afford to upset him. She changed her manner. 'Driver Sahib, I just feel sad for these people. They have no help and I—actually, I came over to say thank you for helping on the bus.'

'I just drive it.'

'I mean your help with that villain. The one leering at that poor old woman.'

'Who?'

How could he forget so quickly? Should she repeat the whole incident now? But something made her stop. She seemed to be pushing him away. 'It doesn't matter. I also like to forget bad things.'

'Did you want something?' The driver narrowed his eyes.

'Actually, Driver Sahib, I came for some advice because you must know so many people. Maybe—' She hurried to take out the newspaper cutting from her cloth bundle. 'You have seen this man, yes?'

The driver took the cutting and unfolded it. He didn't say anything for a moment, then handed the paper back. 'Have I seen the man in the newspaper? That's what you came to ask me?'

'Yes, I just want your advice. Maybe where to start looking for him and—'

'You want my advice?' He looked past her. 'You are new here and already you are prodding for trouble, so listen carefully. I don't know why you have come, or why you are asking me these questions. But two-faced-agents are everywhere. Scammers are everywhere. Those you can trust won't know anything. Those who know something can't be trusted. That's my advice. Keep quiet about this unless you want to end up in jail.'

'Jail? But I am only looking for this man because...he is like family. He was my husband's best friend.'

'Then your husband was not the man you thought. You're not blind.' The driver seemed annoyed. 'You can see the photo. Asking me whether I know that man could get me into trouble.' He stared at her and then stepped back. 'Are you here to trick me into saying something?' He looked around. 'Who sent you?'

'No, I...' She should have shown him the family picture she had, but that was taken so long ago. How would he have recognized Kashif? Their dear friend had changed so much. He was gaunt and stern in the newspaper photo. But she knew Kashif well. She could tell it was him. She was sure of it. 'I am alone in this town,' Dilkhush explained. 'I just need to find someone who has seen this man in the newspaper.'

'Then watch out,' the driver said. 'You are being stupid and your questioning is careless. This is not a child's game. It is not for people like you and me.' He gestured towards the paper. 'And if you are really his family and need to know anything, be ready with big bribes. But me, I know nothing. I know no one.' He flicked his bidi and walked away.

Dilkhush folded the newspaper and was about to slip it back into her cloth bundle when she glanced at the face in the big photo on the same page. The man in that picture was the one that the foreign soldiers had shot. Could the bus driver have assumed she was asking whether he knew that man? No wonder he had reacted badly. But that would be silly. Why would she be looking for the person killed by the soldiers? No, she was sure the driver had seen the right photo, of Kashif. Still, she found him again and tapped him on the arm.

The driver turned around only for a moment. 'I said keep away from me. You're trying to get two-faced-agents to catch me saying something. I don't know anything or anyone.'

'No, I only wanted—did you look at the right photo?' Dilkhush unfolded the paper.

The driver almost tripped as he hurried away. 'I don't know anyone. You hear that, all you two-faced-agents listening in? I won't change my answer. You can't make me tell a lie whether you show me the photo again or not. I never knew that man. I don't know anyone who knows him. I don't know any of their plans. Stay away from me.'

Dilkhush felt shaken. The driver's eyes held such terror that he didn't even look at the photo the second time. Should she be scared? What if Kashif was a person to be feared now? She hoped no two-faced-agent had heard them. Her task suddenly seemed even more difficult. That must be why the driver said she needed big bribes and someone she could trust for information.

The priest had only given her enough money for the bus. 'Don't come back until you have walked fully on the path of equivalence that God intends for you.'

Dilkhush didn't even understand what that meant, only that the priest was a stingy man spouting forgiveness without knowing what that really meant for her. The villagers never paid her money so she had no savings. It shamed her to even consider leaving Jantapur without doing anything. But she had nowhere to go.

She only needed to find Kashif to help her. Together they could somehow avenge their loved ones and balance everything out. Nothing else had helped. If she left now, she would have to face life alone with her angst until she died. And where would she go anyway?

'Hello, hello,' a voice said from behind her.

Dilkhush spun around.

4

Master of Bribes and Bargain
Services with 101% Heroine

'DALYA MBBS,' A boy said. 'You can call me Dalya.' He winked and gave a lopsided smile.

Dilkhush was glad to see it was only a youngster, not an earwigging two-faced-agent the driver had warned her about.

'You must be a heroine from out of town. Otherwise, I would surely remember a beauty like you.'

Such insolence. He seemed barely twelve or thirteen. Fourteen at most. 'I'm old enough to be your mother, you rascal.'

'I still think you are a pretty heroine.'

Dilkhush coughed hard into one end of her sari.

'And you are also from a poison gas town, *hehn*? You also get the coughing. We can join forces, your town, my town, you and me, hero and heroine, leading everyone to some peace, some victory, yes?'

Dilkhush looked him up and down. The boy's trousers barely touched his ankles, his rubber slippers were too big for his feet, and his pinstripe coat was too bulky for his skinny bare chest. A large bag weighed down across his shoulders.

He acted out firing two pistols and blew smoke off each imaginary gun. 'Liking what you see, Heroine?' He winked. 'I am Dalya MBBS. Not MBBS Doctor, but Master of Bribes and Bargain Services. Anything you want, I can get it for you - and cheaper than anyone else. Cent per cent guarantee, and finest quality.'

Dilkhush tried to move away. Master Bandit of Bamboozles and Swindles. The driver's warning hadn't even had the chance to dry up and there was a scammer. Little did he know she had no money. Could he get her some money, super MBBS that he was?

'Go on, try my services,' Dalya said. 'You must be visiting some family, no? Sweets - fifty per cent cheaper from me. Cent per cent guarantee.'

'No, thank you.' Dilkhush walked towards the mirror stall. The seller there had helped her when she first arrived as a young bride with Suresh, scared and nervous, full of doubts about herself. He had changed her life. She thought of him with warmth in her heart.

Dilkhush dressed up in her bridal finery often, during her first year of marriage. She checked her reflection in her cracked, gold-encased mirror. Normally, she hid it from others. But once, she took it out in the open without thinking. She turned her head to look at her eyes, then shifted again to see her lips, and again to straighten her tilak. A final check to dab a handkerchief over her upper lip. Her bangles clinked with each small movement.

The mirror-seller approached her, addressing her as a celestial apsara. 'Exquisiteness shouldn't be distorted by a broken mirror.'

Even though she knew he was only flattering her, Dilkhush liked hearing the praises. She would have accepted his offer of a brand new mirror in exchange for hers, which he called 'vintage'. But hers was a gift from her late mother. Still, the smiling seller was so charming he finally slipped the gold-encased mirror from her hands into his. A few days later, it looked completely new and shiny. Not like hers at all, although he assured her it was the very same one. 'I haven't made a replica to give back to you, have I?'

The newly inlaid mirror had the word 'apsara' curled around the edge. Dilkhush was marvelling at the gleaming workmanship when her eyes fell on her reflection. For an instant, her mind mixed up the golden object of admiration with her own reflection. Her green eyes, sharp nose, and upward curving mouth were all the same. But somehow, in that moment, they looked different – as if they belonged to a stranger. Is that how she looked to others? Not scarred and ragpatched as she felt inside?

From that day, when she was alone for long enough, Dilkhush tried to recreate that moment. She purposely admired the mirror and without blinking, switched to look at her own reflection to feel the warm miracle again. Because of the mirror-seller's stunning workmanship, Dilkhush's admiration of the mirror grew, and that started to change the way she looked at her own reflection *and herself. For a few years, she stopped doubting and despising herself. She cooked, dressed, spoke and laughed without fear of rebuke and rejection from others. She could even feel Suresh looking at her with different eyes. Such was the mirror-seller's miracle.*

Surely he would remember the woman he called an apsara, and help her change her life again. He could smile widely and give her money for the bribes, or find Kashif himself. Dilkhush looked over the stall counter, in case the mirror-seller was asleep on the floor.

He wasn't there. And he wasn't at the neighbouring ice-and-syrup stall either. At the bangles counter a bare-chested man heated metal on a coal furnace before banging it into circular shapes. Another man added silver strips and stuck on coloured beads with mirror pieces. Women bustled around, trying on the finished bangles. They looked at her with suspicious eyes. Widows didn't need bangles.

'I see you are looking for a mirror.' Dalya was back.

Dilkhush turned to find him right behind her.

'Don't buy from that no-good seller. There are better mirrors in the market. Come.' The boy hopped on the spot as if he was a horse. 'Believe me. Other sellers aren't thieves and won't act like a king doing you a favour. I haven't got a certificate for best MBBS for nothing. Trust me.'

'Trust a broker? Tell me, this mirror-seller gives you less commission than others?'

'Ooof, ohh, ahhh.' Dalya bent over and clutched his

heart. 'Heroine in looks and Saraswati in brains. My mother is looking for a perfect wife just like that for me. You know what this could mean for us?'

Dilkhush didn't react. If she were his mother, she would look for a wife who could train him to control his words. Not every thought needed to come out of his mouth.

Dalya seemed to be waiting for a response. When he didn't get one, he straightened his body. 'Okay, okay, you caught me, heroine. That seller gives no commission. But it is more than that. I don't want to gossip, but...' Dalya looked around. 'This man swindled our old, wide-smiling mirror-seller.'

'What do you mean? That mirror-seller isn't here any more?'

Dalya lowered his voice. 'People found that old smiler gagged and suffocated one morning. By the afternoon, this new seller had appeared, saying he was a relative. True story. Can such coincidences occur? Don't trust him. I am the expert. Let me take you to better people.' He thrust his arm out and swung it back. A set of rosary beads unravelled around his wrist and fell into his palm. 'See, expert, hehn?'

Expert time-waster. Dilkhush didn't reply. She thought about getting back on the bus again. But she had no home any more. The villagers didn't want her. The mirror-seller wasn't there. She hadn't done what she needed to and couldn't trust anyone she didn't know; not even the MBBS boy. He didn't seem as innocent any more. If he were a two-faced-agent, saying the wrong thing could get her - and even Kashif - into trouble.

'Heroine.'

She turned to Dalya. 'You can go. I don't need any mirrors.'

'What about turmeric and honey for your cough?'

Dilkhush shook her head and looked around the bus station. If it was God's will for her to return to Jantapur and get balance using revenge, Kashif could be somewhere right there, maybe hiding his face, covering his nose and mouth with the scarf, as he had done in the newspaper photo. They only needed a quiet talk with each other. She would know what to do then.

Dilkhush saw the bus station still functioned doubly as a job junction. She could get work there and earn money for the bribes to find Kashif. But that would take time and she needed to find him fast - those who were in charge during the gas leak were only likely to be there for the big anniversary. She thought of Naseema Bi. Perhaps she could help. But the old owl barely had any money before the leak. Now, alone, without her husband, she was likely to have even less.

Soon after arriving in Jantapur, Dilkhush and Suresh went to see Naseema Bi and Ashraf Mia about renting a room. The old owl and her husband showed them the bigger of the two rooms they had.

'You are newlyweds,' Naseema Bi said. 'You will be having children as well, so better you keep the bigger room.'

Ashraf Mia smiled as he nodded. 'What my owl is

trying to say is that you will feel better about paying rent if you have more space than us.'

Dilkhush smiled in embarrassment. Why did people talk so openly about newlyweds making children?

Ashraf Mia carried on. 'And if your future children can fit into your big room as well then you will feel you can stay here for many years. No need to move.' He laughed.

Suresh shook his head. 'Please, that is too—'

'No, no, son. Now we are all going to be living together we can be honest like this, yes? No shame in knowing we are all the same.'

Suresh doled his head.

'We are only helping and loving and caring and sharing.' Ashraf Mia hugged Naseema Bi. 'Like this, once you move in, there is no need to move out.'

She laughed nervously and prodded him. 'You don't have to say everything that comes into your head.'

'No thought should be wasted.' Ashraf Mia patted Naseema Bi as if to settle her.

He was also clever with money in the market. He spent time looking for vegetables that were the oldest and would banter with the seller as they haggled. Every now and then, laughter would erupt from his belly and engulf all those around him.

Dilkhush often heard him say the same lines to different sellers. 'Arey brother, you should be thanking me. In only a few hours, these vegetables will turn bad. Then it would be lost profit for you, lost dinner for me. But I will take them and pay a little as well. This way we both benefit. Now come, put them into my basket. I better go and cook them before they turn.'

Not only did Ashraf Mia win people over, no one could dispute his logic. Other sellers joined the chitchat as well. They all seemed to know he was always looking for the cheapest vegetables, but they still wanted to laugh and haggle with him, sometimes even trying to lure him to their stalls for newly ripened vegetables.

'Ashraf Mia, try this aubergine. Look, it's so fresh. The taste is still there.'

'Thank you, brother,' Ashraf Mia would laugh. 'You just call me to your house for dinner and I will expect no less than this new-bride aubergine.'

All the sellers who heard would laugh.

Ashraf Mia laughed at his own words too. 'As for my cooking, my old hands shake so much now that I drop too much spice in the pot. Then everything tastes delicious, old or new.'

He also bought boxes of syrupy sweets with too many flies in them that others didn't want. 'I just remove the flies. Then I can afford to give my old owl this treat that she loves so much.'

'You are so nice to her.' Dilkhush hoped Suresh would have such feelings for her when they got older.

'Don't be fooled by our Naseema Bi,' Ashraf Mia said. 'Everyone thinks she is strong. And she never wants me to mention our son to tenants.'

Dilkhush wanted to ask about their son, but Ashraf Mia was an elder. She couldn't simply ask.

'This is real life, my child,' he said. 'We are not acting

or waiting for applause. I know she needs help. And me as well.'

'Why?' Dilkhush couldn't help herself. She hoped it wasn't rude of her.

His eyes wavered. 'I—I—'

'Sorry, I shouldn't have—'

'No, my daughter, there's nothing to be sorry about. It's good you asked.' He remained silent for a few moments. 'It hurt that our son lived away from us. Then... he died in a car accident.'

Dilkhush didn't know what to say.

He shook his head. 'No pain is greater. I should not be alive. It should be Maaz standing here.'

'He was alone? Not married, no children?' Dilkhush realised she may have rubbed salt into the wound.

Ashraf Mia cleared his throat. 'He had a wife, but there were no children. She remarried after some time. Poor girl. Young widow.' He wiped his eyes. 'So now there is no one left for us.'

He looked at Dilkhush. 'You and Suresh will be good medicine for our Naseema Bi.' He patted her head. 'Suresh is like our son. Quiet and responsible. And you... our old owl hears the noises from the groups of girls living around the neighbourhood, all laughing and teasing each other. She always wanted that in her life. You will hear them too. Maybe you will bring that for her. They all eat together, work together, sewing, cleaning, cooking. I can't give her that.'

'You look after her so much though.'

'That is natural. But I told her the best thing is to get

29

tenants and treat them like our children. Then we can also get some life in our home.'

Dilkhush realised why the old couple wanted her and Suresh to have the big room and stay there with a growing family.

Ashraf Mia laughed nervously. 'But your Naseema Bi. She didn't want tenants. She said it would be enough to listen to everyone around us. No Maaz meant no one else.'

'No one can replace your own son,' Dilkhush said. 'This is just for soothing your heart, isn't it?' She was worried. Should she tell Suresh that Naseema Bi didn't want tenants there?

'Exactly right!' Ashraf Mia said. 'I have to slowly, slowly remind my owl that we are getting older. Feelings are not things. They can be changed or soothed. But we have to help with that too, otherwise life passes by. Then what is the point?'

'You are hoping we help her come out of her melancholy. Won't she mind that?'

'Oh, she was not happy with me in the beginning. But with our old tenants, after a while she started to behave as if they were our own children.'

Dilkhush hoped she and Suresh could live up to all they wanted. 'What were they like? The previous tenants?'

'Good people. You only need that. Then you can call it pretending, or adopting, whatever. Treating them like our children helped her. What is the harm then? Pain is not something to be revered. But they had to leave. Big *job for him in Hyderabad. It was very hard. Of course, we smiled for his sake.'*

Dilkhush somehow felt comforted by their sadness and their need to be like parents to her now. She decided not to say anything to Suresh. She would simply try and make the older couple happy. They would never have any complaints.

When they were closer to the house, Ashraf Mia turned to her. He asked her not to share any of what he had said. 'Everyone has a shyness about such feelings.'

Dilkhush remembered it all so clearly, even after all these years. She wished the gas leak had been a nightmare. They could all still be living together. Jiyaa would be married with children of her own. Her husband would look after her well, letting her visit every day, whether there were problems or not. In-laws needed to see that a girl had her family's support. But this was all wishful thinking. If she went to their old house now, the owl would cling to her, and Dilkhush wasn't staying in Jantapur for long. She decided it was best not to go.

The noise around the bus station seemed to get louder. A group of women passed by, carrying shallow baskets filled with stones and rubble. They went to and from a construction site repeatedly. Dilkhush watched them. She would have no chance.

These construction jobs were passed between families first. Dust in building sites made workers sick often. Families had to be ready with replacements to continue earning without a break, or face outside

31

competition. There were always more people than jobs available.

Without money or work, how was she to raise bribe money to find Kashif? But could she even get any work without family or friends to pass on jobs to her?

'Shall I take you to your relatives now?' Dalya was still loitering, which surprised her.

'No, thank you. I thought I said I don't need—'

'No charge. It's just so I know where to find you, in case you need something.'

Dilkhush became suspicious. He was so interested in her, even where she was staying. What if he had overheard her speaking to the driver, and got the wrong meaning, about who she was looking for?

'Everyone knows me,' Dalya said. 'I am very trustworthy. Ask your relatives. You'll see.'

Dilkhush joined her palms together and placed them on her forehead. 'I don't need anything, please. I understand I am only a fresh target for you, but let me say clearly, I have no money. That is what you want, isn't it? Or is there another reason you are still here? I am asking politely, please leave.'

'But—'

'Please go. I have work to do, and you are bothering me.' She kept her voice stern.

Dalya made circles on the dirt with his open-toed slippers. 'Sorry. I thought...maybe for once God had sent an angel to me, some good luck.' He looked up for a moment and walked away, slippers slapping against his soles.

Dilkhush suddenly felt sorry for him. What if he wasn't a two-faced-agent, but simply a boy trying to make a living? Who didn't know about children like that? Her opium-stealing orphan, Makodi, would also be surviving like that in the village. In Jantapur for only moments and already that vile snake of hers had reared up.

Dalya sang loudly. 'I walk in front, in front, you behind, you behind. I turn around, you hide, you hide. Such is the world, I don't mind, don't mind.' He turned around and she looked away.

Dilkhush was annoyed at herself for never asking for payment from the villagers. She had worked hard all those years and had let them justify their behaviour however they wanted - that bad treatment was expected for a widow; that they were being benevolent by giving her work in the first place; that she was a witch with a cursed fate, so paying her would demean her service; that she needed to repent for her sins. But none of that served her now that she needed money. Her eyes skimmed across the job junction.

Sellers, old and young, men and women, sang praises about their wares. 'Beautifying Bleach', 'Calming Cola', 'Palatable Pots'. Recruiters rattled off numbers as they raised and dropped fingers and fists, pointing at one person, then another. Along with bus and film timetables, there were several other hand-painted signs for soap, soda, and ministers' promises with large, smiling photos. One of these signs had a picture of an honest looking face that Dilkhush couldn't believe belonged to a politician. Her father used to say that lies showed up in people's faces, and that was why government workers have so many lie-lines. But how could any lies come from that gentle face she was looking at in the poster? The man's eyes seemed so familiar, but she couldn't understand why.

Maybe he was an actor she recognised, standing in for the real politician. Perhaps the actor looked more trustworthy—that way the party could win votes. Actors and actresses pretended to sing in films when the real voices were of Lata Mangeshkar and Kishore Kumar. So why not use models who looked better and more trustworthy than the real people in power?

The words below the handsome politician's photo said, 'Yes, they did. Now it's your turn.' It could be a sign that it was now her turn to do something. She was already there taking a chance on revenge, but she needed help. Was there another sign more useful to her? She swept her gaze across the job junction.

Many notices were nailed almost on top of one another, trying to be seen just like the jobless people around the station, pushing and shoving each other to get attention from whoever was making the best promises. Enticing brags about jobs clashed with one another around the bus station.

'MOST EXCELLENT TAILORS NEEDED. SEW A SUIT OVERNIGHT OR ELSE GOODNIGHT'

'MASTERFUL PUPPET MASTERS TO PULL AT HEARTSTRINGS OF SHOP BUYERS'

'Sweetest talkers wanted: For arranging marriages of oldest age, lowest caste, scheduled caste, darkest skin, call centre jobless, business bankrupts. Recession-cessation, men must marry, women must hurry'

Dilkhush had no other way of getting the bribe money. And maybe working somewhere would help her carefully ask about Kashif. She joined a heaving crowd of women. Many were holding up sample pieces of embroidery in the air. She didn't have any and wouldn't be able to prove her craft to a recruiter. How would she get any work then? A woman in front had a bagful of samples. Dilkhush inched towards her and slipped her hand into the woman's bag.

'Eh, this thief is stealing your embroidery,' a young woman shouted.

Dilkhush hurried away, but a commotion started.

The woman with the embroidery looked in different directions. 'Arey, coward, where are you? Come here and show yourself.'

The young woman who had raised the alarm pointed and Dilkhush hid behind a stall. There were enough people milling around that she didn't have to worry. Not all of them would have seen or heard anything.

'Don't worry. We are all jobless-worthless here.' The woman with the embroidery samples seemed forgiving as she looked around. 'Don't hide. I have plenty. Take a piece from me, but give me money for it. And any work you get, pass some to me. Otherwise, you will need to bribe the police to get out of jail. Come and show your face.'

Crowds of people moved around the chaos of the bus station. Dilkhush didn't feel the need to leave her hiding place yet. She didn't want to go to jail. She knew she should not be alienating others. The priest's words rang in her ears again. 'Any stupidity will get you a fast ticket to eternal suffering. Follow God's rules, not your own.'

Even if some of his advice was true, how was nectar supposed to emerge from the sewage in her mind? Her thoughts felt so jumbled sometimes. She knew she should prostrate to the Almighty's will. Otherwise, he could organise suffering with a mere click of His fingers. But what kind of God was that - happy to unleash His wrath while telling her to control her own?

Wasn't He taking revenge on her for not listening? He was so sure only pain could teach her lessons that He didn't even try kindness. What power did such a God really have? How cruel He was to savour her difficulty rather than help her through it. She realised such thoughts would displease God, and she needed to mend that. It was best to focus her mind elsewhere to stop this ranting in her mind. Only a split moment later, something caught her eye.

A boy was trailing behind his mother. A dog ran up and nipped at the boy's ankles, before sinking its teeth into one of his rubber slippers. Dilkhush stared for a moment and wondered whether this was really happening. Was the God she had just berated giving her a chance? She had to act fast. This was a boon. She could show people at the job junction that she was not a thief trying to steal embroidery samples. Someone would see her true qualities and give her a job. She headed towards the boy.

5

No One Saw You, so It Can't Be True

S HE COULD CLEAN the bitten boy's wounds and that would make her look good in people's eyes. Someone was sure to give her work then. It was a simple ruse. But the boy began yelling and crying. The dog was not letting go. His mother turned and saw what was happening. She ran back, waving her hands frantically. The boy tried to hit the dog with his bag. It let go of his slipper and snarled at the mother before jumping and trying to bite her arm.

'Get off, you devil,' the woman cried.

The dog backed off for a second.

The boy got up and tried to run, but the dog turned around and clamped its mouth down on his foot. One of the boy's dirty slippers became smeared with blood. Dilkhush heard people complain about mad dogs on the streets. 'So frightening for the children.' But no one helped. Her father always said crowds made cowards out of people. Someone had to do something. How could they only watch? The dog carried on biting and snarling. The boy sobbed as his mother hit the dog with her bag. Why didn't someone help?

Dilkhush chided herself. *As if the gur-gur drilling of your eyes into that beast's head will help. When your daughter was dying, did it help when people just watched? Is this what you have learned? To hope someone else will do something? That boy will be chewed to pieces by the time you do something useful. Go!*

Dilkhush pushed an arm through the loop of her cloth bundle so it hung from her shoulder. She ran towards the dog. 'Get off,' she yelled, but backed away quickly when the dog looked up at her. Its coat was mostly eaten away, leaving pink skin, mottled with grey marks. Even if it suffered from madness, Dilkhush had to chase it away. She looked around for more help. A gangly man in white trousers and a tight-fitting green shirt saw them. He ran towards a white car, but the car sped off, leaving him there. Dilkhush turned to look at other people.

A few men came forward and shouted. They began kicking the dog, but it dodged their kicks, still gnawing on the boy's foot. The boy clenched his throat so tight, his veins stood out. Tears ran down his face. His mother copied a man trying to kick the dog's backside. She missed and lost her balance. A gargantuan man in a black shirt and red neck scarf searched the ground.

Dilkhush was much smaller than him and was about to leave him to do the job, when she decided she would lose all respect from others and herself. She was the one who had been brave so far. Why should she back out now? God had given her the chance to show the embroidery job seekers she was not really a thief. She picked up a fallen branch to push the dog's jaws away from the boy.

But by then, the gargantuan man had swiped the dog's head with a child's cricket bat, catching an ear.

The mutt yelped and jumped away for a moment and then sprang towards the man. Dilkhush hurried over and poked it with her branch. She stepped back when the dog turned towards her. The boy had pulled his foot away, but the beast suddenly turned on him again. Dilkhush hit it, catching its jaw with her branch. As she retreated, she tripped on her sari and fell down. The dog lunged at her.

She was squinting because of the sun. Her breath was uneven. Even in those fast movements, Dilkhush saw the dog had orange-brown eyes with a red lump in one eye. Was its madness from some poison? The gas had made Suresh angry with her all the time. Suddenly the dog whined and staggered for a moment. The gargantuan man had hit it hard on the head.

He was holding the cricket bat high as if to bring it down again. The boy ran to his mother and Dilkhush hurried to get up. The dog snarled weakly. She saw a red thread tied around one of its paws, as if it had just attended a holy *puja*. Was this to confirm that God had sent the animal to help her regain some standing?

'I'm alright,' Dilkhush said to the gargantuan man. 'Don't hit it again.'

A few others, who had not helped before, came and kicked the dog. Blood dribbled from its head. A gust of wind blew. Dust rose in a small cloud and for a moment the colours on everyone's clothes became a beige blur. The gargantuan man threatened with his bat again and the dog whimpered away. People whistled and howled as it left.

Dilkhush threw her branch aside and dusted herself down. She wiped her face and neck with her sari. A few people looked at her, and she quickly covered her face. The dust settled back to the ground and the crowd heaved again around recruiters who didn't seem pleased with the disturbance.

'Any excuse to run away from work, isn't it?' said one recruiter. 'Come on now, hurry and make a line.'

A few people shouted at each other. 'Eh, get back in the right place. You weren't in front of me!'

'Why did you leave then?'

'Okay, okay. Forgive me, God's guardsman. I wanted to see what was happening.'

Dilkhush saw the mother and boy sitting on a stool by the mirror stall. She went over to them. 'You should take him to the hospital. He might get a disease from the bites.'

The mother stroked her son's hair and shook her head. The boy's foot already had a handkerchief tied around it, but blood had seeped through. 'Without money most hospitals won't even help a dying child, let alone one bitten by a dog. And what money do I have to pay a doctor? He's all right. Just scared.'

'I wasn't scared,' the boy said. His tears had left a clean trail down his dusty face.

Dilkhush nodded. She couldn't force anyone. She was about to rejoin the embroidery job queue when the young woman who had seen her trying to steal a sample spotted her. 'No thieves are allowed here.' The woman shook her head vigorously. Those around her also turned Dilkhush away with mere indications of their fingers.

'But I am not a thief. I was just trying to get a better chance. I need work desperately.'

'What, and we are here just for show?'

'I made a mistake,' Dilkhush said. 'I didn't even take anything. And you can see I am a good person. I helped that boy.'

'What boy?'

Dilkhush pointed to where the incident had occurred. She described everything that had happened with the dog, the boy, and his mother.

'I have been here all this time and didn't see anything,' her accuser said. The other job seekers talked amongst themselves.

Dilkhush tried to get their attention. 'Maybe you saw it all happen?' She realised there were a lot of people in the job junction, so not everyone would have seen her. But some of them must have. She needed them to vouch for her actions.

'No one saw you, so it can't be true,' the accuser said.

Dilkhush stood for a moment. She turned to look for the boy and his mother. They were nowhere to be seen. Nor was the gargantuan man. He could have assured the others about her. The dog had gone. She looked for the branch she had used, but couldn't find it. Dilkhush realised what might have happened but didn't want to think about it. She quickly put it to the back of her mind and went to join other lines.

But the message had spread that a thieving widow was stealing wares and jobs, and making up lies about attacks and dogs to make herself look better. There had to be so many thieves in such crowded places, but she felt singled out. Her white sari announced her widowhood and she was there for work. That was enough to confirm to recruiters they were snubbing the right person. Who would trust a thief with work? Whichever line she approached, job seekers checked with others whether she was the widow culprit. Recruiters shook their heads at her. 'No thieves allowed here.'

Dilkhush felt defeated. She had only just arrived and already the gates had closed on her. How was she to raise money for any bribes? Is this what God had brought her there for? To taunt her? She wished something went her way. After all her struggles, she deserved a little luck. But she went from line to line without being able to join any. There were so many gods and goddesses around her, couldn't even one help? Was it more satisfying to sneer at her? Or was there one Almighty they were all afraid of? Suddenly, a screeching voice sounded.

Dilkhush didn't believe it. She listened out again.

'Hear, hear,' the voice said. 'Jobs for outsiders, jobs for outsiders. Get in line if you're an outsider. Don't crowd or push like animals or I'll throw you out. And don't waste time if you live in Jantapur. Good money. Outsiders only—' The voice coughed and restarted.

'Jobs for outsiders only.'

Bodies in vibrant clothes rushed over. People in green, red, mustard patterns and weaves, swarmed around the voice despite the instructions to line up. Men and women jumped off buses that had been waiting to fill up.

The voice shrilled again. 'Good money. Very good money. Only for outsiders. Make a line here quickly.'

Dilkhush knew this was her chance. The job was for outsiders only. No one would know anyone else there. Were her prayers being answered?

Maybe there was a kind God after all. She had doubted Him needlessly. Only He could work such miracles. She hurried towards the line. Her foot landed on a wobbly wooden plank hiding a puddle, which drenched her foot.

She slipped in the hurry and grazed her ankle, but didn't bother to stop or wring her sari. She could do that once she was in the queue.

The voice became louder. 'Not like that, you primitives. Haven't I already said I want a queue? Line, line! Why do you keep coming at me and pushing and shoving like a herd of deaf goats?'

6

Bilayati from Blighty

DILKHUSH STOOD ON her tiptoes and saw that the generous recruiter was the gangly man she had seen trying to run away during the dog attack. His tight green shirt was stretched across his rib cage. She had been sure the thin voice belonged to a woman. But it was him. 'Outsiders only. Jobs for outsiders. Very good money.' He had been a coward, running to the car as the boy was being attacked, but she had to let go of such thoughts. She needed the job and would have to bow down to him.

She might have a better chance competing with outsiders, whatever the job. The recruiter was promising good money, so naturally people jostled each other and scrambled to form a line, crowding around him to grab his attention. Ebb and flow. A few people bickered about no one else following the instructions.

'Good money. Job for outsiders. Come on now, quick, quick,' the gangly recruiter continued, still not saying what the work was.

Dilkhush finally secured a place. 'Thank God. Even getting a place in the line is difficult, let alone getting the job and then doing it.'

A car horn blasted. Beep, beep, beep. Then again. Beep, beep, beep. The gangly recruiter ran over to the white car. It was the same one that had driven away during the dog attack. One of the tinted windows was rolled down. The woman inside spoke to the recruiter and pointed at the crowded line.

She looked Indian, but fair, like most high castes. She was obviously rich, judging by her different clothes, hair, and car. Dilkhush wished the recruiter would hurry up. She still had a lot to do after getting the job - getting paid, bribing for information about Kashif, planning with him.

A hunched man with red eyes walked up the queue. '*Bilayati se darna*,' he said in a raspy voice. 'Fear the people from foreign lands and beware the jobs they offer. Why don't their own people do them? Look at me. Think about how we suffered. You are outsiders, but you are still our brothers and sisters.'

Someone asked the hunched man, 'This job is working for *bilayatis*?'

Dilkhush needed the money and reminded herself not all bilayati people were the same. She wasn't betraying Jiyaa by wanting this work, whoever it was with. She called the hunched man over and spoke in a low voice, but people in the queue leaned in to listen.

'The British used to say they were going back home to Blighty, and we started calling all foreigners bilayati...

Blighty. But British bilayati people are different from Amrikan bilayati, who are different from Italian bilayati, different from French bilayati. Not all bilayati are the same. Just because—'

'Remember my words,' the hunched man said. 'Bilayatis can only be loyal to their own, not to us. They can use us and spit us out.'

Dilkhush shook her head. 'But it is about what kind of people. Even our own use us and spit us out.'

'Eh, you, deluded beggar,' the recruiter ran back to them and the woman in the car rolled up her window. He shouted at the hunched man. 'Get away from these people. All the time you are sniffing for something. Go on, get out.'

Three short horns sounded again, and the recruiter returned to the car. He spoke to the woman inside and twisted back to look at the line, before hurrying back. 'Now listen hard,' he shouted to the crowd. If you are old, over thirty-five years, go please. I have no use for you. There is heavy lifting to do in this job.'

A woman in front whispered, 'Why do they need heavy lifting? What kind of a job with bilayati people needs heavy lifting?'

If the woman didn't want to work hard, she should leave, Dilkhush thought. That would leave one less person to compete with.

'And why do they want outsiders only?' the woman asked. 'Why not people from this town?'

'Maybe they're too weak from the gas,' Dilkhush said. Then something dawned on her about her own words. This recruiter's bilayati bosses were assuming the locals were not suited to their work, maybe because of illness or weakness from the gas, or local suspicions about factories. It must be a factory job, needing heavy lifting. But everyone living there already knew what had happened in the town before. No wonder this recruiter wanted outsider hire-fire types instead. Less trouble.

A woman nearby started to argue with a moustachioed man. 'Get off, you sweat on a lizard's pubics. I was here first, straight after I got off the bus. You weren't even standing there. Don't try and take advantage of the commotion.'

The man didn't respond. His long green kameez flapped in the breeze and occasionally touched the dark girl standing behind him. She was holding his hand and picking her nose. The woman shouted towards the head of the queue, where the recruiter was making gestures for a straight line.

'Sir, look. This man is not an outsider. I have seen him walking his goats by the big lake, and now he is pushing into the line in front of me.'

The man shouted back. 'So idiot, if you have seen me in the town, you're also not an outsider. I know you walked two kilometres to get on the bus to pretend you are not from here. Unless you were a local how would you know about this everyday job? That's why you were pretending to come to the town on a bus.'

The recruiter hurried towards them. 'There is just one trouble after another with you people, isn't there? Don't you understand anything?' He tapped his green biro on his clipboard. 'We don't want any of you who are from Jantapur. Shall I start taking photos so I can tell you all apart, to know you have been here already?'

The quarrelling pair stared at the ground. Others leaned over to look. A man behind the recruiter used his fingers to denote a square shape around his face, doling his chin side-to-side, smiling widely, and mouthing, 'Photo, photo please.' He started doing different poses for the imaginary picture. Angry. Sad. Happy. Crazy.

'No matter how much you lie or cheat, you will not get the job.' The recruiter's voice was loud. 'Go on, go home, bloody blood-sucking parasites. I need people who can follow orders, yet you are already lying about being outsiders. How can we trust you will do as we say? What is the point of giving people like you good money when I can see right now that you will just create trouble?'

Dilkhush also thought the pair had been stupid. Anyone in the junction would have recognised them. Like her, they must also have really needed work.

The recruiter looked at the pair – first the man and then he focused on the woman. 'Why did you even bother? You look like you will collapse under a dust speck, let alone what we have in mind. You have to lift heavy weights and be very careful. No dropping anything accidentally in the wrong place like idiots. Otherwise, you will get fired straight away. You are not an outsider, and wouldn't pass in any case, so you better go now.'

Dilkhush's heart raced. The job sounded exactly like

what her husband had described. Suresh's words ran through her mind.

'The grinding machine stopped working, so they got desperate hire-fire types off the street to crush the chemical into powder with sledge hammers. Then when the pouring-melting machine for that powder didn't work, the workers carried heavy sacks to the reactor, opened the manhole and poured the powder straight in. One worker emptied a sack and then accidentally dropped the sack itself into the tanker as well. The idiot was so scared of being dismissed, he climbed in to try and lift the sack with his bare feet. Complete duffer. He could have died. Luckily he only got himself suspended for a day or two.'

If these were gas people, why had they come to this town only? Were they up to some tricks, milking whatever was left there? The people in the town could end up sick, as before, or dead. How could they know it would be safe this time?

The recruiter was still shouting at the quarrelling couple. 'Get out of here, you bloody useless parasites.'

Both the man and woman pleaded, still pushing each other, their voices overlapping.

'Please Sir. I have to—'

'It wasn't my fault. It—'

'...feed my children and—'

'...it... it... it was this donkey who—'

'Shut up,' the recruiter shouted. 'Get out of my sight. How many days will I keep having this same damn problem?' His nostrils flared.

Dilkhush wanted to flare her own nostrils right back at him. Who did the bastard think he was, treating them like dirt? She knew his sort - swearing and acting big with poor people, then wagging their tails at the rich. Hadn't Suresh's warning been clear from all those years ago? These people dressed to look decent, but were wicked inside, trapping others into dangerous jobs they would never do themselves. And they were knowingly targeting outsiders.

No one would even miss outsiders. No one would complain if they died in any accidents. Hadn't that happened to their friend Rafiq? Suresh thought it was all because a cheap part had failed. She realised nothing had changed. She had to warn everyone. This would be an added bonus to her good deeds there. Others at the junction were sure to notice how she saved all the outsiders from this factory job. She would become a heroine.

The fighting pair walked away from the line, still yelling at each other.

'And listen more,' the recruiter shouted, walking down the queue. 'Stay if you know how to make chis-bis-burga-shurga. Otherwise, leave the queue. You useless people know nothing. We will have to teach you everything, do half your job, and even then you will complain that we treat you badly, pay you badly. If you can't live by our rules, then go. We have no need for the ungrateful and useless.'

The snake inside Dilkhush began to stir.

'And if you can't speak English, then leave. English is a must.'

'Oh, you need English speakers for these jobs now, do you?' Dilkhush shouted. 'Standards have been raised to only let literate people do heavy lifting, or have the chance to get sick or die? The illiterate are not even good enough for that any more?' She started to walk away from the line.

'Eh.' It was the gangly recruiter.

Dilkhush turned around.

He ran his eyes up and down her before scribbling something on his clipboard. 'Are you an outsider?' he asked.

She didn't reply.

He raised his voice. 'You are an outsider ready to work?' He waited for her to speak. 'I asked, are you here for a job?'

Dilkhush remained silent.

'Fine. If you want to go, then bloody go. But why stand in the damn queue like a beggar in the first place? And then, when I am asking a question, you become deaf?'

Dilkhush wanted to slap him. Who was this man to insult her left and right? Her ears throbbed again. She saw people's mouths move, but couldn't hear anything. The snake inside her hissed and unleashed.

'Deaf must be your mother. Deaf must be your mother's mother.' Her ears burned. Spit sprayed as she shouted. 'Deaf must be your mother's mother and her whole family. Deaf must be your entire ancestry. What do you think? Just because I don't want to put my life into you people's hands, you think you can insult me? Who gave you that right? You think I am stupid? You are stupid. You think illiterate people can't think. My English may be crooked, but you think I will sell you my life for a few extra paisa?

'Go find naïve, inexperienced people who believe more money comes at no extra price. Go find desperate people who look at you as a God because you have that damned clipboard and a job. Just because you have the power to put food in their children's mouth, they don't say anything about you running like a dog to that mistress of yours sitting comfortably in her car. Left you when there was trouble here, didn't she?'

The recruiter's eyes flickered. 'What the hell are you talking about, you delusional bitch?'

The mistress's car sped off.

The recruiter looked at it and turned to Dilkhush. 'Good work! You had a chance with that job. But not any more.'

'I don't want your job,' she shouted. 'There can be no good reason you are looking for outsiders only, promising them good money. What is wrong with the locals? They know the likes of you too well? I don't care for this gold nectar you are dripping in front of us, promising notes that flaunt Gandhi's picture whilst flouting his principles.'

'Eh, Mother India,' the recruiter said. 'Don't lecture me. Does this look like an election stage? Get out if you don't want to stand here. I was asking you because you spoke English, but look at you. Firing faster than a whore's cunt filled with an elephant's trunk. I want a competent outsider. Not one with all her screws loose. Go on, get out of my sight.'

'Who wants to be in your sight, you sewage rat?'

Some people around her sniggered.

'Get out I said, you bastard bitch.' The recruiter's face was turning red from shouting.

'Your father owns this job junction, does he?' Dilkhush spat. 'I have no need to stay. It was you who called me back as if I am a useless-waiting-around-person. I have important things to do, just like your clipboard clack-clack things.' She began to walk off but heard his loud slurs.

'See that?' the recruiter said. 'Try and give you people a chance and you bite at our cocks like deranged dogs. As if you people can even survive without—'

'Deranged dog, your father,' Dilkhush shouted back. 'And your father's father. Deranged dog your entire family, you rich people's bloody chamché. We don't need parasites like you preying on us.' She went to join another line.

'What do you think you are doing?' the recruiter in the other line asked. 'Already you were branded a thief, and now you have shown your insanity talking to that esteemed recruiter like that. We don't want the likes of you here.'

'But I was only explaining to the outsiders that they might end up getting sick or dead. They shouldn't be fooled. I saved that boy from the dog as well. I promise I am a good person. A good worker.'

The man wagged his finger. 'Out of the line.'

Whichever job line she went to, Dilkhush got a similar reaction. She didn't know how to correct the stupid mistake she had made with the embroidery pieces. She had tried to save the boy and now even saving other people with a warning wasn't enough. Why were the recruiters turning her efforts against her?

'You are giving everyone here a bad name,' a job seeker said. 'We all need work. So what if they are bilayati with difficult work? If you scare them away, all of us will lose. We need money even if you don't.'

'I need money too, but these people might eat you and your family.' The job seeker turned away from her. Dilkhush didn't know why they couldn't understand. Maybe the outsiders didn't know anyone who had suffered from the gas. 'I don't want people to... you don't know what it is really like afterwards.' She realised she had not thought it through. Her years of pain meant little to them.

The local job seekers and recruiters knew each other, and everyone needed work. Her fighting against predatory recruiters meant nothing. Pointing out there could be more harm to people in the town if things went wrong at a factory was even more foolish. She didn't know it was a factory job. If it was, the recruiters were more powerful. Not only would they all call her a thief and a liar, but also a troublemaker, endangering chances for work. And what could she give anyone? Not work. How would they feed their children?

After seeing this, what recruiter there would give her a job? Why was she ruining her own fate? She had to explain to them that her shameful behaviour was because of her losses. But others in the town must have suffered like her. How had they managed better than her? She started to walk away and bumped straight into the wrinklewretches from the bus. The old couple flinched again, and Dilkhush scowled at them. Her blood started to boil again.

'Stay back, my child.' The old man's voice was soft. 'We have downtrodden karma that curses everyone who touches us. You are already an unlucky widow. Don't get more polluted by us.'

They shuffled away. Dilkhush watched as the crowds engulfed their frail bodies. She had been wrong about their flinching. If the old man had not spoken so quickly, she would have lashed out at them. She seemed to have no control over her rage. Should she leave the town before she caused more damage to her own karma?

Dilkhush stood under a tree, hidden from others, collecting her thoughts and clinging to any sense she could make about what had just happened.

She needed to find help. A kind soul.

Naseema Bi.

7

Everything Seemed the Same,
but Everything had Changed

DILKHUSH WINCED AT the thought of going to see the old owl. After losing Jiyaa, Suresh had died within months, coughing out blood. All of their friends had perished. And she felt she had no other choice than to abandon Naseema Bi because of the old owl's behaviour.

After the night of the gas leak, Dilkhush even lost that almost burned, blackened being that came out of her own swollen belly. The ogress doctor said, 'It's no good. This one's gone. And the insides of your body are now decimated by the gas. Your womb has no more chances.' Dilkhush couldn't bear it and begged the doctor, but there was no way of putting life back into her child.

In an instant, she felt disgusted with herself, and even the baby. She became ashamed of her own reaction, of what her body had done, of what it had failed at doing in protecting that child inside her. She wanted to erase it all from her mind. Yet Naseema Bi's pained face had always been in front of her, constantly reminding her that the gas leak had happened. That it was all true. Dilkhush couldn't even pretend she was still heavy with child, or that she couldn't see Jiyaa around her only because the girl was at school or playing outside.

Instead, the scabs on her wounds were constantly being ripped off, every day. She had to leave. The old owl was not her responsibility. Other tenants could easily take her place and keep the owl company. Dilkhush knew she would be breaking Naseema Bi's heart. They had both lost everyone, and who knew what would remain now? But she ignored her worries about the owl and went to the Holy City, without saying anything. She was afraid the old owl would have come with her otherwise. Dilkhush thought she would learn to get peace in the Holy City with all the thousands of gods, prayers, holy waters, and sages.

Now she had no choice but to face Naseema Bi, after forsaking her. She had to overcome her reluctance. After all, the old owl had been like family. There could even be joy in seeing each other and maybe fast forgiveness between them.

Dilkhush walked slowly, making a plan. If Naseema Bi had savings, she could ask to borrow some. She would find a way to pay it back, but first she needed money to find Kashif quickly. Of course, she couldn't tell the old owl about that, but she might be so happy there may be no questions. There would be no need to say anything about her plans, or that she and Kashif would have to leave soon after they took revenge.

Otherwise, the old owl's heart would break again. She would pay Naseema Bi back, Dilkhush promised herself. Maybe she would even try and find a place for all of them to stay, away from the town. She looked towards the old owl's house when Dalya appeared.

'Heroine, you are still here? I am back after an errand, but I saw you with that dog. You are truly a heroine.'

So, he had seen her with the dog, but luckily not shouting at the recruiter. Maybe he could help her find work. He could vouch for her honourable action of saving the boy from that dog, and confirming she wasn't making it all up. But Dalya explained that he kept out of the way of recruiters. 'They have a lot of power here. They hold livelihoods in their hands, *nahn?*'

Dilkhush excused herself and walked away.

'OK, bye Heroine,' Dalya said after her.

What use was that MBBS title if he couldn't actually help her? Dilkhush decided she had to rely on Naseema Bi. The cemetery was going to be on the way to the old owl's house, but she was not yet ready to visit Jiyaa's grave. Nothing had changed. Maybe after she and Kashif had finished their deed, she might deserve her daughter's forgiveness.

If only she had agreed to leave the town after the smaller gas leaks, they would all have returned to Suresh's parents. They could have avoided the massive leak, and would still be alive. But Dilkhush had only thought about herself at that time. And where had that got her?

A lifetime with her mother-in-law would not have compared to the punishment she ended up facing. If Dilkhush had known it was so dangerous, that the gas would kill her own children, she would have left Jantapur immediately. It was her folly for believing the leaks would stop. In avoiding her mother-in-law's daily punishment, she had lost everything. At least her mother-in-law would have died one day and her torture would have ended. This anguish had no end.

'Stop your ooh-aah,' her mother-in-law said, pulling Dilkhush's hair and digging in her claw-like nails. 'Filums and newspapers have mothers-in-law who burn brides to death. Am I doing anything like that? If you had any decency, you'd burn yourself to death and let my Suresh marry again. What bad luck I have that a whore like you and your conniving village chief of a father softened my son's brain. Whatever bribe and dowry your father gave us will never be enough.' She unleashed such taunts several times a day with beatings and burns from hot frying spoons. The witch claimed this removed the evil inside Dilkhush. She found other ways too, with cruel words, heavy pans, and poisonous concoctions.

Before their marriage, Suresh had taken the unusual step of asking to speak to Dilkhush. He knew about the allegations the villagers had made, and how sensitive her father had become of his teenage daughter being alone with a man. It was the growing rumours and gossip in the village that had forced her father to act fast and get her married. Suresh was a townsman, not a villager.

He had seen Dilkhush before, when he had come to fix her father's machinery.

He told her he believed her, that the lower caste boy Dilkhush had been caught with one night was only consoling her, wiping away her tears. Nothing else had happened. She had only gone to relieve herself under a tree that night, and the boy had overheard her sobbing. Her mother had died, and Dilkhush hadn't wanted to cry in front of her father.

Suresh had become her saviour, but his mother spared no cruelty. So, some time after their marriage, without saying anything, Suresh found work at the gas factory in Jantapur, far away from his parents. His mother accused Dilkhush of black magic and hit her on the head with a rolling pin. But nothing took away the excitement. And in Jantapur, Naseema Bi and Ashraf Mia were their godsend landlords.

The old owl praised Dilkhush's cooking as well as the way she dressed and looked. Naseema Bi loved all the noise from neighbours' houses and helped Dilkhush make friends. She kept their courtyard open for all their new friendships. 'These girls from around the neighbourhood with their laughter and singing will keep us all happy.'

Dilkhush had doubts about herself, but then the mirror-seller worked his magic and somehow she felt like a new woman. Their house became full with lively, jovial people simply visiting, wanting help or coming for Dilkhush's famous dinners. Naseema Bi seemed happy too. Whenever Suresh announced a warm night by the lake or to the open-air talkies, the old owl first made sure *they ate well and then prepared Dilkhush so she was like a new bride again.*

She combed her long hair lovingly, rubbing oudh oil into its thickness and holding it over lit jasmine incense, so the fragrance infused each strand. 'Better your Suresh gets distracted by this sweet smell of you, even if he is watching the thrusting hips of those actresses. With men, you have to use gentle ruses like this.'

Dilkhush was sorry not to have come earlier. She got ready to see Naseema Bi and practiced explanations about why she had left. She couldn't tell her the truth, to spare the owl's feelings. And she would also have to gradually explain why this was a very short stay. But could she be so callous as to say nothing until she got some bribe money? As Dilkhush walked through the streets, it felt almost dreamlike. She passed busy groups of people and wished she were a part of them.

Some men played cards in front of a chaiwalla and drank their tea from small glasses. A few people queued for the street-side dentist. Others stood at various feeding stations, next to piles of dead leaves and grass, which goats chewed on as their owners talked. Several puppeteers practiced their shows. Some people painted murals. Another group practiced their dance plays. Everything seemed the same, as if Dilkhush had never left. Yet everything had changed.

Before she realised, she was outside the cemetery. What kind of God had chosen her child to end up in a hole with a pile of other bodies? There wasn't even a separate grave for her daughter.

'You let her die.' Suresh's accusation echoed in Dilkhush's mind. Before she could manage her thoughts, she noticed Dalya coming out of a building with coins. He put the money in a plastic bag, which he slipped into his satchel. Then he headed to an old woman sitting on a makeshift wheelchair. Her body was covered in boils.

The wheelchair was a wooden-backed seat tied to a board with small wheels. Dalya pushed it onto the street, but the wheels struck a stone. The old woman almost lurched out. He hurried to her and settled her back into the wheelchair. Then he went back into the building and came out with a rope.

Dalya secured the old woman to the chair with the rope and kneeled down in front of her. He patted her boil-ridden hands. Her hand shook as she reached out to touch his head. When they were out of sight, Dilkhush went towards the building to ask about the coins. The sign above said, 'Gas Survivors Clinic.' She wondered whether the clinic was giving Dalya money for his mother. Dilkhush's family had got nothing, not even any treatment for Suresh. Their house had been looted after the gas leak, and she didn't have any copies of their birth certificates or any papers to prove anything.

Some time later, Dilkhush rushed out of the clinic. A high-pitched ringing sounded in her ears. What had she done? She dropped to her knees. Her plan had already unravelled. God had only been mocking her by bringing her to Jantapur. Her thoughts became woolly. Everything was a blur. She should end her torture. There was no need to carry on with life any more.

8

The Truth and the Story About the Truth

DILKHUSH SAW DALYA leave the clinic with coins. Maybe she could also get some. But how could she just walk in and ask for money? She waited for Dalya to leave with the old woman he was pushing on the makeshift wheelchair.

As Dilkhush gathered the courage to go in, she overheard a heated discussion nearby that mentioned costs. A man and woman were standing by a car and eating kulfi.

'Yes, I hear you,' the man said. 'And I don't want to sound like a broken record. But you know how many additional costs there are now for a clean-up of the site? Look how far it has all spread.' He shook his head. 'In fact, there is a lot of money for anyone who wins that clean-up contract, but there are issues. Otherwise, you think we would still be here? There's too much at stake. So, no one will budge.'

'What about the UN helping? Or—'

'But who takes responsibility for all this then?'

'Idealism is fine,' the woman said. 'But be realistic.'

Dilkhush didn't understand everything they said, but if they wanted to be realistic, they could look at her. Should she tell them that?

'I am realistic,' the man said. 'But idealism is necessary as a goal. The other way can lead to compromise upon compromise until the original well-thought plan has vanished, replaced with half-baked solutions.' He looked at the woman and chewed his lower lip. 'But I understand your point.'

The woman nodded. 'So then, technicalities. Originally, there was a Disaster Claims Act for compensation, right?'

Dilkhush wondered whether the coins in Dalya's hands had come from some claims compensations. Is that what these two were talking about? She and her family had got nothing after the gas leak. Maybe she could find out more if she eavesdropped a little longer.

The man kicked the pavement as he ate his kulfi.

The woman half-glanced towards Dilkhush, and carried on talking. 'But it was violated.'

'What was?'

The woman rolled her eyes. 'Don't play dumb. The Claims Act was violated. The survivors did not appoint the government.'

'No, but it's the government. They decide what to do. And anyway, it was a different government then.'

'Yes, but—' The woman sighed. 'Let me give you an example to explain my point, OK? So,' she paused.

'When there is a dictator, harmful action is challenged by other countries, isn't it? This wasn't about a dictator, but still about rights. If it is a human rights issue—'

'But nobody challenged it.'

'Because it looked like the government was doing the right thing, with the right intentions. But they cannot claim paternal duty and then have incompetence, or corruption, or conflict of interest that makes them fail in that duty. What track record did they leave? And no-one has straightened that out till now. So in the future how can anyone trust—'

'Hello? What world are you living in?' The man dropped his empty kulfi cup in a plastic bag nearby.

Dilkhush's mouth watered. It had been so long since she'd had a kulfi.

'Don't you see?' The woman touched the man's arm lightly. 'The Act becomes void because it is misrepresentation.'

The man laughed. 'Misrepresentation is many governments summed up, which means no one will point the finger.'

'Come on.' The woman folded her arms.

The man raised his eyebrows. 'Seriously?' He shook his head. 'Look around. How many foreign companies invest here now? How many want to make billions more? Even companies here want that. It's the reality. Whether we like it or not.'

Dilkhush realised they were talking about a different reality to hers. Yet, she heard in their voices, that maybe they did see people like her, in whatever form they explained. But how did that help her?

The woman pouted. 'That Claims Act was supposed to be to the best advantage of the survivors. But it went against any rights they had.'

The man grimaced. 'Check the wording. The Act probably protects the people in charge.'

The woman finished her kulfi and licked her lips. 'Hmm. It was a good try though.'

The man gave her a sideways hug. 'Our newspapers scream corruption scandals every day. Even our Bollywood films. It's become part of our culture. Investments still come, maybe because of corruption. Even you and I don't want India to lose out.'

The woman became serious again. 'I think they are removing some clauses and laws. What if they are ones that can help us? Business can be done with humanity.'

'Maybe that works with the trader on the street. But not when there are billions on the table. There will always be a choice.'

'Thousands died, Ash. And these people in the clinic, they're still sick. What can stop or reverse the damage? Does anyone know? Can anyone help them? Isn't withholding that help violating their right to life, right to dignity?'

'Are they really removing laws and clauses?'

The woman nodded. 'Someone here has to go through each one. Someone trustworthy. Otherwise, even useful clauses and laws can be cut out and the job finished up that way. Change the law, change the outcome.' She paused. 'Maybe Salman?'

'What is he now? Everyone's saviour? He is busy already with all that campaigning.'

'But—'

'You know him.' The man shook his head. 'He'll just say "yes", whether he can manage it or not. And we will still be sitting here in twenty years' time, same thing, waiting to pick him up, birthday or no birthday. And he will be doing even more than now. Still staying late everyday. And you and me, we will still be here arguing about this thing.'

'Don't say that,' the woman scolded. 'Not twenty more years! Someone must have the balls to become history's hero.'

Dilkhush waited a while longer to hear more but they didn't say anything about compensation again.

The clinic was bright inside, flooded with sunshine from an inner courtyard. As she oriented herself, she saw people sitting on chairs against a wall.

Inside one of the rooms, a doctor was checking an old man's cough. In another room, a group of children of all ages crowded around a table and matched shapes and holes, sometimes with difficulty. Across from Dilkhush, there was a young woman in another makeshift wheelchair. She was by a corner table with a pile of newspapers, cutting out pages.

Her wheelchair was similar to the one Dalya had been pushing - a normal chair tied on top of a thick board with wheels. The young woman looked up. She was short, and her arms and legs were deformed with missing fingers on her hands. Her neck sat almost inside her chest, and her face seemed too big for her body. She had bright red make-up on her cheeks and lips. 'Can I help?' she asked, smiling widely.

Dilkhush asked her how she could get money from the clinic. 'Like the boy who just left with coins. Maybe it was compensation money?'

The young woman didn't know anything about that. 'But if you are asking because you are gas-affected, we can do a check-up and help you with many things. It's free. We have doctors, nurses, and therapists. Many of them are gas-affected as well. We do TB care, Ayurveda, and allopathic medicines. Then there is yoga. We also have inhalers for breathing problems. And if your children are affected, we have speech therapy and physiotherapy for them, with sports and special education. A minibus can collect them. Look.'

She pointed towards a wide corridor where children with various physical and mental disabilities were crawling or walking with difficulty. Each group had an adult helping. Dilkhush was not happy asking about the money again, but she had to. 'I saw someone walk out with coins from here. I wanted to know how he might have got them.'

'I honestly don't know about that,' the young woman said. 'But I can go and ask someone for you.' She called a boy over to wheel her towards an office. He was small, and managing to walk, although he struggled to push her wheelchair.

Dilkhush looked back at the children in the corridor. One of the boys practiced walking by holding on to a wall. A woman sitting nearby nodded. 'Well done, Raju. Now, also try to walk a little without the wall. Just one or two steps. That is fine for now.' Another woman helped stretch and bend the legs of a girl who lay on the floor, staring at the ceiling. 'Come, try with me Priya. A small stretch. We will do it slowly,' the woman said in a soft voice. She looked up and saw Dilkhush watching. 'You are waiting for Jaadu?'

How did this woman know she was waiting for a miracle?

'That lady in the wheelchair, Jaadu. You are waiting for her?'

Dilkhush nodded.

The woman smiled. 'She will come back just now only.'

Dilkhush smiled back weakly and turned to a notice board pinned full of newspaper pages. The sign above it said, 'Our story in the News.' Several pages had photos of the clinic, the flare tower and tanks rusting, overgrown grounds, sacks of chemicals still in the stores. The headlines demanded a clean-up. 'Disaster entrepreneurs welcome to clean-up and turn our misfortunes into their fortunes.' Dilkhush looked closely. Pinned to the notice board was also the same newspaper page she had in her cloth bundle. The headline was the same:

'#TRUESTORY. TOWN POISONED FOR 30 YEARS. CONTRIBUTOR @SALMANJANTAPURI.'

Underneath was a photo of a crowd of people

reacting to some news. 'Will all in charge at time of Jantapur gas deaths attend 30th anniversary or reject it?' Dilkhush read the words again, slower this time - 'Will all in charge at time of Jantapur gas deaths attend 30th anniversary or reject it?'

How had she missed seeing the main part? She had seen only what she wanted to and made the journey to the town. She looked at all the details of the newspaper. Kashif was not even in the picture. She had misunderstood it completely. The article was not about everyone attending the anniversary, but questioning whether those in charge would attend, to see the full effects 30 years after the leak.

Dilkhush was sure she had read the article several times. Why had she only read into it what she wanted? It couldn't be true. Her mind had to be playing tricks on her again. Was this all her life could ever be? Living inside fantasies to get through each day? She looked at the other headline on the same page. Had she misread everything? But the other headline was the same as she remembered, and in the other papers too. They were all celebrating.

'#*GOTCHA*: TERRORIST SHOT BY OUR HEROES'

'#ALLOVER!'

'#JUSTICE_AT_LAST!'

'#HEROESFORPEACE'

Each headline had the same photo of foreign soldiers holding big guns and standing over a man they had shot. The man had given orders that killed thousands of innocents, so the soldiers had killed him in return. It had taken them only 15 years. It was 30 years for Dilkhush, and she still had not managed anything like that. She looked at the Jantapur headline again.

It was the only one she had mistaken. Her mind had fooled her. She had come all this way, believing she had seen Kashif in the photo of the Jantapur crowd. Because that had the promise of ending her hopelessness.

Had she been so desperate after being kicked out of her father's village? She had seen the photo of the soldiers, and believed if Kashif was there too, they both could also take revenge. But those soldiers had guns in their hands. And the newspapers rejoiced their victory.

Even if Kashif was there, how would they do anything like that? And as if she, of all people, could help him. With what weapon? Her snake of rage? It was all a botched-up fantasy plan. She should never have come. Now she was in a worse situation, with no money to go back. Her thoughts felt fragile and started to disintegrate. She tried to get hold of them and keep herself steady.

The photos in the papers stared back as if to ridicule her. Her plan to return seemed absurd now, yet there was nothing else left. How small she felt looking at those pictures. Even if she and Kashif took revenge on anyone, they would both end up in jail, and hanged for murder. There would be no cries of victory in the newspapers. At the back of her mind, she felt there could be no peace from any killing, whether for revenge or not. But that felt unjust.

Dilkhush got up. She should leave the town. But the young woman in the wheelchair came back.

'Someone will come soon.'

'It's okay. I have to go.' Dilkhush backed up towards the door and accidentally bumped into a freestanding notice board, almost toppling it over. She turned around to steady it.

'Don't worry.' The young woman smiled. 'It happens all the time. But please don't go. Let me at least get some water for you while you wait.' She quickly sent the boy. 'I don't recognise you, but you are asking about compensation. So you must be gas-affected, yes?'

Dilkhush didn't speak. She was becoming afraid of the collapse happening in her mind.

'I can understand you might be worried about coming, but we are here to help. You shouldn't be concerned or embarrassed for having only a little money. It is for people like you only that we are giving free treatment. There is no cost at all. This is from the humanity of others. Many people come here and get better. If you suffered from the gas leak, we can see whether we can make your life a little easier.'

Dilkhush just stared. The woman's words surprised her, but they did not hit a nerve any more. What was the point in making her life easier, or in prolonging her life? 'I don't have any money to get my bus back.'

'Where are you from?'

Dilkhush looked at her. How cheerful she seemed despite her state. She must take so much care putting on that make-up everyday. Who got her dressed and into her chair?

'One minute.' the young woman said. 'There must be someone who can help. I will be back in a moment.' She beckoned the boy over again. He brought water and then struggled again with the young woman's wheelchair. Dilkhush gulped the water down. Kashif had been a false hope. Her legs suddenly felt heavy and she sat down, exhausted.

The young woman's words were soothing. What if there was someone who could help her? Someone who gave her the courage to go to Jiyaa's grave and at least try to get forgiveness. Oh, now she was listening to the priest! Choice whore!

Dilkhush ignored the snake inside her. She had to try the priest's way after all. A bell sounded. She looked around the clinic. A few children swapped rooms. One looked over at her and struggled across slowly. She stayed frozen in her spot. He hugged her legs. Dilkhush started to get up when a woman came to him.

'Come on, Bheem. That's not your mummy. It's not time for her yet.' She looked at Dilkhush and doled her head side-to-side. 'His mother sits there when she comes to pick him. He can't see well, so he must have thought—'

'It's okay. No harm.'

'Because that's where his mother sits for him.'

Dilkhush nodded. 'I understand.' When the children were in their classes, she got up. Her legs still held the memory of the boy's innocent hug. She walked towards rows of notice boards with plastic covers, under which there were hundreds of black-and-white photos of children. Was the boy on one of them? But each photo had a face and a numbered label. A sign at the bottom said, 'May they Rest in Peace.' Dilkhush looked around. There were several notice boards with photos of adults and children, sectioned by areas. Her heart raced as she recognised faces from her old neighbourhood. They were photos of people who had died from the gas leak.

She had seen so many children then, somehow separated from their parents. Their bodies had been placed in a line under the banyan tree outside her house. That's the tree she used to sit under to teach the street orphans. The men collecting the bodies after the leak had asked around. They tried to place the dead in the right neighbourhoods, so relatives didn't have to scour for lost ones.

It didn't seem so long ago that she had watched parents run to the lines of bodies and break down when they saw their child lying there. Officials carried on with their work, putting stickers with a name and number on the foreheads of those already identified. Someone took photos of each of the dead.

Without warning, Dilkhush came upon a photo of her daughter on the notice board. She felt nauseous. She had never placed Jiyaa on the ground outside. Had Suresh taken her for officials to stick a number on her and take a picture? They had no right. Jiyaa looked in her worst state then. Otherwise she always had her mischievous smile and twinkling eyes. Rosy cheeks that were so plump, no one could resist pinching them. Jiyaa always ran over to give hugs and trusted everyone. How would anyone know that from this picture? They couldn't tell what gem of a child had died from the gas.

Dilkhush started to force open the plastic cover on the clinic notice board to grab her daughter's photo when her eyes fell on a picture of Naseema Bi staring at her from a few photos down. The same neighbourhood. That meant the old owl was dead.

Dilkhush looked away, ashamed. Her throat felt thick. She had planned to use the old owl to borrow money, and to have somewhere to stay until she decided what to do. But even the owl was gone. Suresh, Ashraf Mia, and thousands of others had died, with all of their photos probably pinned up on these notice boards. Why had she expected Naseema Bi to be stronger? In the photo, her face was etched with pain. Her mouth and cloudy eyes were both dry and open.

Dilkhush knew she should have returned sooner. She had sentenced them both to agonising isolation and now needed forgiveness from the old owl as well. Her karma was worse than she thought. It might never get resolved, and she would never see Jiyaa again.

Had Naseema Bi even been buried with the appropriate rituals? She had snubbed that important duty at her peril. Dilkhush looked at the old owl's photo again and begged for forgiveness. She needed help from God. Her eyes searched. Around Naseema Bi's picture were photos of girls and young women. Dilkhush's eyes landed on one labelled Omera. Her heart dropped even further into her stomach.

Was that really Kashif's daughter? How Dilkhush had spent months, searching for a unique name that was fit for the firstborn of her beloved Simran and Kashif? It was Omera who had heard Jiyaa's baby cries and saved her. It was Omera who Kashif had pined for. He had refused the loss of his child; refused to believe what Dilkhush had seen after the gas leak. This photo exposed her disastrous mistake and sealed her fate. There could be no resolution for her now.

The photo and label showed Omera as a young woman when she died. Her grown-up features were barely recognisable. The cause of death was suicide. Dilkhush turned away.

She had been in tears when she told Kashif she had seen young Omera on a burning pyre during the mass funerals after the gas leak. He had refused to believe that and kept looking for weeks afterwards.

What viciousness in her had made her see Omera dead? She had been so sure it was her. What a way she had repaid the girl, when it was only because of her that Suresh's mother had failed in her deadly tricks. Dilkhush felt defeated. She wanted it all to go away. This was not what she had returned for.

Dilkhush had lost so much blood in childbirth that she was too weak to get up. But she knew her witch of a mother-in-law thought girls to be unlucky curses. When the witch insisted on taking the newborn away to clean her, Dilkhush cried out for her to stop. She tried to run after her, but collapsed. The witch bolted the door from outside the room. She came back saying the baby was too weak and had died.

Dilkhush screamed for Simran, who was unwell herself. Otherwise, she would have stayed during the birth. Yet Simran came. And she told Kashif not to worry about her. She took Omera to look for the baby. It was Omera who heard faint cries and found Jiyaa. The witch had sealed the baby into a pot with dough and hidden it under nearby bushes. But the child's will to live was strong enough to be heard, even as she was losing air in the pot. When Simran and Omera returned with the baby, Dilkhush sobbed and snatched the girl into her bosom as she took in the smell of her newborn, kissing the softness of her child's skin all over.

She was sure then that her baby would grow up to be something special. She had been saved from death for a reason. So she was named Jiyaa, to signify the life inside her. Yet Dilkhush was terrified. She felt such a strong love for her daughter. It had physically pained her to be away from her even in those short moments. Her heart could never be intact because it was inside her daughter now. She knew she would never be able to bear it had the witch succeeded. Omera had not only saved her baby's life, but her life as well. Dilkhush gave her prized gold-encased apsara mirror to Simran to keep for Omera's wedding trousseau. 'It is the only valuable thing I have to give. Omera has blessed me, and I am forever in her debt.'

Now, there was Omera's photo, grown-up, alone, having taken her own life. Dilkhush scoured her mind. There had to be something she could do to mend her wrongs. She couldn't have come all the way, after all these years, only to find out that any chances to be with Jiyaa's soul were already lost.

The God who had not spoken to her all these years continued that punishment. The past rushed at her, snarling. God was only mocking her by bringing her back. Dilkhush rushed out of the clinic. What had she done? She dropped to her knees. Her plan had unravelled. There would be no resolution for her. What was the need to carry on with life now?

9

It wasn't a Memory. It hadn't Happened yet

DILKHUSH REALISED SHE may never reunite with her daughter's soul. The truth of that was in the clinic. Her failings may have been unintended, but they had led to suffering. There could be no good end for her.

She couldn't make her thoughts line up straight. How had her eyes deceived her about Omera? Of course, Kashif had been devastated with her news. He probably sensed his daughter's heartbeat, alive and well somewhere. He had already lost Simran to the gas. Why would he have given in to Dilkhush's horrific claim? Yet, she struggled to understand how she had been mistaken.

After Dilkhush and Suresh had buried Jiyaa, they walked from grave to grave, pyre to pyre, looking for those they still hadn't found. Corpses were piled up to be buried together in cemeteries or burned in cremation grounds. Hundreds of fires crackled. Along with the sickening smell of burning flesh was the chanting: 'Ram's name is the truth.' Suresh hurried to help others with the dead, and left Dilkhush to walk home alone. She didn't feel his absence until she stumbled upon one of the mass funeral pyres. She saw something that halted everything around her. Dilkhush had never expected to see Omera's body burning on that pyre. It should have devastated her.

Instead, she felt numb and thought about Omera being Muslim, and that she should have been buried. As if the cremation was the most shocking part. She looked around for Suresh, but he had disappeared from sight. When he returned home, she told him and they went back to where she had seen Omera. But they couldn't find her. Suresh looked for hours. Her body must have burned already. Other corpses could have been piled on top. Kashif didn't believe them. He looked for his daughter for weeks with Suresh, until they were both haggard with exhaustion. When Kashif put his life in danger, fighting with the police about looking for his daughter, Dilkhush decided she had to go to him.

She was almost grateful that she was not alone in her sorrow. 'How can you and I accept our loss?' she sobbed to Kashif. The words meant nothing to either of them. They united in their grief for a night. But he left the town straight after, telling them to convince Naseema Bi that he had died. Otherwise, the old owl would look for him.

Dilkhush knew now that even if she found Kashif, she could not face him. Omera had not died as a child. Father and daughter could have been together all these years. She had stolen away their time. If Kashif was ever in the town and had seen Omera's photo in the clinic, he would want to punish Dilkhush, not help her. The only blessing was the possibility that Naseema Bi and Omera had found each other and stayed together. Maybe then at least the old owl wouldn't have died alone. But that did not help Dilkhush's karma

Had she lost her mind and imagined seeing Omera on the funeral pyre to take away all of Kashif's hope, because she couldn't stand another child being alive while hers had been snatched? Could she have been that callous? The night they shared had driven him away from Jantapur. If he had stayed, maybe he would have found Omera. Or if Dilkhush had returned earlier, she would have had the chance to put things right. She could have seen Omera alive and found Kashif. Poor Naseema Bi didn't know he hadn't died. It was too late.

It was one thing to pretend for years that she was living with her own family, as if they had left Jantapur before the gas leak. But this. She hadn't even known about her sins that had inflicted pain on others. She had dragged herself through years of emptiness, using a little opium, but mostly her imagination to bear each day. And for what? God had brought her back there under some guise, and then snatched away all her hope for resolution. He was jeering at her, pointing out the cruelty she had meted out.

A grey horse clipped-clopped on the road in front of her, pulling a cart with a bulging load. Its owner was sitting on top, holding long reigns. Pictures of deities were painted on the horse's body. It was the priest who had sent her there so she could face the truth that was in front of her now. '*Give forgiveness, get forgiveness.*' She finally understood. But how was there any possibility of balancing her karma now?

God had brought her there to show why she was still suffering. He had exposed her dark deeds and sealed her fate away from her daughter forever. She asked Him to give her any other punishment. She would do anything to change what had happened. To do right by those she had left her cursed shadow upon. She even asked to forget what she had just seen in the clinic. She could live in ignorance. Coward! That would not change what she had done.

God remained silent. There would be no easy way out for her. She had to face her karma. Dilkhush ripped off the ragpatches of wounds inside her, one by one, wincing each time. Ever since she had reached the town, she had wanted to keep away from Naseema Bi. She had reluctantly decided to seek her out. Now all she wanted was the old owl's hand on her head.

She looked at others around her - the man sitting down for a shave, the boys with goats chewing dry grass, the women carrying vegetable baskets on their heads. How did they seem to have simple lives with children alive, maybe even thriving? And she had nothing, no one. No miracle could come and right her wrongs. Then, a final devastating karma tried to resurface from deep within her, but she panicked and buried it back down. She had faced too much already. Dilkhush pleaded with God. 'Help me, please. I'm drowning.'

Nothing happened. The snake inside her started to hiss awkwardly. It had taken a beating from what she had learned in the clinic. Its head seemed almost cut off, hanging at an angle. A beggar sitting across the road seemed like a jeering reflection of her, except he was outside what she felt inside. His body was covered with fraying skin and moth-chewed ragpatches that stuck to oozing blood and pus. She was like that inside, where no one could see, raw, with peeled patches of tattered memories.

After a long time, Dilkhush pushed herself off the ground. She had lost. She wiped her face with the end of her sari. The sun was lower in the sky now, with a pink-purple hue. It seemed unreal, as if she was in a trance. The reflection of the colours seemed to bounce off the oily skins of those around her, off bicycles and glasses on stalls, as if they were all in a painting.

Even her white sari seemed to have swaying colours reflected from the sky. It seemed as if she was walking in one of her bright, larger-than-life memories, except this wasn't a memory. It hadn't happened yet. She was creating it with each moment. A calmness took over, as if the venom from the dying snake inside her had seeped in and deadened any feelings.

Dilkhush felt disconnected. She waited outside the cemetery for a while, but couldn't bring herself to go in. Her daughter lay there. A deep gnawing scratched inside her. Before any final farewell, she had to fulfil her duty with the sacred remnants amongst the roots of the peepal tree.

Dilkhush had planted it in Naseema Bi's courtyard because gods lived in those trees. She had wanted those gods to look after her loved ones. If another family lived at Naseema Bi's house, she would explain that she needed holy leaves and roots from that very tree, to bury at her daughter's grave. So that those gods could look after Jiyaa's soul. No one would question that.

At the cemetery, to finish her final duty, she would explain to her precious loved souls that she had failed. She had not resolved her karma, and there was no chance of that now. Their souls may never be together again. Dilkhush choked back her tears. She wished there was something she could do to change her fate, but she didn't know how.

She decided that afterwards, she would go back to the peepal tree. She would take her last breath hanging from there, in her old courtyard, in front of the remaining gods of the tree. What other choice had they left her?

10

Being One of the Strangers

O N H E R W A Y to their old home Dilkhush passed Jantapur Talkies. She stared at the layers of movie posters, some of which were peeling away from the walls. One film had multiple posters pasted across repeating rows and columns. *Jab tak hain jaan.* Jab tak hain jaan. Jab tak hain jaan. Jab tak hain jaan. Jab tak hain jaan. Jab tak hain jaan. Jab tak hain jaan. Jab tak hain jaan. Jab tak hain jaan. Jab tak hain jaan. Jab tak hain jaan.

She stared at them. However many times those words were recited, being alive didn't mean anything when she felt dead. All she could picture was Simran collapsed outside those talkies on the night of the gas leak, bleeding between her legs.

'You give this to Omera when she gets married,' Simran croaked. 'You will be her mother now.' She held out the gold-encased mirror, but Dilkhush shook her head. She was heavily pregnant and also carrying Jiyaa in her arms. So she couldn't help Simran, but she still had hope.

'No, you will give the mirror to Omera yourself. I will go and bring back medicine. You are going to be fine. You'll see.'

Now Dilkhush thought Simran the lucky one. She and Omera were together.

She reached the steep incline towards the old owl's house and dug her toes into the ground to avoid slipping. Her breath was strained. Women in various coloured burkhas bustled around, holding bags of food or clothes, talking, or arguing with sweeping arm gestures. A street mother breastfed her baby under the veil of a red sari.

Three children played with tyres, rolling them down the hill, and a girl shuffled and slipped behind them. She was walking with knees bent inwards, holding onto tree trunks and other children. A boy with a large bulging eye looked on. His head seemed to weigh down the left side of his body. Dilkhush missed a step and almost tripped, but stopped short of the ground. She thought she could smell the poison trapped in the soil.

When she reached their old house, she stopped. It was unkempt from the outside. She looked around before knocking. The door seemed to give, as if unlocked.

Dilkhush realised that could mean no one lived there. For a moment, she was relieved. Then she realised what that meant. She was almost at her end. Taking her own life would ensure her soul would never reunite with her loved ones. The priest had assured her of that throughout the years. Even though she was sure now that her karma left no hope of reuniting, she panicked. She did not feel ready. She had come with entirely different plans for heavenly outcomes of resolution and reunion. What if she took her life now and was wrong to do that?

There would be no turning back. How could she trust herself any more? She hesitated and scrambled around in her mind for guidance and any other path that she might have overlooked. She asked God to give her just one sign to indicate there was still a way to be with Jiyaa. She waited a long time, but nothing came. Dilkhush took a deep breath and pushed the door.

Instead of opening ajar, the door pulled askew - as if it was locked after all, just not properly. She tried again. It didn't give way. The lock was simply misaligned. Dilkhush let out a sigh. She had been stopped from taking her own life for the moment. It could be the sign she was waiting for. She knocked again. There was no answer. After trying several times, she walked around the outside of the wall and looked through a crack.

No one was in the courtyard. Newspapers and pieces of rags were strewn all around. The peepal she had planted was now a large tree with a thick trunk. Her breath caught. She had planted it straight after losing her blackened stillborn. The ogress doctor had said there would be no more babies. There was only that tree left now.

'Can I help?' a voice asked from behind her.

Dilkhush turned. An almost skeletal man was standing nearby. Instead of answering, she shook her head and pulled one end of her sari over her face. She didn't want any neighbours to recognise her or tell her stories about their hardships or Naseema Bi's difficulties while she had been away.

'Suit yourself.' The man pushed his own door and locked it behind him, loud and hard.

Dilkhush sat on the step outside the door. She would wait there until the new owners arrived. But she felt unsettled about what she was going to do after meeting the new owners. She had to get the peepal leaves and dig at the roots. If the delay caused by the locked door was a sign from God, what did it mean? It was not clear.

If she took her life, that would be final. There could be no returning, no regrets. She didn't want to do that only to discover later that she might have had a way of being with Jiyaa, and of making up for her sins with others. She had to take a little time to be sure. Taking a bit longer now would not harm her as much as being wrong with no possibility for return.

She should have visited Naseema Bi before. For so many years, her thoughts had become muddled. She had taken whatever refuge she could in her brother's cattle pen. Dilkhush only saw glimpses of her daughter over all that time, often for a few mere moments before they slipped away.

Even now, as she sat outside her old house, she wanted to soothe her wounds, savour the image of her daughter's sweet face smiling back at her. She wanted to show Jiyaa how much she was trying.

Soon Dilkhush became aware of whispers around her, asking who she was. She turned her body towards the door and covered her head and shoulders with her sari. Pans clanked nearby and water gushed out of a tap. Laughter erupted from groups of girls in the neighbourhood, sharing jokes with each other, some that made Dilkhush blush. They sang songs and teased each other shamelessly.

It was like the raucous banter she remembered from before, when she lived there with Naseema Bi. Was she a traitor for wishing she could be one of them in the neighbourhood, or even any of the other strangers nearby, working, cleaning, complaining to each other, collecting cowpat, making dung biscuits to burn for fuel?

She wished she could easily slip into their lives, feeding their stranger children, sleeping with their stranger husbands, with stranger hands roaming over her body. She heard a boy tell a story in a high-pitched voice. There was applause. Jiyaa had loved puppet shows. Even picking the cloth in the market and stitching the puppets had been a pleasure because of her daughter's delight. Dilkhush pulled her knees to her chest and rested her head against the wall. She soon nodded off, waking up with a jerk only a few seconds later. She wished it was time for the new owners to return. Her eyelids felt heavy and she gave in.

Her dreams and visions came in translucent patches. Jiyaa kept giggling and running away. Dilkhush kept waking up and dozing off repeatedly. Each time she awoke, the light had not changed much, although the sky seemed to gradually become duller. She closed her eyes and thought again about how it would have been if there had been no gas leak. She had never been able to imagine Jiyaa's grown-up face. She had only seen her young face. But that didn't stop Dilkhush from trying. She had felt sure that one day she would know what it was to be Jiyaa's mother all through the years.

Even now, she could simply be sitting outside the house because she had forgotten her keys. Jiyaa would have her own children and would visit and laugh at her silly mother locked outside. They would be so close.

Dilkhush would have relished that and been equally scared at explaining to Jiyaa before her marriage what happened between a man and a woman. It would be their special mother-daughter talk. Jiyaa would have been dressed in a red sari at her wedding, a veil over her head, afraid of leaving home to go and live with her husband.

Dilkhush would make sure her in-laws were kind to her little girl. She would tell Jiyaa to confide in her about everything. The new family would join them for dinner every day, as their own friends had. Their banter and laughter would help Dilkhush relax and know that her daughter was safe and happy. That was all she wanted as the girl's mother. That was all any mother would want. Her dreams were interrupted.

'You are not a commoner,' Dilkhush's mother said. 'You can't go to see the travelling puppeteer with the other children. Behave like a landlord's daughter!' Her mother lay back down on the string charpoy bed in their courtyard.

Soon her mother seemed asleep. Her father was out of

the house. So young Dilkhush went into their bedroom and dressed up in her mother's princess pink sari. She put on a bright red lipstick before wearing her mother's gold jewellery. Then she pretended her father's head-pagdi was her husband. She held the pagdi and walked around an imaginary fire seven times, smiling as she got married. Her pretend husband fed her a sweet and she giggled shyly at his teasing.

Then little Dilkhush got an idea.

Many of the pregnant women in the village walked with one hand constantly on their backs. Dilkhush stuck a pillow under her sari and turned sideways in front of the mirror, with one hand on her pillow belly, and one on her back. She looked like a pregnant bride, which pleased her. She was about to pretend to get her baby out to nurse him when her mother came in to get some opium pellets. There were none left and her mother instantly became angry. Dilkhush hurried to undress.

'Get it all off, you curse of a child,' her mother screamed. 'Want to be a pregnant bride and bring shame to our family?' Her mother picked up a peacock feather hair clip and flung it at Dilkhush, but missed. A gold-encased mirror followed. As it smashed to the ground, it landed on a lizard's tail, cutting it off clean. The severed tail continued wriggling as the lizard scuttled off.

'You are horrible,' Dilkhush cried. 'I hate you.' She ran away with the hair clip and mirror and hid between the hookah and wooden almira before finding shelter in their cattle pen.

A jagged edge of the broken mirror sliced through the

pad of her thumb and her blood dried into the cracks. She looked at her broken reflection. Dilkhush didn't dare return to the house and instead, lay down amongst the cattle.

Soon her mother shrieked and complained she had stepped on a broken piece of mirror. She hunted Dilkhush down and dragged her to their courtyard. The moon shone bright as she tied Dilkhush's wrists and ankles to the four corners of the charpoy. She stretched the skin on Dilkhush's forearms and pierced them with the mirror shard she had stepped on, scratching the words 'vile curse' on both arms. All the time she warned, 'Don't you dare cry.' Dilkhush was already biting her lips, not letting any sound escape. She stared at her mother and blinked back her tears. Her thoughts collided into each other.

'This will teach you,' her mother said. 'Who will ever marry you with that intolerable fury inside you? Better you die than shame us with such behaviour.'

After she left, Dilkhush tried to free herself, but the ropes cut into her skin. Her hands and feet felt numb. She wanted to ask God for help but was scared she had such wickedness inside her that even He had abandoned her. In her mind's eyes, she tried to see her mother hugging her and feeding her with love, and then putting her to bed. Instead, she could only imagine her mother pushing her away. She had to try harder. Dilkhush's flesh fell away and her insides became knotted fibres ruffling in the wind. They soon became covered with blood. A rogue piece from her mother's princess pink sari fluttered over and stuck to her. An image of her mother appeared and ripped off the pink patch. Pus oozed and smelled. The sari piece floated back to her. Dilkhush didn't know whether it had come to protect these putrid insides or to hide them.

More fraying patches appeared. They were from familiar things: her father's whip, her mother's veil, her brother's torn underwear that she wiped the floor with. Dilkhush became repelled by her insides. She hadn't been aware of them before. How could she expect anyone to accept her, especially her own mother, who knew her inside and out? As she began to lose consciousness, she was glad God hadn't rescued her. She was finally going to hell as her mother had said. At least no one would see what she had become.

But she didn't go to hell that night. Her father returned drunk. Dilkhush was surprised he could bear to touch her as he untied the ropes. Would he flinch when he saw her insides? She held her breath and pretended there was nothing wrong with her.

Her father barely glanced her way, simply giving her a puppet from the show. He hadn't noticed anything. She realised she could get away with being around people if she pretended there were no patches, or blood and rags and pus. Other people would only see her outside body, like her father did.

She went to the cattle pen and lay against the warmth of a goat. Her tears blurred everything. When she looked at the bloody words scratched on her forearms, she saw they weren't spelled correctly. For some reason that bothered her.

In the days that followed, Dilkhush secretly drenched

her arms in a bowlful of water and let the scabs soften before picking them off. Otherwise the scratched words would be visible to others. She sneaked into the kitchen and used the knife to scratch designs around each letter on her forearm to disguise the scabbing words.

Her skin felt so raw, she had to tie scarves around her palms, all the way up to her elbows, using her teeth to hold one end and tighten the knot. When anyone commented, she said, 'Donkey, didn't the priest tell you? Or maybe God thinks only I can hold the weight of the world in my arms. That is what all these bandages are for.'

She tried to ignore the heckling from the other children when the village priest rejected her claims. One of the scarves accidentally came off, and a boy told everyone what he saw scratched on her. No one wanted to be seen with a vile curse.

Only a few days later, she found her mother hanging by her princess pink sari from the peepal tree in their courtyard. A ladder lay on the ground. Dilkhush could hear the slight creak of the branch and her father's heavy breathing as he came in and rushed to drag the charpoy under her mother. He stood the ladder against the branch and climbed up with a sickle.

He told Dilkhush later that her mother would be forgiven and guided by the gods in the peepal tree. Neighbouring villagers whispered around them for many months.

'That tortured woman! She cut off her soul completely from her family. God only knows what those wretched children did to deserve this.'

Little Dilkhush realised then that she must have done something for her mother cut off all ties between their souls. The village children teased her as the girl whose mother chose death over her. The peacock feather hair clip and gold encased broken mirror became Dilkhush's most precious possessions. They were valuable gifts from her mother. She showed them to others to prove how much her mother loved her. Many of the children didn't believe that and she ran fast from their name-calling.

Dilkhush woke up. Her heart was racing. Her hands were sweating. She looked around. The people living in Naseema Bi's old home hadn't returned yet. She tried hard to force the bad memory aside. She had happier ones too. Why couldn't those come through so vividly instead? Her thoughts had to be grabbed, wrangled, and directed.

Just then, a tune she hadn't heard in years played on someone's radio, and it softened her heart. It was her favourite song, *Baarish*. How deeply it expressed her feelings of being with Jiyaa. She hummed and sang along. Her voice was gentle, as if she was singing to her daughter.

Bheege ye pal saare sunke teri baatein
Bheege mere subh-o-shaam
Bheege ye pal saare
Pyaari ho ye raatein
Honton pe ho tera naam

As in the song, each sweet moment with her daughter felt like it had the fresh smell and wetness of rainfall. Seeing her play and hearing her little stories, every morning and evening was filled with the freshness of rain drizzle. How charming the nights were, with only her name on the lips.

Dilkhush closed her eyes and let herself go inside the song with longing. Her memories mingled in.

Jiyaa was swimming with Suresh in the lake, near their favourite picnic spot. As she looked on, Dilkhush's heart burst with joy at the life she had got. She had so much. Everywhere she turned, there was love, except when her Mother-in-law was around. Her own love for Jiyaa and her daughter's adoration sealed her life. She couldn't want any more from God. If they had a son as well, Suresh would be happy. A son to look after them in their old age, after Jiyaa got married and left home. Suresh was as much in love with Jiyaa as she was.

It sometimes scared Dilkhush that something would go wrong. How could she have so much happiness in her life? Jiyaa shouted out to her. 'I love you Mummy.' Dilkhush's whole body danced inside. Just then, her cherished song sounded in the background and as Dilkhush sang along, a light drizzle of rain started, as if the song itself had conjured that up. Soon, they were all dancing in the rain. Dilkhush picked Jiyaa and sang to her.

Halki si baarishein
Yunhi barasti rahegi

Betaabi chhaahat ki
Pyaasi tarasti rahegi

Dekho jugnuo ki
Raatein bhi jhilmilaati hain
Kyu na phir ham dono
Taaron mein ghar basaayein

Aur bus , bheege ye pal saare...

Dilkhush never wanted to let go of her daughter. 'How this light drizzle will continue, as will the thirst from this anxious yearning. Yet look at the fireflies, twinkling in the night as well. Why don't we also make a home in the stars together? Then these moments with the freshness of rainfall can be there too...'

She put Jiyaa down and together they collected water chestnuts and then ate with all their friends before going boating. Ashraf Mia's weight made everyone nervous. The boat wobbled as he climbed in and out, or stood up in the middle of the lake. But they spent an hour safely in the water. And then suddenly a massive wave came in the lake and overturned the boat.

None of them had expected it. How could it even happen? Dilkhush could barely swim and kept going under, but she kicked to get to the surface and search for her daughter. 'Jiyaa, Jiyaa.' She pulled her child to the shore and helped her spurt out water. Dilkhush hugged Jiyaa tight as she opened her eyes and smiled weakly. 'I love you, Mummy.'

Dilkhush came round with a start. Her breath was heavy. She reminded herself there had never been a wave in the lake that had crashed on them. Even her happy memories were getting tainted in her mind. Baarish was still playing on the radio. If only rain had also fallen on the gas night. Suresh told her the gas would have lost power against water. But there hadn't been a single drop anywhere to help them. She was left with her fate.

Dark thoughts about the happenings in recent weeks descended, as if she needed reminding that if she didn't end her life in Jantapur, she had no other place to go.

'For the sake of my future children, and the children of our village, kick this vile, haggard witch out,' Dilkhush's sister-in-law screamed, beating her chest and wailing from the roof terrace after another miscarriage. Her brown sari fluttered. 'That whore, Dilkhush, devoured her husband and daughter. What chance did they have by coming into her life? You all know better than me her vileness even as a mere girl.'

Some of the villagers murmured amongst themselves and tried to speak out. But the angry woman talked over them in a louder voice. 'Didn't her own tortured mother hang herself to cut off her soul from this wretch? God only knows what curses she has rained upon us by now. We have had droughts, our animals have died, and our children have become sick. Wasn't she a whore with a Dalit boy even before marriage? Now this orphan, Makodi, who runs our village errands, is also under her black spell. I lost a child again, a son, from the water that orphan brought me. It has to be because of Dilkhush's evil magic. If she stays, I will have to suffer another dead child. Beware of who you are harbouring here all these years. You will suffer as I have.'

Dilkhush had kept quiet through the years, but now her sister-in-law was blackening the orphan's name because of her. This was the third severe accusation she had made against the innocent girl, and no one had the courage to stop her. The allegations could ruin Makodi's life. No one would take her as a wife when the time came. The snake inside Dilkhush stirred. She spat out at her sister-in-law. 'If I had such powers, would I be living in your cattle pen? Instead of hollering blame at me and this orphan about your lifeless womb, thank God that He doesn't want to burden a newborn with your razor tongue.'

Dilkhush realised then that she had lost all mending chances with her brother, but she still pleaded with him to let her stay. No villager sheltered her either. She had tilled their parched land, washed their pots, ground their millet, and cleaned their huts. In whatever manner they had treated her, she had accepted. But her brother and his wife were the moneylenders. As Dilkhush left the village, the orphan ran after her.

'Please, let me come,' Makodi said. 'I have no one else. I want to be with you. I can't say that in front of the villagers, or your sister-in-law. Otherwise they will laugh and taunt if you don't take me.'

Dilkhush looked into the girl's black eyes and shook her head. 'Take my work from them, Makodi. These villagers will take your labour for free. Without me casting a shadow over you, one of them may give you a sari when it is time. Maybe even arrange your marriage. I can't give you any of that.'

'But you like me.' Makodi stared at her. 'You care for me.'

'That is why I can't jeopardise your future.' Dilkhush hugged the girl. 'God willing, maybe one day we'll meet again.'

Makodi held out two opium pellets. She had stolen them for Dilkhush from her work with the poppy grower. The pellets helped with heartache. Everyone knew that. Makodi slipped her hand into Dilkhush's. They walked together to the village outskirts.

For the next few days and nights, Dilkhush slept under bushes and stole from the snack dhabas by the roadside. When she reached the nearest town, her soles were blistered and bleeding. The priest she knew at the Hanuman temple shook his head. 'You couldn't have listened to me and left by yourself? You had to wait to get kicked out. That viper inside has shown how it can ruin you.' He lectured her again as usual. The same chastising. 'You claim you want to reunite with your daughter, but you don't do what is needed. It seems you will die without changing anything for her or your soul.'

Dilkhush didn't tell him what she thought. Forgiveness and resolution were only words to him. Other people's acts had caused her daughter's death yet it was she who had to prostrate and make amends. What kind of justice was that? One evening, Dilkhush left the temple. She slept on a train platform for several days, alongside vagrants, thieves, and beggars. But they were suspicious of her.

One beggar, who wore plastic bags on her feet, accused everyone of stealing her clients, so Dilkhush sat far away to avoid taking anyone else's share. When she became a familiar figure, she sat on the platform with the others amidst passing trains and flickering lights. She listened as they told each other stories, laughing, complaining. They were like a family of strangers. Most days they built a small fire and boiled water from the station tap, adding onionskins or garlic leaves and millet flour.

Dilkhush realised she had become the person she used to look at with pity. She couldn't have brought Makodi there, with no real place to sleep, relying on the scraps of passers-by forever. She had lost everything. Memories about her old days in Jantapur and even the village seemed unreal. She found it difficult to resign herself to her new life, yet had little else to go to. Early one morning, she was still laying on the platform when, out of nowhere, she felt a sharp kick from behind.

'Eh, get up.' A policeman was moving everyone from the station. 'Get your things and move out. The minister is coming.'

Dilkhush had become used to the kicks from some of the village women, but the policeman doing it felt worse. Her viper hissed. She moved away from the policeman. 'So what if the minister is coming?' she shouted. 'What have we done to you or him that we should move?'

'Talking back? You better get out of my sight right now, before I lose my temper.'

'You think I would stay here if I had somewhere else to live?'

'Making everyone else responsible for your own karma. Shame on you.'

'Shame on me?' she shouted. 'Shame on you! It is you who pretends you are protecting the country, but treating us like pigs. What disgusting putrid insides you must have that even your outsides that try to disguise it are abhorrent.'

'Bastard bitch.' The policeman lifted his baton. 'Get away from here.'

Dilkhush spat at him. Suddenly, the policeman's eyes changed and he raised his baton. For a moment she thought he was only threatening her. She flinched and was about to move away. He brought down his baton hard on her arm. After that, it was as if a wild animal inside him had been unleashed.

He beat her repeatedly across every part of her body until he was sweating. 'Think because you have these full breasts you can behave badly? Lucky for you that all I am doing with this baton is hitting you.' He wiped his forehead before restarting the beating, but his baton snapped. 'Don't ever insult me again, understand? You RESPECT me!' He shouted to another policeman. 'Get someone to jail her before the minister comes.'

Dilkhush's eyes swelled up. She kept them closed and as the policeman left, he kicked her in the stomach. She let her body go limp. She hurt all over and wondered whether she would die. She imagined seeing Jiyaa in the sky. Instead, the beggar woman with the plastic bag shoes returned and found her. With the help of others, she moved Dilkhush to crouch between a wall and the back of a toy stall for days. None of them saw any minister visiting the station.

Over the next few days, Dilkhush barely managed to hobble to and from the station latrine, sometimes falling, and lying there until someone saw her. The beggar woman brought her water, slippers, rotten tomatoes, and cooked rats. Dilkhush managed to suck the vegetable juices slowly through puckered lips, but refused the rat meat.

'Look at how the starving get fussy nowadays,' the beggar woman said as she ripped pieces of meat from the small bones. Another beggar dragged himself over and picked the bones she had thrown away. He broke each and sucked whatever was left inside. 'If I had cooked this, I would have added cumin,' he said.

'Yes, you should be cooking for the prime minister, isn't it?' the beggar woman said. 'Cumin, my foot.'

Several weeks later, Dilkhush saw the policeman again. He was laughing and eating at a stall on the platform. A boy ran to get tea for him. Passengers came off the train and asked questions. He helped with an air of authority. Dilkhush went to the nearest women's police station to report what had happened with her. A woman would understand better.

She relayed the incident. The policewoman was reading a newspaper and looked up for a moment before turning her attention back to the paper. 'No bruises, and you want to report an attack by a policeman? If we spend our time with such fantasies how will we ever catch real criminals?'

Dilkhush lifted her sari to show her bruises, but not many were left. She should have come when the wounds were raw, but she could barely walk then. She was about to lash out when the policewoman's newspaper caught her eyes. She reached across and snatched it. A part of it ripped. Dilkhush ran out with it and kept running as fast as her body would allow. When the policewoman's whistle blows were out of earshot, she hid and read the article that had caught her eye. Although part of it was torn, she could make out enough.

'...all in charge at time of Jantapur gas deaths attend 30th anniversary'. The date for that was coming up soon. There were photos of people Dilkhush didn't recognise. There was also a photo of the reaction from people in Jantapur. It was that picture that had caught her attention. She recognised Kashif immediately. The image was blurred, but she knew it was him. She was sure, even if a scarf was tied over his nose and mouth. She recognised his eyes and that hardened and haunted look in them. It was exactly the way she felt as well. Dilkhush held the paper so tightly the ink smudged on her fingers.

On the same page was another headline and photo. It was of foreign soldiers standing over a man they had shot.

'#GOTCHA: TERRORIST SHOT BY OUR HEROES.'

The article started with joyous news about the world's

most dangerous man being shot dead. He seemed to have caused thousands of deaths. The lengthy revenge mission to find and destroy him was outlined. Dilkhush realised it meant there was hope for her and Kashif. Towards the end of the article was something from the Holy Geeta. 'Krishna told Arjun to destroy evil, even if they are your flesh and blood. You should never be a coward!'

Dilkhush did not bother to read further. If the Holy Geeta included words about equilibrium, as the priest said, it also seemed to include words about destroying evil. Those who knew more, who had better means, understood the role of revenge. Forgiveness wasn't the only route.

That this was on the same page as the Jantapur article had to be a sign. Those in charge during the gas deaths would attend the thirtieth anniversary. And Kashif was there. The newspaper was proof that God was giving her permission and aligning things. The soldiers had big guns, but that didn't matter. They had shown her revenge was acceptable, instead of forgiveness. And she was thankful for that.

Dilkhush folded the torn page carefully into her cloth bundle. Later that day, she went to show her family of strangers at the train platform. She didn't want them to feel she was abandoning them after their help. All she was doing was planning to avenge Jiyaa to gain peace and resolution, to be with her daughter's soul.

But at the platform, she discovered that a group of policemen had rounded up everyone who lived there, then beaten them and put them in jail. An old beggar who hid in the latrine came out. He told Dilkhush it was she who had brought them trouble by making a report. The police had initially come to look for her.

Dilkhush waited there for two days, but none of the beggars returned. Everyone had dispersed because of the police threats. She slumped down the outside wall of a house by the station, but their security guard came to move her along. At the ticket office, she saw there was a bus to Jantapur the following day. She made a plan to get money for the ticket.

The priest squinted at her. 'And what has brought about this change of mind? I have been telling you to go back for years, yet now you realise.'

'I was wrong. You have always been right. I could have lived all this time with the relief of forgiveness. I could have taken that chance to be with my daughter already.' Dilkhush feared if she didn't make it to Jantapur soon, Kashif could avenge his family and leave. She may never see him again. 'If you can lend me some money, I will go directly to Jiyaa's grave to give and get forgiveness, like you said.' She was lying about that, and also about the amount she needed for the bus. The priest stopped another temple-goer and double-checked the bus fare before giving Dilkhush only enough money to reach Jantapur.

That night she stole an empty plastic container from a young boy who sold used bottles to travellers. At a nearby water pump, Dilkhush filled the container and washed herself under a bush, still with her sari on. She slid a neem leaf between the cloth and her body to remove the *dirt that had collected on her skin.*

Dilkhush averted her eyes from shadows passing by. As she dribbled water over her hair, a rickshaw put-putted past and someone whistled. She squatted to hide. Afterwards, at the back of the platform she peeled off her dirty, wet sari and wrapped the dry one around. She had to stop thinking about the friends she had lost at the train platform. There was no family of strangers left there. She had a chance of finding Kashif and being with the souls of her real family again. Dilkhush got ready to return to Jantapur.

A whining sound woke her with a start. She felt disorientated and looked around. It was almost dark. She was shivering. Dilkhush tried to remember where she was and realised she must have been waiting outside Naseema Bi's old house for hours. It was darker now. The ground was cold and her body ached. She got up and stretched, and then realised the whining sounds that woke her were the sirens signalling the end of the day at the factories in the town.

Soon the neighbourhood would become busier as people returned home from work. The new owners should be back soon. She stood for what seemed like a long time, but felt exhausted and sat down again. Dilkhush closed her eyes and promised herself it would only be for a few moments.

All of a sudden, something jabbed at her thigh.

'What?' a voice above her said. 'What is that?'

Something feathery brushed Dilkhush's face, and

a hard prod followed. It felt like someone's foot. She rubbed her eyes. For a moment, she thought another policeman was about to beat her, so she swung her arm out, but didn't catch anything. Dilkhush tried to refocus her eyes in the dim light. She got another jab on the thigh, and tried to get hold of the foot. When she looked up and strained harder, her heart almost jumped. She reached out again and grabbed the foot, which was pulling back to kick again.

Dilkhush didn't want it to end, whatever it was, a dream, a fantasy, or reality. She wanted a last chance to make up somehow. Was this real? It had come from nowhere. She looked up again, and her eyes softened.

The foot she was holding belonged to a very old wrinkled Naseema Bi.

'Who's that?' the old owl asked. She pulled her leg back from Dilkhush's hands. 'Come on, speak up before I call my next door burly goonda.'

Dilkhush didn't want to break the spell, and smiled. It would be just like the old owl to pretend the skeletal neighbour was her burly goonda. She wanted to call Naseema Bi's bluff.

11

Old and Wretched be
Your Enemies

'COME ON, SPEAK up, whoever you are,' the old owl said. 'What are you doing outside my house?' The owl paused for a moment. 'I am not some aged woman living alone that you can come and scare me. 'Eh, burly goonda,' she shouted towards her neighbour's house. 'Come and help me with this intruder.'

Her neighbour's door opened and the skeletal man Dilkhush had seen before came out.

'What is it, old owl?' The neighbour looked at Dilkhush. 'I saw this woman, but left her. She seemed like one of your rescues.'

It was truly the old owl. She wasn't dead. Dilkhush's heartbeat raced. What if this was one of her illusions, like those she had tried with her daughter? It didn't matter. She would eke out as much joy as she could from this encounter. After all, how much time had she given Naseema Bi even in her own mind?

The old owl had aged badly, not like she would have

in a good dream. She was lurching bow-legged with her left foot dragging slightly behind her. A few coriander stalks were in one hand and a long radish in the other. She was wearing the same flowery green salwar kameez Dilkhush had stitched for her during their first Eid celebrations together. There were several patches on it now. Without warning, Dilkhush jumped forward and put her arms around the old owl.

'Naseeeeema Biiiii.' She could smell the old owl's sweat, but didn't mind even a little. She quickly touched the owl's feet and then buried her face in the crook of the old woman's neck. 'My dearest, dearest old owl. Tell me I'm not dreaming. Tell me you're alive and well. I knew you wouldn't leave me alone to suffer. You are here, my very own, my dearest old owl.'

'Arey, who is this?' Naseema Bi asked, half-laughing. 'Of course, I am here and alive. I have been alive since I left this morning. Nothing has changed.'

Dilkhush saw that many of the old owl's teeth had fallen out and one of her grey eyes had clouded over completely. She stepped back. 'It's me, Naseema Bi.' In a split moment, the old owl adjusted her grey eyes to see better. Dilkhush thought she caught a distant flicker of sorrow. Almost immediately, smiles broke out on both their faces.

Naseema Bi shouted, 'Ya Allah, ya Mollah, you? You are here? My Dilkhush? My daughter, my life, long-lost, beloved piece of my heart, sliver of my moon. Is this a miracle I am seeing, or have you finally come after all these years? I knew you wouldn't have forgotten me.

I am your mother, after all. God listened to my prayers. May Allah bless you with all the happiness you deserve.'

She held Dilkhush's chin. 'How the years have tried to age you, but see how your loveliness has resisted.' The old owl pulled her closer. 'But you have become so thin. And your eyes have still not regained any life.' She looked around. 'You are not married again? You haven't brought a husband or any children?'

Dilkhush shook her head. Hadn't the old owl seen her white sari? 'Of course not.' There was a moment of silence.

Naseema Bi shook her head and smiled. 'What a time you have come at, so exactly and precisely, you won't believe. God works his miracles in mysterious ways, I tell you. Come, come. Let us sit inside. I will explain everything.' She looked at Dilkhush. 'Still you are the film beauty I remember.'

'That's absurd, Naseema Bi.' Dilkhush hadn't looked at herself in a mirror in a long while, but she knew it was only the old owl's loving eyes that still made her seem beautiful. 'I am old and wretched.'

'Old and wretched be your enemies,' the owl said.

Dilkhush's eyes became tinged with wetness. She hated herself for not visiting her daughter's grave, yet dropping tears here. She was indulging herself in the old owl's failing eyes. 'Oh my Naseema Bi, I have missed you. I don't know why for all these years I punished myself by not coming back to you. Will you forgive me? I was convinced I had lost all chances.' She pinched the old owl's arm.

'Ouch, what are you doing?'

'Sorry Naseema Bi. At the clinic, your photo was with the rest of the dead. You even looked dead. I want to make sure—'

'My photo is with the dead again?' Naseema Bi laughed. 'That Jaadu girl! I will beat her. She wants people to think I am a ghost, haunting them when they see me. Such tricks she plays with me. Wait till I see her. This time she will get a proper scolding. Imagine, you could have believed it and left the town without finding me here. It is my good luck that you refused to accept it and waited for me.'

'What else do I have left than to come and see you? And my peepal tree is still here. I came to...' Dilkhush stopped herself. She took a step back. 'I found it too difficult to accept that you had died.'

'Exactly. So you came here to check. See, people have to think like you.' Naseema Bi shook her head. 'But others might not. Now, since when are things exact? Sick people are assumed well, alive people never to have lived. And now with Jaadu's tricks, treated patients are presumed dead. You and I know that is not true now, don't we? Believe me, God has not decided to call me yet.'

Dilkhush hugged the old owl and then hesitated. 'Naseema Bi, there was also a photo of Omera. She had grown into a young woman. Was that a mistake as well?'

'Omera?' The old owl smiled. 'Our Omera? Remember how you first discovered that name for her? You were such a genius. Now, that name has become very common. Who would not like to be named Omera - one who inspires others?'

'So the photo wasn't of our Omera? Kashif and Simran's Omera?'

'Which photo?'

'At the clinic. A young woman's picture, staring back.'

'I don't know which photo. But our Omera—' Naseema Bi held Dilkhush's arm. 'Don't you remember? You said you saw her. On the funeral pyre.'

Dilkhush nodded. But she wasn't sure any more. What about the photo she had seen in the clinic? If she had made a mistake, she would have to bear Kashif's wrath for keeping them apart.

'I also miss Omera and Jiyaa,' Naseema Bi said. 'And Suresh, Simran, and Kashif. And your Ashraf Mia. You aren't even dead and I missed you.' She laughed. 'So I can understand that everywhere you look, you see them. In every photo.'

Dilkhush let Naseema Bi carry on talking. She wanted to blurt out her plan to find Kashif. Something niggled inside and stopped her, but she wasn't quite sure what. For some reason her revenge plan did not have the same intensity and certainty as before. Perhaps it wasn't Kashif in the newspaper photo either. She had suddenly lost all sense of urgency. She could make up to Naseema Bi at least, to help towards her resolution. The old owl was still talking away. Dilkhush noticed a black mark at the corner of the owl's mouth. She held one end of her sari to wipe it, but it didn't come off.

'No, don't worry. It's nothing,' Naseema Bi said.

'I fell down. This is just a mark from that. These idiot eyes can't see very clearly now, and something must have got stuck inside when I hit the ground. You don't worry.' She continued to chatter. It was as if the years between them had never been lost. 'I think about you every day,' the old owl said. 'I pray that away from my eyes you have not died. And you haven't, but who knows what plans Allah has for all of us. And now, here you are, piece of my moon. You must stay here with me. You are not in some hotel-botel are you?'

Dilkhush shook her head. 'I want to stay right here with you, my old owl.'

They hadn't even gone inside the flat when Naseema Bi shouted towards a nearby alleyway. 'Eh conman. I have an important task for you.' She turned to Dilkhush. 'This is fate. I tell you, this is fate. I will arrange this work for you. It will be so magical.'

Dilkhush was disappointed the old owl already wanted to see less of her by arranging work so soon. But she understood Naseema Bi was only trying to help. Everyone needed money. And it would also help pay towards food for both of them. She still needed to find Kashif somewhere, whether or not he was in Jantapur, whether or not it was him in the newspaper photo. Money for bribes would be useful.

And if those in charge came for the thirtieth anniversary, her plan was still possible, only without Kashif's help perhaps. She only knew he was alive the last time she saw him. That was still something.

'What important task do you have for me?' a familiar

voice asked from the alley.

Footsteps ran towards them. Dilkhush turned around to find Dalya, MBBS. 'You?' she blurted out.

'Arey *vah*, Heroine,' he said. 'You have been following me all this time, hehn?'

She frowned.

'Stop wasting time,' Naseema Bi said to him. 'Run and arrange an interview time for that job at Volog Colony for my lovely daughter.'

'Oho, your daughter? Where from, heaven? I haven't seen her all these years, this secretive daughter who—'

'Go quickly now,' the old owl said. 'And listen, I don't want anyone else to get that work, you hear? Tell them she cooks world-class food.'

'Naseema Bi,' Dilkhush said. 'I don't know if I—'

'What, my moonbeam? Don't be shy. You cooked for all of us, yes? And we all said how it was so tasty. Better than any restaurant. Now between all of us, twelve, fourteen people, we have eaten in so many places. And still, yours was the best food. You have to show people like that. If you say you cook at home only, they don't understand the true meaning.' She turned to Dalya. 'Run. And make sure you get an interview for tomorrow only, before anyone else gets there. And listen, that extra *razai* I gave your mother to keep for your future wife, I need it back.'

Dalya argued about him being the owner of the razai now. He wanted to agree a fee with Naseema Bi. 'My mother could find a wife for me any time, and then we will need it.' When he discovered it was for Dilkhush to sleep on, he gave a lopsided smile. 'For the heroine? Then you can have it for free. No charge. The razai was for my wife, after all.'

Dilkhush thought he was showing too much familiarity because of their earlier meeting at the job junction. She should stop his insolence, but she liked his spirit and didn't want to break it. She had upset him earlier already.

Dalya held his hand out to Naseema Bi. 'Money for this errand at least.'

'I'll give you one tight slap. That's what I'll give you,' the old owl said. 'Telling me that you are lending me my own razai back for free and asking for money before you have done anything. Bring that razai and get the interview. Then we'll talk.'

Dalya ran off mumbling. 'Yes, yes, give me a slap. Such treatment I take from all these town people, taking advantage of my useless backside because I will do any job for money.'

Naseema Bi turned to Dilkhush. 'Now, don't take the wrong meaning. I don't want to hurry you into work, my moonbeam. But trust me when I say it is a miracle that you have been brought here at this precise moment.'

'What do you mean?' Dilkhush asked.

'From all the possible times in all the years, how could such a coincidence happen that you have come now, unless it is truly by God's will? It is a sign. You will think all your prayers have been answered. Truly. There is such a very special reason waiting for you here in Jantapur. You must get that job. I promise you that suddenly your soul will dance. You will start living your name and have joy in your heart all the time.' Naseema Bi fumbled with the keys that were tied to the end of her scarf. She grunted as she put some pressure to unlock the padlock.

Dilkhush entered the courtyard behind the old owl. Her final memories there flooded into her mind and she had to struggle to fight them off.

12

A Boy came to View for Marriage

DILKHUSH NOTICED THAT the courtyard was not how she had seen it through the crack. There were no newspapers or pieces of rags strewn around. Her eyes fell on the peacock mural she had painted on the far wall of the courtyard for her first Diwali in the house. Simran had helped her. They were such close friends that Dilkhush thought they would never part. The paint around the peacock was flaking now and the wall surface was crumbling, but the peacock itself looked like it had been recently painted.

'I tell the girls to prepare the mural for Diwali every year,' Naseema Bi said. 'Just like you and Simran did.'

'The girls?'

'I didn't say? I have nine others sharing the house.'

Dilkhush remained quiet. She had hoped they would be alone.

'It is not possible for an old woman like me to manage otherwise,' Naseema Bi said. 'You don't mind, do you? I was so lonely. Some of these girls lived around the neighbourhood at the time of the leak, and they lost parents, husbands or children. Some were born long after the gas, and lost their parents to gas sickness. Their own bodies are defective; they can't have children, so no marriage. They were young with no one to care for them.'

'They needed someone,' Dilkhush said. 'It was kind of you to take them in. You did that for us as well.'

'So you understand, don't you? I needed someone.'

Dilkhush looked apologetically at the old owl, but neither said anything about her leaving Naseema Bi.

'Over the years, I collected these girls in the house. One by one. It's true that we are so full now. But how can I turn anyone away? What do we care for crowding and comfort when we are with loved ones, isn't it? You will stay, won't you?'

Dilkhush stared at the peepal tree in the courtyard. It was so big now.

'Please say you'll stay,' the old owl said. 'And I promise, this job I found for you will change everything. You won't believe at what a moment you are coming, my daughter. Time-to-time, exactly and precisely. You must have such grace from Allah that he sent you back now only. Another time and the same gift would not have been waiting for you. What a memorial you must have built to create this lifewalla chance. We must get some sweets to celebrate.'

'What lifewalla chance? I don't understand.'

'Not yet, because you haven't seen this chance that will give your life that oomph. Oh, my moonbeam, joy and only joy will be in your heart soon.'

Dilkhush didn't believe it. There had been little joy in thirty years. How was that to change? And Naseema Bi seemed so excited Dilkhush didn't want to reveal she hadn't built a memorial of any sort. 'What is it about this job that will suddenly make me feel alive?'

'Sit, sit.' Naseema Bi shuffled around the courtyard. 'Let me tell you.' She picked up a saucepan in one hand and a paper bag of tea leaves in the other. 'Only a few days ago, I was thinking about you. The job is temporary, looking after a bilayati family who are visiting Jantapur. They are here especially for the thirtieth anniversary events. They have already been here a few weeks and you missed all that time. But you still have some left. You will see. When you start working there, you will be your happy-laughing self again.'

'Here, let me do that.' Dilkhush took over making the tea from Naseema Bi. She poured water from an earthen pot into the saucepan and lit the fire. After the tealeaves, she added sugar and cloves, black pepper, cinnamon, and bay leaves to the water. She put extra cardamom in, the way Naseema Bi used to like it, and waited for the tea to boil.

'Their flat is not so far, these bilayati people.' Naseema Bi crossed her legs. 'You know that new pink and white complex near Bharat Bhavan, called Volog Complex? Oh...' She slapped her forehead, which made a loud sound. 'How can you know? These are new homes across the bridge gates, with sitting toilet and sleeping bath. These people who stay there have so much money, they don't need to stand or walk for anything. I went myself for the job, but I had zero luck.' Naseema Bi clicked her tongue. 'It was good money, so naturally I knew I would fail.'

When the tea started to come to a boil, Dilkhush added milk from a plastic bag that the old owl handed to her.

'But now I know why I didn't get it,' the owl said. 'That job is for you only, my moonbeam. Even if I had got it, the minute you came, I would have given it to you. Only two things to remember. They didn't like the fact that I have lived here all my life, and...do you still have your cough?'

Dilkhush nodded. Why didn't these bilayati people like those who had lived their whole lives in Jantapur?

'Just swallow any coughs until these people become dependent on you,' Naseema Bi said. 'Then they will accept it. It's for a short time only, but if they like you, who knows? They can take you back to bilayat with them.'

Dilkhush didn't say anything. She had no intention of going anywhere yet. She had the chance to make up for leaving the old owl. Naseema Bi had confirmed the girl in the photo was not Omera, so there was no extra burden on her karma. She might be able to do enough for the old owl to gain resolution and reunite with Jiyaa.

'But there is more special news.' Naseema Bi grinned. 'Come, come, let the tea simmer.' She gestured for Dilkhush to sit on the charpoy. 'Let me tell you all the tricks you need to know.'

Dilkhush massaged the old owl's swollen ankles. 'You are chattering about it, but I don't know why it should be so special for me to work for them.' Hadn't they learned that no one should be worshipped and trusted mindlessly?

'I have no Inglis,' Naseema Bi said. 'But you, with your teacher job, can impress them. And don't think, "Why should I do a servant's job when I am a teacher?" First see why I am sending you there. Remember, in life things can go up and down. Sometimes what seems like lowly work comes for a reason.'

Dilkhush got up and blew on the tea to stop the skin forming. In spite of how she had lived in the village, she felt ashamed of taking servant work in Jantapur. She used to teach in that town, even if it was only under the banyan tree outside their home, and all for free to street orphans. 'Maybe I can find some teaching work here, Naseema Bi, or sewing. I can—'

'No, you don't understand. Listen to me. The best thing about this job is...' Naseema Bi stopped speaking. 'Are you listening?'

Dilkhush turned to her. 'Yes, yes. You are saying, "listen to me, the best thing..."'

'You are only repeating the last words I said. I am not going to tell you what the best thing is if you don't listen.'

'Okay, okay, I am listening, Baba. See?' Dilkhush already felt her load get lighter in the few moments she had spent with Naseema Bi. She pushed her ears forward, as if to capture every word the owl said.

'Stop that, you rascal.' The old owl pinched her

cheek. 'You think it's a game, but no. The best thing is what this family has, and I found out because I saw it with my own eyes, however faulty they are.' She paused. 'There are four generations of them—'

'Lucky for them.' Dilkhush said, irritated. 'It would be special if I had four generations in my family too, but there is only me. And I count for nothing.'

'I can be your surrogate mother,' Naseema Bi said. 'Then we have two generations. Some of my girls would be Jiyaa's age now. Three generations. If even one of them had a child, maybe adopted also, we can have four generations ourselves. It is more possible that way than for me to find a surrogate parent.' She clapped her hands. 'My joke. Anyway, the special news I want to give you is not actually about their four generations.'

Dilkhush strained the tea and changed the subject to the old days. The old owl didn't wait for the tea to cool down. Instead, she took a saucer, dribbled a little tea into it and slurped from there. Afterwards, as they talked, Naseema Bi brought musk from her room and dabbed it behind both their ears. 'I am not one of those who believes that after your husband dies, your life is finished. Why should that be? No sweets for widows, no colours, no perfume, no smiling. What nonsense. We all come alone and go alone, husband or no husband.' She started to comb her own hair.

Dilkhush took the comb from her and slid it slowly down the old owl's thinning strands. 'Now I am here, you don't have to strain to do anything.'

Dalya returned with a razai rolled under his arm. He

was out of breath. Naseema Bi gave it to Dilkhush to sleep on later. He also brought a permit. 'Here Heroine. With this you can cross the bridge to the rich area at the time it says. You have to be at the bilayati family's home at twelve midday sharp. They won't hire anyone who is late. And they like eating this chis-bis-burga-shurga, so you have to know how to make that.'

Dilkhush froze. Chis-bis-burga-shurga? The job had to be the same one the gangly recruiter was shouting about at the job junction. Dilkhush had screamed at him, certain it had been a dangerous factory job. Now Naseema Bi was saying it was a servant job for a bilayati family. What was the heavy lifting then? What was this chis-bis-burga-shurga? That gangly recruiter was sure to remember her. He wouldn't give her a second chance after the way she had attacked him. She was glad Dalya hadn't seen her shouting at the man that morning.

'Dalya, find out what is this chis-bis-burga-shurga from these people in hotels,' Naseema Bi said. 'They must know. I'll give you five paisa afterward.'

'Five paisa?' Dalya frowned. 'What a feast I will eat with that!'

The old owl mocked threatened Dalya with a slap. 'You raggedy-waggedy tail of a stray dog. Only one question you have to ask the hotels. "What is chis-bis-burga-shurga?" That's it. And still you are complaining. At least I am giving you work and money. Shall I call another boy, hehn? How will you feed your poor mother then?'

'No, no,' Dalya said, hurriedly stretching out and prostrating at Naseema Bi's feet. He looked up at

Dilkhush and winked, soon turning back to the old owl. 'Don't shower all your riches on anyone else. Only me. How else will I build my kingdom for the heroine wife that I want? I will go and come back like lightning with answers.' He got up and shook his head. 'Why don't these people like keema-dhal-pava-kachori? That's more straightforward. Chis-bis-burga-shurga!'

'But if life is straightforward...' Naseema Bi started a singsong.

The boy joined in and completed her line. 'If life is straightforward...then how will Dalya make money?' They both laughed as he ran off.

'Call him back, please,' Dilkhush said. 'They won't give me that job. I have done something. I don't want a job with bilayati anyway. I will find something else.'

'You don't worry,' Naseema Bi said. 'I know it sounds like a big job with bilayatis, so you're nervous. But put your faith in me. This job is the very reason you are back here in Jantapur at this moment. Believe me. I don't want to ruin it by telling you why yet. But you will know when you get it.'

Dilkhush felt uneasy as they chatted. The recruiter would take one look at her and kick her out. She didn't know what Naseema Bi meant by this job being the very reason she was back. The old owl didn't know about her dark plans of revenge that had driven her to return. She tried to keep her mind on what the old owl was saying and answered her questions, sometimes honestly. Most times she lied because she was ashamed.

The moon seemed brighter in the sky when Dilkhush

heard the metal latch of the main wooden door click. A few girls and women, some in their late teenage years, others in their twenties and thirties, trickled in through the wooden door, in ones and twos, each holding an item of food and herbs.

One girl, who had wrapped a shawl around her neck three or four times, held out a packet. 'Biskuut today, Naseema Bi.'

'Oh Shaila, very good. Give me one just now. I can dunk it in whatever tea is left.'

Shaila opened the packet and Naseema Bi took a biscuit. 'Mmmmm.' She dipped it into the tea that was left in the saucepan, but the biscuit broke in half.

'Rascal,' Naseema Bi said to the biscuit. 'Wait there. I'll get you later.'

Shaila offered Dilkhush one too.

'Yes, yes, take one,' the old owl said. 'You need it after such a long journey.' But Dilkhush didn't have anything to give in return, so she shook her head.

Another woman came in, bringing an animal leg in her hand. 'Hit the lottery today,' she said. 'A group of bilayatis from the Palace Hotel came for a massage and each gave me five hundred rupees on top of the massage price.' She smiled, showing her buckteeth.

'Why?' Naseema Bi asked. 'Did you give them some special treatment to get such big tips, hehn? I told you to be careful of such generosity, didn't I?' She turned to all the girls. 'I want you to always be vigilant. Whether girls are looking good or not, what men want is not on your face. Even a little shoulder can excite a man who has not seen a woman's body. When they give you big tips—'

'Oh, don't worry, Naseema Bi,' the masseuse said. 'I didn't do anything wrong. Only rubbed the bottle of oil in front of them and that...that...that...uh...seemed enough.' She breathed heavily and then squealed with laughter. The other girls joined in.

Shaila covered her mouth with one end of her shawl as if in shock. Two girls exchanged glances and giggled.

'But I know that's not the only reason I got the tips. Those were for looking the other way when their milk ran over their lingums and they were trying to hide themselves. The trick is to let them know you have seen something and turn away only slightly.'

'Oh, you're so baaaad.' The girls squealed.

Naseema Bi shook her head. 'You filthy, filthy girls. I should sew up your mouths and make sure you cover yourselves completely. In my day—'

'Yes, yes, in your day, no one had sex, of course,' the masseuse said. She pretended to pull a veil across her face and then hurried to cover between her legs as well. 'In your day, Naseema Bi, you all came from God's gaze only, didn't you. Emasculate contraption.' The girls laughed and teased Naseema Bi.

'Such insolence.' The old owl picked up a sweeper and began to swing it at the girls without really trying to touch them. They all ran around dodging her and giggling. 'You're lucky,' the old owl said. 'I am so good to you. You can't speak like that forever, you know. Wait until your husbands hear such talk.'

Dilkhush felt even more like an outsider now, watching

the girls with the owl. She was surprised Naseema Bi was not strict with them. But she remembered how playful they had both been together, how they had also exchanged wicked jokes, how Naseema Bi used to hold her hair out over incense smoke for her nights out with Suresh. She may do it with these girls now. Her own hair didn't need that any more. It was so rough as well. As a widow, she couldn't wear it loose, and wore it pinned into a small bun.

Dilkhush followed the masseuse with her eyes, listening to her scoff about husbands, before disappearing into the larger bedroom.

That used to be her room, where she lived with her small family. It didn't seem so long ago. The other girls followed the masseuse inside. Dilkhush felt there was something about the girl. She peered into the room and saw some of their reflections in the mirror on the wall.

She remembered standing in front of that mirror herself and straightening her tilak, putting on her sari, checking it was even at the bottom. The girls stretched their legs, took off their earrings, and changed into their salwar kameezes, a sweep of red, green, cream, blue, pink. A few of the girls smiled at her as they came out into the courtyard, but mostly they chatted amongst themselves.

'Dilkhush is from here only,' Naseema Bi said to them. 'Come and talk to her. Don't you think she looks like a proper film heroine? Like that Sharmila Tagore? You will have plenty of time to get to know her. She is staying with us for a while, aren't you, my moonbeam?

Her brother and sister-in-law will want her back with them soon, but we will try to keep her here for a while. She has come after so long.'

Dilkhush felt embarrassed, but was grateful to be amongst all the girls and women. She wondered how long Naseema Bi would let her stay.

'Sharmila Tagore?' A dark girl looked over. 'It's true. You look just like her. Only you are thinner.'

'Everyone wants to be thin,' Naseema Bi said. 'We wanted to be fat remember, Dilkhush? To show we could buy rich food.'

The dark girl hurried towards Dilkhush. 'An ageing, thin heroine living with us. I feel famous just sitting next to you.'

'I am not a heroine.'

'My name is Preeti,' the girl said. She had a wide nose, two missing teeth, a receding chin, and a harelip.

Dilkhush knew Preeti meant joy in Hindi, but she couldn't help saying, 'You know, in English your name means beautiful.' She regretted saying that immediately because she thought the girl unattractive. But still so innocently heart-warming.

'Beautiful?' Preeti's laughter was loud. 'You see? That proves I was never meant to be born English. No one would have given me that name then. Just look at my face.' She asked Dilkhush in full speed about where she was from, how long it took for her to get to Jantapur, and whether she had been anywhere else. 'I want to go to Bombay one day. Have you been to Bombay? I want to meet Preeti Zinta, the real beauty with that name.

I know I can't be in films with a hero. But you think I can be with a villain?'

She looked at Naseema Bi. 'Your guest is so shy. No stories, no jokes. Very serious. No chattiness. I will make her less shy. She will have a lot of thoughts then and will be able to say a lot more to join in with us.'

'Preeti,' the old owl said. 'Silly girl. The less a person says, the more thoughts are going around in their heads. Haven't you learned anything from me? Empty vessels make the most noise, like you.'

Preeti laughed. 'True, Naseema Bi, true. But even in an empty vessel, you need at least one thing that can make noise. I must have at least one thought.'

The other girls laughed. 'Yes, going to Bombay and meeting Preeti Zinta is your one thought all the time,' one of the girls said. The others giggled.

'Technically, that is two thoughts.' Preeti laughed. 'But you have to dream.' She started to dance with a veil around her face and hum a tune.

The door opened again and immediately the girls chorused. 'Ehhhh, Jaadu's back.'

Dilkhush recognised the girl from the clinic. The small boy from there was struggling to push the makeshift wheelchair again.

'I'm home!' Jaadu said.

Behind the small boy was a young man, who helped him push the wheelchair. They both waved goodbye to the girls.

Naseema Bi turned to Dilkhush. 'Here, this is our Jaadu, clever girl in the clinic. She invented that wheelchair. Now, so many people in the town have it. No need to wait for expensive foreign ones. She wanted everyone who came to the clinic to see how she gets by if there isn't enough money for the real thing. Poor girl. She thinks it makes a point, for people to see that the world quickly gets used to blotches like us. But I told her, no one thinks like that. They see what a sorry sight she is, but what a clever chair. Then they go and have their soda.'

Naseema Bi looked over at the girl. 'Arey, Jaadu, my miracle girl. Come and meet my daughter. I haven't seen her for so many years, but she is still the same beauty. She was here with me on *that night*.'

'*That night*? Oh, very good,' Jaadu said. She quickly added, 'I mean, very bad. But lucky that you are still here, that's what I mean.'

Dilkhush didn't think of herself as lucky. She wondered if the girl's parents had named her Jaadu because it was magical that she had survived, or magical she didn't seem bitter.

Preeti wheeled Jaadu's chair to the *charpoy*. 'How was your day? Tell us everything. Did you save anyone today? Did you make a pass at that new doctor? Shall I come and help you make a match with him? Have you got any new foreign volunteers? Any Indian ones at all?'

Dilkhush noticed Preeti used a hard 'd', when she said Jaadu's name, rather than a soft one - making the girl's name mean fat, rather than magic.

'Jaadu works at the gas clinic for a reason,' Naseema Bi said, using the soft 'd'. 'Seeing her encourages people

133

who are ashamed of their deformities. It helps them to come and speak to her.'

'I saw her at the clinic,' Dilkhush said. 'She is doing such good work with the newspapers.'

'Yes everyone, please call me Jaadu Mother Theresa,' the girl laughed at her own joke. 'What can I say? We are with sick people all day, so you have to make life interesting for them and us.'

She looked at Dilkhush. 'Yes I remember seeing you at the clinic today. We were worried about you. By the time I fetched someone, you had disappeared. You were asking about compensation. But we don't deal with that side or any other legal things, only treatments and help. Sometimes you may hear people talking about such things around the clinic, maybe the patients or those who visit us. You could ask them. But we wouldn't know about these things.'

Dilkhush nodded. She didn't want anyone else knowing she had gone to the clinic to ask about compensation money. But Jaadu carried on.

'Still, I asked about Dalya's money that you saw. When you said MBBS, you meant him, yes? He had come to the clinic.'

'It doesn't matter,' Dilkhush said.

'No, no,' Jaadu said. 'Let me tell you at least. He only came to pick up his mother and changed his notes for coins. He said he heats them up and puts them on her boils. She likes him to burst them that way. Not with a hot needle.'

'Are her boils from the gas poison?' Dilkhush had

seen how bad they were. She was afraid everyone got them in old age if the gas affected them.

'Maybe from the gas, maybe not,' Naseema Bi said. 'What I know is that Dalya looks after her as if she were his own mother.'

'She isn't his mother?' Dilkhush asked. Dalya had to have a kind heart.

'He was her miracle. She was alone, and had lost everyone, sick for years from the gas and nearly dead inside. She told me that one day she felt so bad, she wanted to kill herself. So, she was walking towards the derelict factory, when out of nowhere, Dalya came out of a slum home crying. He was only a year old. His father had died only months before. His mother died just then. He stumbled out of his home and because he was crying, she put her arms out and he hugged her. She didn't even know what had happened to him. But he became the reason for her to live life. All these years later, she is still here. He tends to her every need, and her boils, as if she was his own mother. He kept her alive. Miracle boy.'

'Like Chandni was for you,' Jaadu said. She turned to the other girls. 'True story.'

They laughed. 'True story.' One piped up. 'But even us. We keep Naseema Bi alive too. All this pampering and scolding she had to do for us. That gives her reason, yes?' All the girls laughed and agreed. The old owl nodded her head. 'True true true story,' she blink-winked.

'So let us start for today.' Jaadu gathered everyone's attention. 'Listen up. Today's winner I heard at the chaiwalla.'

The girls turned towards her. 'Yes, give us a few laughs.'

Dilkhush looked over at Naseema Bi. The old owl's eyes were wide with anticipation. She seemed so happy.

Jaadu cleared her throat. 'Okay. A woman is arguing with her husband because he won't fight for her with her lover. "You won't fight for me? Are you a man or a mouse?"

'"What do you mean, am I a man or a mouse?" he says. "I have not two, but *four* balls between my legs, what do you think?"

'"That doesn't make you a man, you idiot." The wife jeered at him. "It just means this other man is banging your arse." Get it?'

The girls began laughing and hooting.

But Jaadu continued, raising her voice. 'Not finished, not finished. So, the husband says, "*THAT* is hardly a big surprise, with you as my wife. I'd rather have another man bang my arse than you bang my balls."'

Dilkhush hesitated to smile. The joke was so vulgar. Naseema Bi patted her arm and wagged her finger at the others. 'Why are you girls so dirty today? What will our guest think? Can't you tell some of your more innocent jokes?'

Dilkhush was saddened. She had gone from being the old owl's daughter to being a guest.

'These are the men's jokes from the chaiwalla,' Jaadu said. 'I am only re-telling them.'

'So the husband let her go with her lover?' Shaila asked.

'Yes,' Jaadu said, cocking her head to one side. 'He let her go.'

Shaila stared at her for a moment, and then her face changed. 'Stop it. You are teasing me. I thought they were fighting about the lover. Anyway, I am not bothering with you.' She started playing with her shawl. 'I don't get these jokes.'

Then Preeti put her hands in the air. 'Okay, listen. My mother asked me the other day—'

'What?' Jaadu said. 'Your mother in heaven, that mother? How did she speak to you? Through a jantar-mantar-magic phone?'

'Yaar, it's a joke,' Preeti said. 'Why spoil it? I am talking about the wisdom of mothers.'

Naseema Bi looked at the other girls. 'Yes, yes, let her tell you all about the wisdom of mothers. You will learn something.'

Preeti cleared her throat. 'The other day, a boy, a bit heavy, so heavy his parents had to help him sit and stand, came to view me for marriage. After they left, my mother asked me, "Did you like the boy, Preeti?"'

Some of the girls around Preeti started giggling.

'So my mother asked, "Preeti did you like the boy?"

'I said, "Mummmmmyyy, he is a bit plumppp."

'And you know what my mother said, "Look *beta*, whether a TV is 51 inches or 15 inches, the remote control is always only 6 inches." Get it? Click click?' She wiggled with her little finger and then made an action as if to shoot a gun.

They all burst out laughing.

'Vah, vah,' Jaadu said to Naseema Bi. 'You are right. What wisdom mothers have - that remote control is no bigger than 6 inches, no matter the size of the TV.'

Naseema Bi made a face at her.

Jaadu and Preeti began talking to each other. Dilkhush felt awkward. They were talking about people she didn't know, and looked at her now and again to be polite. She knew they were younger. They could talk about anything they wanted, dirty or clean, not like her. She had to be careful. But she didn't know how to be with them.

She tried to tell herself they were the same as the women in the neighbourhood before, or like Simran, maybe like Jiyaa would be if she had grown up. She, too, would have joined in if she had been around such laughter. But she would still be her innocent child. Like Shaila, she wouldn't understand crude jokes, Dilkhush hoped. But there was no harm in only laughing.

Just at that moment, the masseuse came up to her. Although she had changed her clothes, she wasn't wearing plain colours like the other girls. Her salwar kameez was a vibrant red and black with sparkling sequins. She scowled at Naseema Bi and sat at her feet, handing her a comb. 'So you have already set up an interview for your new daughter, I hear. You didn't waste any time, Naseema Bi. Especially with that bilayati job with good money.'

She seemed annoyed at Dilkhush, pouting like a child. Was it better to explain the job was the old owl's idea?

'Arey, my child.' Naseema Bi touched the masseuse's cheeks. 'We don't even know for sure whether these bilayatis are linked to the gas. And we still have to make a living. Do we have such luxury to choose? Even I tried for that job, didn't I? If I could speak Inglis, I might have worked for them myself. Their money can help us, and we can still be wary for our own sake. How will you get peace for yourself with such a grudge? You think it hurts anyone else other than you?'

'Vah, vah. They are here for the anniversary because they were somehow connected. Should I forget that? Because this woman wants to work there? I hope she fails. I curse any work they need doing, and anyone who dares to help them after what their people did to us. They should know what it feels like to suffer, and not get what they want. Why should we offer ourselves? Let them do all the work they create... clean up all their own dirt.'

'Hush, hush.' Naseema Bi stroked the downy hair on the masseuse's arm. 'We can't curse the fate of others. Good girls don't do that. And you can't blame all rich people or all bilayati, or even the families of gas people here or in foreign. Those themselves responsible are the ones to hold something against. And they each know inside what they did. Dilkhush is going for the work with that particular family for her own reasons. What if you had to work with the families of people you suspected were bad? What if there was no choice for you? Sometimes there are reasons, to feed yourself, to do it for your children.'

'What children can I have after the gas? Who is going

to marry me again?'

'Dilkhush is just trying to do something for her daughter,' the old owl said.

The other girls quietened. Dilkhush wanted to ask Naseema Bi what the job had to do with her daughter. She was embarrassed about all the finger pointing, and wanted to cancel the interview. From what the masseuse and Naseema Bi said, it was dawning on her the job might be with a gas person's family, and that alarmed her. Why would such a job mean doing something for her daughter? Had the old owl lost all sense? Then she realised something. What if working for the family was God's way of helping her avenge Jiyaa? Is that what the old owl meant?

Dilkhush asked Naseema Bi's reasoning in a low voice, so the others didn't hear. The old owl used charm and logic, mixed with her sweet words to convince her. 'I can't say anything yet. But I wouldn't push you into this unless I thought it would bear exactly the fruits you need. Trust me.'

The masseuse interrupted. 'Anyway, why is this woman here at all? We don't have room. You can't keep bringing more people here. Where will we all sleep? How can you say "yes" to people without asking us? Isn't this our home as well?'

Naseema Bi sighed. 'It's not like that, my moonbeam. Why are you being like this today? What is eating you? This is not like you at all. Dilkhush is not a stranger. She used to live with me. She is dying to go back to her own family, but she came to visit me especially. She can only stay long enough to do this job for her daughter, that's all. The bilayati family might even take her back with them, so the crowding in the house will be temporary only.'

Dilkhush sat on the charpoy. She didn't want to go anywhere. Why was the old owl saying she would go with any gas people?

The masseuse looked at her. 'So after all these years, you come here to visit your Naseema Bi. Where were you before? It is strange that you came at the exact time this bilayati job came up. And straight away the old owl gets you this interview. All this time you didn't think of her? Or did it occur to you that now the old woman is nearer to dying age, she could help you. That you can have her house? Or are you here to swindle some of her savings?'

'Of course not.' Dilkhush knew she shouldn't have abandoned Naseema Bi. 'You don't have to worry about me. I am not going to be here long. I have to go back soon.'

'See, don't be jealous,' Naseema Bi said, gently scolding the masseuse. 'What does Dilkhush need with my home? Her brother has been taking good care of her all these years. That is why she hasn't been here. She has only come to pay her respects for the thirtieth anniversary, isn't that right Dilkhush?'

The masseuse scoffed. 'We'll see. When it's too good here, we'll see who leaves. And however long she stays, she better pay rent just like the rest of us.'

'Of course,' the old owl said. 'Whether this job is for

two days, two weeks, or two months, as long as she stays, she will give some for rent. She never said no.'

Dilkhush nodded. 'Of course, I will pay. I don't expect favours.' She had learnt her lesson with the gangly recruiter and the women in the embroidery job queue. She didn't want to alienate any of these girls, in particular this one that the old owl seemed to dote on. After all, this was now other people's home, and they were doing her a favour by letting her stay. 'Just because I have known Naseema Bi for so long and used to live with her myself, doesn't mean I will take advantage. We used to pay rent before, and I will pay again.'

The masseuse smirked. 'You may have rented from Naseema Bi before, but I have been looking after her for thirty years, since I was a girl myself. If I were Naseema Bi, I wouldn't be forgiving and forgetting so quickly that you left her in the first place.'

The old owl shook her head. 'What is there to forgive? She is my daughter.'

The masseuse looked hurt. 'I've been your daughter all these years. I've been struggling with you.' She walked away into the large bedroom.

Dilkhush was worried that she would be forced to leave at some point, and had no place to go. But she couldn't say anything straight out. 'Naseema Bi, if it is a problem for me to be here—'

'Don't worry. She's a little sensitive.' The other girls started to banter with each other again, and the old owl took Dilkhush aside. She seemed to find it difficult to find the exact words to explain. 'This girl is very special to me. After the gas leak, when you left, I went to look for you. I thought maybe you were laying on the roads somewhere. For months, I went out every day, shouting, "Dilkhush, Dilkhush." I had given up on you and was so terribly lonely.

'It was many months later, that I found this girl. Someone had found her at the train station under a wet sack, but she wouldn't live with them. She couldn't remember where she was, or who she was. But she was living in the alley outside, and I had given up looking for you. I said she could stay with me. Poor girl. All she remembered was that her mother died on that gas night. And she never found her father. We don't know where he is. Even if he is alive, she never saw him again.'

Dilkhush's stomach lurched. Something was amiss.

'The girl didn't speak in the beginning, for a full few weeks,' Naseema Bi said. 'The first time she uttered anything was when I called her Omera by mistake. She said she despised that name. Silly me. Just because something about her reminded me of Kashif and Simran's daughter, but my eyes have not been good after the gas. Who knows what I saw in her. No one wants a different name to their own.

'I never called her Omera again. Such a beautiful name you had found for Kashif and Simran's daughter, but for me it was sentimental. For this girl, it was someone else's name. I even told her what it meant.' Naseema Bi paused. 'She hated it but didn't tell me her own name. So I called her Chandni. Everyone is a piece of the moon for me. And she didn't mind that name.'

Dilkhush walked towards the room that Chandni had gone into. She saw the young woman looking at her reflection in a small mirror, and was taken aback. It was Dilkhush's own gold-encased mirror with the word 'apsara' curled around the edge. Chandni turned towards her and their eyes met.

Neither said anything. Dilkhush had given that mirror to Simran. She had even refused to take it back on the night of the gas leak, when Simran had tried to insist. She had been sure her friend would remain alive. It was to be given to Omera for her wedding trousseau. What if this wasn't simply a jealous girl afraid of being replaced? Didn't she feel she might have recognised something in the masseuse?

Could this be Omera? It was too much of a coincidence. No. Kashif had not found her despite his intense searching. But Dilkhush couldn't shake off her suspicions. Why was her mind trapping her into this torture when she had just gained some relief?

She knew making up to Naseema Bi, and getting assurance she hadn't wronged anyone else, was too easy. She tried to recall the woman's photo in the clinic. Was it possible Omera's picture was also misplaced into the wrong section, like the old owl's?

The girl had convinced Naseema Bi. But not her. Dilkhush felt burdened with guilt. The only way would be to find Kashif and reunite father and daughter, and face their resentment for their lost years. They both might even eventually feel indebted to her.

144

13

Once a Very Lucky Bug
Lived on a King

'Come on now girls,' Naseema Bi said, banging a spoon against a saucepan. 'If we don't start cooking, we won't eat until midnight. And Dilkhush has to get up early for an interview.' She directed the girls to chop coriander, marinate the meat for the next day, boil the water, and salt it for the potato and lentils. The girls giggled at each other.

'Yes, officer Naseema Bi,' one girl said.

'How many potatoes, SIR?'

'How many lentils, SIR?'

'How many farts, SIR?'

'You want to taste the sole of my *chappal*?' Naseema Bi laughed.

'But from all those lentils, there will be farts. Just tell me how many you need for full digestive relief, and I will know how much lentils to use.'

Naseema Bi became busy with the girls, so Dilkhush couldn't ask her about the mirror, or whether she ever suspected Chandni was actually Omera. The chitchat amongst the group grew.

Dalya, threw open the door. '*Yaar*, that chis-bis-burga-shurga is nothing but burger and chips, nothing special. Chips-bips-burger-shurger, just make like meat petis with fried potatoes. That's it.'

'*Baas*?' Naseema Bi asked. 'That is what these bilayati people go crazy about?' She turned to Dilkhush. 'You can make that in a minute. Potato and petis. Your cooking was always first class. You just put the fried potatoes into the mixture for the petis. And it will be ready.'

'Separate, separate,' Dalya said. 'Not potatoes inside petis. Fried potatoes that look like my fingers. Long and thin chips. Not fat or not mashed with petis. They will complain otherwise and might not keep you. Don't listen to Naseema Bi about making up your own ways. And you know, one man told me that you have to put a lot of tomato sauce and chillies to make that food more tasty.' Dalya went and sat cross-legged with the other girls.

Naseema Bi doled her head side-to-side. 'You will be perfectly ready. And if there is meat, spice it like vegetables only. If you are concerned about touching the meat, just use a spoon.'

Dilkhush became worried about the job. It was meant to be so important, yet she didn't know anything about it. She wanted to ask how small the petis should be for burgers and how long the chips should be.

Dalya was busy laughing and joking amongst the

girls. He took a metal glass, cocked his head back and held it above his chin to dribble water into his mouth. Dilkhush didn't interrupt him. She would have to try her best. If she didn't get the job, she was sure Naseema Bi would understand and help her again.

They all sat on the ground to share dinner from four large steel plates. Dalya got up to go and eat with his mother instead. Chandni stood up too, still chewing her food. She made a food parcel for him and his mother.

'Dalya, you rascal rogue,' Naseema Bi said. 'When your mother finds you this perfect wife, how will you steal away from them both to spend any time here? Your new wife might not like that.'

'Then you find me the perfect wife who will like you as well. We will move in here with you. No missing anyone.'

'And your mother?' Jaadu asked. 'She refuses to come and live here now. Why would she come then?'

Dalya laughed. 'You are right. But she refuses now because you are all corrupted. When my wife will be here, she will sweet-talk my mother and train you all to stop misbehaving.'

Naseema Bi waved him away. 'Go, go, Dalya. Your mother will be hungry. Until she finds you a wife, you'd better go and look after her.'

Chandni nodded. 'Yes, you go. Our old owl has a new favourite she wants to spend time with.'

Dilkhush ate only enough to stave off her hunger. The lentils and potatoes were delicious, especially after the watery millet meals she had been eating. She knew if she had stayed all these years with Naseema Bi, she would have been part of her enlarged adopted family, not the suspicious stranger she was now. It made her think about her life in the village. She hoped Makodi was eating well. The orphan was capable of scavenging food for herself, but Dilkhush wished they were together.

The old owl and her girls would love her. Even if Omera didn't want her there, the girls might take in Makodi. She would have a home, food, and affection. She could marry Dalya when they were both older.

After dinner, Dilkhush sat alone with her thoughts while the other girls and women talked. Two of them washed up. Out of the blue, Naseema Bi started bragging about Dilkhush's puppetry.

'Now you are here, tell them a story,' she urged. 'Idea! As we are going to sleep soon, tell them that one about the king going to bed.' Naseema Bi nudged Chandni. 'Wait till you see this. Then you'll want Dilkhush here all the time.'

Chandni didn't say anything.

Dilkhush resisted at first. 'I don't even have any puppets.' Then she thought a story could soften the girls in her favour. She used to do puppet shows for Jiyaa and Omera, and both girls loved them. She hoped she could use her stories to ease some of the tension.

Maybe then Dilkhush could check whether there was any chance Chandni was actually Omera, even if the girl had forgotten or wanted to forget. She had to find out how the girl got the mirror. Did she know anything about Kashif still being alive?

'Come, come girls,' Naseema Bi said. 'Entertainment is starting soon.'

The two girls washing the plates and saucepans hurried with their chores, wiped their hands on their dresses, and joined the others who were already sitting down. A few of them hugged their knees to their chests and rested their chins on them. Chandni sat alone, looking at the ground. For her story, Dilkhush painted *kajol* on her hands for eyes and *kum kum* for smiling lips.

She told the story about the bug that lived in the lovely sheets of a king. 'Each night this lucky bug waited for the king to fall asleep before biting him and feeding on his blood.' Dilkhush moved her fingers, pretending her hand was a bug. 'Then one day the bug saw a flea.' She made a hopping action with her other hand. 'The flea wanted to feed on the king as well, but the bug told it to leave. The king was *his* meal.'

Dilkhush put her hands on her hips and pretended to be the flea. 'What kind of a Hindu are you, bug?' She used a crafty flea voice. 'I am a guest in your home and instead of feeding me, you are throwing me out. What tainted karma will you get in your next life? To be thrown out when you need a home somewhere?'

'But this is my home,' the bug said. Dilkhush hunched a bit when she acted out being the bug. 'I worked hard to be here and to be patient each night until the king falls asleep. You don't know his ways. You will become impatient and ruin it for me as well as yourself.'

Dilkhush cleared her throat. 'The flea tried to

persuade the bug and promised him that life would be much better with both of them working together. After a long time, still with doubts in its mind, the bug relented and agreed to let the flea stay. That night, as soon as the king came in, instead of waiting like the bug said, the flea jumped on the king's arm straight away.

'The king was not asleep, so he noticed the bite. He screamed, and his helpers ran in. They first began hitting the king's arm to get rid of the flea. Then when the king slapped them on their heads for hurting him, they took out all of the bed sheets. By then, the flea had jumped off and hidden in a nook in the bed-frame.'

Dilkhush looked at the faces of the girls. They were listening intently. She was glad and started to relax, taking her time with her movements and elaborating the story with descriptions and sounds, almost the way she used to for Jiyaa and Omera. 'The flea had escaped and hidden, but the king's men found the poor bug, which had not even started his evening meal of the king's blood.'

Dilkhush described the king's room, explaining how the bug tried to escape from one piece of jewelled furniture to the next, from velvet curtains to gold-threaded pillows. The girls' eyes gleamed. 'But finally, the king's men cornered the bug and immediately rushed forward. Bang, slam. They killed it. What do you think the flea did? Did it feel sorry for the bug? Or sorry for its own greed and carelessness that led to the bug's death? No. It went on its way to find another body to suck on, not even thinking about the bug whose life ended up as a red splodge in the king's room.

'So, now, we come to the moral of the story. You must follow your instinct and not abandon those you trust for someone persuasive, whose character you do not know. The End.'

Dilkhush bowed.

The group began clapping and whistling.

Chandni stood up. She raised her voice above the sound of the cheering. 'So you have told us a story about being wary of an outsider like you? After all, how can we know what your actions have been in the past? And why you are really here. You, too, could have left someone to die, like the flea did.'

Dilkhush was speechless, and now certain that Chandni was Omera, and that she knew about her broken promise to return with medicine for Simran as she lay on the road that night of the gas leak.

Preeti laughed. 'Yes, yes, we must be careful because this heroine-lookalike outsider seems very dangerous, isn't it?' The other girls also laughed, but stopped when they saw Chandni's thunderous face.

She went into the large bedroom and shut the door. Preeti turned to Dilkhush. 'But it is true that this story has a very sad ending. We get enough of those in real life. Can't you do it filmi style, that the bug and flea fight and kiss and fight and miss and finally fall for each other and get married, and feast on the king happily ever after? That's so much better, no? And even Chandni wouldn't be upset with such a happy ending.' The girls danced and laughed enacting a marriage.

Shaila pretended to be the flea and Jaadu shouted, 'I'll be the bug.' Naseema Bi laughed and clapped, as she watched the girls hold hands and whirl around the courtyard to celebrate the wedding in their new ending of the story. 'Long live the bug and the flea.' Dilkhush didn't join in, but smiled and kept an eye on the bedroom door for Chandni.

Later that night, while everyone slept, Dilkhush tossed and turned on the razai Dalya had brought. It was more comfortable than what she was used to, so it wasn't that which kept her awake. She was in the same room as Naseema Bi and Chandni. When she turned over again, she saw two girls stirring. Dilkhush didn't want to disturb anyone. She got up and tiptoed towards the door. It creaked as she pulled it open.

She hoped it did not wake anyone and left the room without looking back. Outside, she sat against the peepal tree in the courtyard and was about to say some prayers to the gods there, when she remembered the opium pellets in her cloth bundle. She slipped back into the room. Chandni stirred on her razai and murmured something. Dilkhush hoped she hadn't seen her. She didn't want another fight. Chandni said something again.

Dilkhush couldn't make out the words. She took her pellets and crept outside. There, she tied them inside a handkerchief. If the job interview was going badly, she could put a pellet in some water, like they did in the village, and offer that. It could help her chances. She stuffed the handkerchief into her blouse. Maybe it could also help ease the tension with Omera ...Chandni.

Dilkhush didn't know what to call the young woman who was making it uncomfortable for her to stay with the old owl. Chandni. That was the name Omera now found acceptable, not the unique one Dilkhush had searched for.

Dilkhush wasn't ready to leave the old owl yet. Being with the other girls and women had relieved her heart. She had to pacify Chandni somehow. Even amongst so many villagers around her before, she had felt alone with her memories. Only Makodi had said kind words to her. The orphan was young and didn't know how Dilkhush had lived before. Maybe some day, they could both stay with Naseema Bi in her home.

That way there would be no bad karma for abandoning Makodi either, especially if something terrible happened to her otherwise. Dilkhush needed to build trust with the girls and show she could pay rent, buy food, even for a few days. She would stay away from trouble with Chandni. Then after some time she could bring Makodi for a visit. The girls would surely love the cheeky orphan.

Chandni was not so young to react like a child, yet she seemed compelled to, almost as if she had her own viper inside of her. Could that be what was happening? Had her presence there stirred Omera's snake? Hadn't Naseema Bi said she wasn't like that otherwise? The door of the bedroom creaked open.

Naseema Bi came out of the room and lowered herself to the ground, next to Dilkhush. 'Excited about this magical job?' she asked.

'I am more worried than excited.'

'Don't be. I want it to be a surprise, so I don't want to say anything. You will see when you get there.'

Dilkhush couldn't tell Naseema Bi what was on her mind about Chandni. She would have to find Kashif. She would never get any forgiveness otherwise. But if he was not the man in the newspaper photo, where would she look for him, with no money and no help? And if she found him, would he agree to any plans of revenge if he got Omera back? She shouldn't say anything yet.

If Dilkhush hadn't left, she would have recognised Omera. They would have looked for Kashif, put announcements in the newspapers. Her karma could have become clearer.

'What is bothering you?' The old owl squeezed Dilkhush's hand. 'Whatever Chandni says, don't take it too hard. You used to live in the town before, so maybe she sees the past in you. She had a difficult time.'

'But her anger seems directed at me only. You lived in the town too. The other girls and women as well.'

Naseema Bi nodded. 'It's not simple. Her parents...'

Dilkhush pulled at some threads that had come loose in her sari. 'Is it because of her mother's death?'

'And her father's. All these girls are orphans, but for some reason Chandni can't move forward. We try. See, Preeti is a Dalit. I said there would be no such thing here. The neighbours around here don't all agree, so I tell them to keep out if they don't like it. Then when we have fun, they want to be part of it. If we don't welcome them, they complain about the noise. So we tell them, no

Dalit-balit talk here.

'Jaadu, well, it is God that has made her nature so full of smiles. Shaila, her husband tried to kill her by cutting her throat. Surprisingly, he didn't get too far before she kicked him in his *ladoos*. She wears the shawl to cover her scars. Still, Chandni takes it the hardest. I told you, she was found alive under a wet sack by the train platforms. There were bodies on top of her and all around her. She still wakes up from nightmares.'

Outside, the sound of crickets seemed louder now.

'We even found her a boy, but her in-laws sent her back. She kept losing babies. There is no chance. Nothing anybody can do. Sometimes she gets very angry. I am the only one she has left and when I die— Inside, she is still that scared child, hearing the trains, people dying on top of her. When she finally told me about it, she seemed so... I just hugged her. Nothing else I could do. If she had children of her own, maybe they would distract her.'

Dilkhush played with her loose threads. Even if she could reunite Kashif and Omera, what would the girl think of her plan for revenge? Kashif had lost his wife and parents to the gas. Didn't he need to balance that? A noisy tractor trundled past outside.

'Naseema Bi, can I ask you a difficult question?' Dilkhush squirmed before saying anything. 'Do you think revenge can work? Krishna told Arjun to destroy evil "even if they are your flesh and blood, never to be a coward."'

The old owl shook her head. 'The meaning of that

is very clear. "Even if they are your flesh and blood". This is about killing any evil, any shadows inside your own flesh and blood, inside yourself. When you notice darkness in your thoughts and intentions, destroy that in yourself. That is what it means. Imagine if everyone overcame their own darkness. No one would even be looking for others to kill, isn't it? Such less destruction.'

She patted Dilkhush's hand. 'It's like how we believe about jihad. Same to same. It is our inner struggle to live a godly life. For that we have to recognise any evil within us and cut it out. But you don't worry about such matters. Your memorial for Jiyaa must have been so clear of any darkness, so pure, that it has brought you this miracle, which you will soon see. Maybe you can build a memorial like that for Chandni too, so she can get her parents back. Then she might feel happier about you being here. Maybe all the girls can have one just like yours. Everyone has lost someone. They can all have the same joy you will have.'

Dilkhush didn't understand. She had never built a memorial, and what joy was the old owl talking about? Being with them was a boon that was true. Maybe that is what she meant.

'This is a very good idea of yours, Dilkhush. You can help everyone build a memorial like yours.'

'But I never even...I don't understand what ha—'

'Oh no, I can't keep it from you any longer,' Naseema Bi said, as she put her hand across her mouth. 'Dilkhush, tomorrow you are going to see your own daughter.' A few moments passed.

'Oh, look at your face, Dilkhush. Oh, my moonbeam. Yes, it's true. It's true. You are going to see your daughter tomorrow. Our beloved Jiyaa. She is with that bilayati family. Rejoice, rejoice. After all these years, you will be reunited. Jiyaa is back. Your memorial has pulled her to you at this exact time when you are back here in the town. How can such a coincidence occur if not by God's wishes? She is your miracle. Like Dalya is for his mother and Chandni is for me. You have your own daughter back.'

Dilkhush was taken aback and yet at the same time, her chest expanded about this unreal possibility. She inundated Naseema Bi with questions. After a long while, she finally accepted the old owl's word. And yet, she suddenly felt even more uneasy.

14

I Know your Dirty Secret

THE SUN WAS almost half way up the sky as Dilkhush walked to Volog Complex for her job interview. From the moment she had heard the news about Jiyaa, her heart had been hurrying and scurrying here and there. She had to get the job. She didn't want to appease anyone who might be even vaguely connected with the gas leak. It felt like a betrayal. But the old owl said Jiyaa was there. The night had been restless. This could not be real. Yet, how was she to ignore it?

God could make anything possible. It would have seemed unthinkable that a gas leak would ever have happened in the first place; that it would have destroyed her family and thousands of others for decades, with no end. If that could happen, couldn't God with his almighty powers heal some of that, however incredible and absurd that seemed?

For now, she needed to worry about the gangly recruiter she had angered at the job junction. If he was going to be there, he would not even let her in. She would have to shout past him and tell her daughter everything. She would apologise and ask for forgiveness. Jiyaa would be older now and may even be doing the interview. Dilkhush fretted about her snake and hoped she could keep it under control.

She adjusted the cloth bag across her shoulders. Naseema Bi had given it to her, with reassuring words. 'This suits you better than your torn bundle, my moonbeam. And I have put a key inside for you.' All night and that morning, Dilkhush had prayed hard. She took the peacock feather hair clip as proof to Jiyaa of who she was, in case her daughter was really there and had forgotten her. She must be living away in bilayat now, in luxury that Dilkhush could never provide. Still, she couldn't make any sense of it. How could Jiyaa be there with a bilayati family?

In the village, there had been stories about people presumed dead only for them to get up from their own funeral pyres. If Dilkhush had stayed in the town, she would have been the one to find Jiyaa. It seemed like God's big joke to get her back to Jantapur and have Jiyaa there with some gas leak family.

Dilkhush rebuked herself. She couldn't be sure who the family was, so shouldn't hold anything against them. She put away all thoughts that could jeopardise her chances. Even when she had first heard, and wanted to go immediately to Volog Colony, Naseema Bi had stopped her. 'You must sleep. Save your energy.'

'But after hearing this, I have more energy than ever,' Dilkhush said.

'Going now can be a big mistake.' The old owl held her arm. 'The guards are very strict about who crosses the bridge to the rich area and the exact time anyone goes. If you do something wrong, even small, you can spoil your chances completely. Be patient. It's only a few hours away now. After all these years, why endanger anything?'

Dilkhush agreed reluctantly. She slept with difficulty and fantasised about the reunion when she was awake. What would she say after all these years? She would hug Jiyaa so tight and never let go.

Even as she walked to the interview, her chest expanded. It made her want to laugh and cry at the same time. She felt she was in a haze. Events from the night before swirled around in her head.

Dilkhush became cautious of doubting thoughts that could spoil her intense joy, and tried to manage her unwieldy mind. Groups of people hurried past her but she carried on walking without looking. That morning, the layer of ragpatches around her heart had thinned a little. They hurt less too. Baarish played on a radio again. Jiyaa hummed and sang it softly.

'Kyu na phir ham dono
Taaron mein ghar basaayein
Aur bus
Bheege ye pal saare.'

Dilkhush smoothed her hair. She found a stray strand, and quickly undid her bun and tied her hair up again.

On the dusty street in front of her, a group of people chanted slogans, but she didn't listen to what they were saying. When they came closer, they subsumed her amongst them for a moment. She looked up, and saw one of them staring at her. He was handsome and his look was intense. She could feel her cheeks become hot. The man looked into her eyes, but she lowered her gaze. He smiled and the more he bent to look at her, the further she looked down, until all she could do was try to get past him.

'Sorry,' he said. 'I thought we've met before.'

Dilkhush looked at him, in case it was someone she knew from the old days. He looked familiar, but she couldn't place him.

'You have the most beguiling eyes,' he said. 'I wouldn't forget those.' His voice was deep, like the rumble of rain clouds.

She tried to hurry away, unsure why he would say such a thing to a widow. As she rushed past, their arms touched and she pulled away.

'Sorry,' the man said again. 'I didn't mean to... I'm sorry.'

'I'm late.' Dilkhush shook her head. When she was further away, she turned around.

The man was jogging backward and still looking at her. Their eyes met for a few moments and he smiled nervously. Dilkhush felt her throat tighten. He turned around to catch up with his group. She walked faster, but couldn't help glancing back. She caught him looking back at her too. She didn't know who he was, but she was sure she had seen his face before. The road turned, and she focused her mind on the directions the old owl had given.

She showed her permit to the bridge guard. He looked her up and down, and checked the time and date of her permit repeatedly before making a call to confirm it was legitimate.

Soon, Dilkhush reached the new complex of flats in Volog Colony, behind large silver gates. There were pink and white blocks standing one after the other, ten storeys high. Dilkhush didn't have a watch, but knew from the sun it was not midday yet. She decided to wait for a few minutes until she thought it was time.

There was no one in any of the balconies of the flats, except for a corner one on the first floor. A dark woman was hanging clothes, rolling each item in a towel first, patting it all the way down to dry and then laying it straight out on the edge of the balcony wall. The woman's hair was tied up, revealing an oily face and a wide forehead, streaked with three horizontal white markings. Dilkhush assumed the markings were from a temple visit. She could tell from the cut of the woman's face and her movements that she was a servant, lower caste. But she reminded herself that she, of superior caste, a warrior caste, was also going there to be a servant.

What fortune had she had in life that she should now look down on others? If Jiyaa remembered her, Dilkhush was sure then she would not need to be a servant there. Otherwise, she had to do any work to stay with the family, and slowly convince her daughter of who she was. Dilkhush was about to walk to the gates, when the sound of a beep made her jump.

The horn sounded again, and the security guard hurried to open the gates. A white car rumbled past, and she stepped back. It was the same car she had seen at the job junction. The guard went to close the gates. All of a sudden, a motorbike revved and swerved out from the Volog Colony grounds through a gap between the gate and the wall. Dilkhush did a double take.

The rider wore a white handkerchief across his nose and mouth. Before Dilkhush could stop herself, Kashif's name escaped from her lips. She said it again, out loud. 'Kashif.' The motorcyclist turned his head sideways for a moment, but raced away behind the car.

Dilkhush ran a few steps after the motorbike, but remembered what Dalya had said. Not to be late, otherwise they wouldn't give her the job. She couldn't risk missing Jiyaa. Naseema Bi said even getting permission to cross the bridge was a task. There might be no other chance to get this close to being with her daughter. She had waited all these years. She would have to find Kashif later. After all, she wasn't even sure whether it was him.

But somehow she felt certain that once she got the servant work with the bilayati family, everything would fall into place. She couldn't catch him anyway. He was too fast on his motorbike. Then someone else ran past her from behind the gates. Everything was a blur for a moment, and Dilkhush hoped it was the gangly recruiter leaving. She should try and slip in behind him. But she was shocked to discover it was the villain she had confronted on the bus.

What was he doing there? He would be a shadow to her every move if he worked near the bilayati family. What a curse God had put on her. She knew she only had herself to blame for her reckless attack on the bus.

Dilkhush hurried to the nearest wall and stayed flat against it, hiding in the shadow of a tree. She felt ghosts of her past jeering at her, ensuring she kept collecting enemies and ruining any relief she got.

The villain shouted after the motorcyclist. 'And don't you dare show your face again, you hear?' He looked around before shouting at the security guard. 'Idiot! If the boss hears his family was in danger, what do you think will happen to you?'

'Please don't say anything, Sir,' the guard said. 'The man said he had documents for the boss. There have been so many people, I thought—'

'You are paid to guard, not think.'

'Sorry, I'm sorry. It won't happen again.'

There was silence for a few moments.

'I am not finished with you,' the villain said. 'I have to go and see Madam. She is interviewing someone, so keep your eyes open for a woman. Use your brains this time. And listen, while you are waiting, call that idiot bridge guard about the motorbike. Make sure that rogue is never allowed back across. Take his licence plate number.' He walked through a wooden door into a flat.

Dilkhush panicked. The villain must work for the bilayati family, unless someone else was also interviewing. Then something dawned on her. Of course people like him were there. What other kind would a gas family know? She rebuked herself again. They might not be a gas family. But why else would they have villains around them? The excitement that had swelled inside her started to deflate.

She became frightened. If Kashif also suspected the family's link to the gas, he might have come on that motorbike to harm them. But his revenge should not include Jiyaa, even inadvertently. He wouldn't know she was alive and wouldn't recognise the girl after so many years. Dilkhush had to stay close to her and warn Kashif off. What if he wasn't acting alone? There could be others like him, who might not listen to her. If she told the family about these dangers, they could leave straightaway. She had to get that servant job and go with them.

Dilkhush took a deep breath. She didn't even know whether the man on the motorbike had been Kashif. Or that there was a gas link with the family. But Jiyaa was so close now, it was no wonder she was scared of losing her. Dilkhush chanted prayers and asked God for help.

The first thing for her was to get to the interview. She peered through the gates. Dalya had stressed about being on time at midday sharp. But if the villain saw her, he was sure to make trouble. If she hid long enough behind the wall, he had to leave at some point, even if that made her late. She would try and persuade the family afterwards.

The villain came back out of the flat and waited by

the door. He was dressed in a red shirt, still with a leather jacket. Dilkhush wished she had never said anything to him on the bus. Her stupid anger was coming to bite her now, even if he had deserved her lashing out.

Time went by and Dilkhush waited. The sun got higher. She was in danger of risking the job. Tick tock you leper dick of a dog. She wanted the villain to leave. But he didn't. She checked every few moments. He stayed there. She checked again. Still there. Checked. There. She threw a stick from behind the wall towards where he was standing. The villain looked over, but didn't move.

The priest had been right about her behaviour ruining her chances. The sun passed the midpoint of its arc in the sky. A car left the Colony gates, but the villain wasn't in it. She had to go in. If the villain said anything, she would pretend she didn't recognise him. A shadow came up from behind her. She turned around.

'Eh heroine, are you finished already?' It was Dalya. 'So now you have the job, how much *baksheesh* will you give me for getting you the interview?'

'Nothing.' She looked at Volog Colony. 'I haven't gone for the interview yet.'

'Eh, eh. I set it up. You have to pay whether you do your bit or not. I said not to be late.'

Dilkhush told Dalya to shut his rattling-tattling mouth. 'I can't pay you anything because I can't even go in.' She told the boy what had happened with the villain the previous day on the bus.

He laughed. 'Baas, is that it?' Dalya took out a neck

scarf from his pocket and tied it across his face. 'Let me fix this and you can pay me double. Just tell the interview Madam that you got caught in the preparations.'

'What preparations?'

'Everyone knows about the thirtieth anniversary preparations. Even Madam will understand your lateness because of that.' Dalya ran towards the Colony gates. He danced with one hand behind his head and one on his waist, thrusting his hips forward and back. 'Eh you pervert,' he shouted at the villain. 'I know your dirty secret and I am going to tell your boss you have been harassing old women on the bus, wanting to jump inside their blouses. Don't try and stop me.'

Dalya looked towards Dilkhush and smiled before turning back. She wished she hadn't told him anything. He seemed incapable of keeping anything to himself.

'Don't try and stop me even with a bribe,' the boy mock-threatened the villain. 'I am going to tell your boss. The least he can do is protect old women like my mother.' He ran off.

Before long, the villain was out through the gates chasing Dalya. '*Benchaud*. I am harassing old women?' For a moment, Dalya seemed within reach of the villain, but he sped off.

15

Sloppiness will not Run this Household

The job interviewer was the same woman in the white car that Dilkhush had seen at the job junction. It couldn't be Jiyaa. The woman was too old. She insisted she did not want to be called anything other than Madam. 'Not Bai, not Didi, not Memsahib. Now, you know you are late, but my new idiot recruiter wasn't here to stop you coming for the interview. I might have to fire him too. This place is full of incompetent people.'

Dilkhush hoped the woman did not remember seeing her at the job junction the previous day, fighting with her gangly recruiter. Had he been fired now? 'I am so sorry. I was caught in the preparations.' Dilkhush glanced around for Jiyaa.

'They are a nuisance, those preparations. But I have a good mind to tell you to get lost. You should have left plenty of time for such predictable delays. What does this tell me about your planning?'

'I am so sorry.' Dilkhush didn't want to upset Madam.

'I promise it won't happen again.'

'You have not been part of these preparations at all?' asked Madam. She looked straight into Dilkhush's eyes.

'No, I...' Dilkhush didn't finish her sentence. She didn't know what to say that could help.

The woman took a sip of a golden-brown liquid in a stout glass. Dilkhush recognised the smell. Her brother used to drink it when important people visited their village.

'This kind of sloppiness will not run this household.'

Dilkhush nodded and apologised again. Madam was Indian, but so different from her in every way. She had so much money to live in that place and to live in foreign lands, to have people do everything for her. She couldn't tell how old the woman was because of all the make-up, but Dilkhush liked her smell and how she looked with the black skirt and sleeveless chiffon top. Her eyes were drawn to the exposed dip in the front of Madam's top. She herself used to sew such tops, but always stitched a thin veil for covering.

'Have you finished staring?'

Dilkhush looked down at the marble floor.

'I am not a dragon employer,' Madam said. 'But there is a clear understanding. You are a servant and that is that. If you need to clarify something, you can speak to us. But we are not the same. You will not speak as if we are. You will come here before we wake up, eat after us, and go home after all the work is done. I am not one of these people who pretend they treat their servants like family. And we want eggs and toast for breakfast, no fatty paratha-sharatha. The cleaning has to be proper. I presume you have done such work before.'

Dilkhush nodded. Who wouldn't have? Then she realised Madam probably hadn't.

'Why do you look familiar?' Madam asked. 'Have I seen you somewhere before? Have you come for an interview already?'

Dilkhush shook her head. 'I just have that type of face.' She hoped the Madam didn't remember her from the job junction.

'Hmm. You people do look the same, even to me. Anyway, the cooking is a test. Already you have failed by not coming on time. I don't want a lazy servant who sleeps late and uses excuses every day. But maybe your cooking can save you.'

'I will always be here an hour early. And I will cook the best food.'

'We'll see,' Madam snorted. 'If you had been here on time, both my girls would be eating by now. I don't want them even thinking about going out unnecessarily for food or anything else. It is dangerous outside.'

'I will cook very quickly. Today I was late, but that is the last time. I will prepare lunch and dinner sharp whenever you need it. There will be no reason to go out. And I can stay late and clean after dinner. I can be here as long as you want.'

'You don't have children, do you?' Madam asked. 'No one to send off to school in the morning and distract you? No one to get sick and keep you home? I will cut your wages or kick you off your job otherwise. The boy told me you were a widow and came from outside. You have no history in the town, do you? That is the only reason I gave you an interview straight away. I don't want any *lafdas* with men or any of your crying over beatings either. I have heard about you widows who have relations with more than one married man and get into trouble with the wives. These things are in the papers all the time about women who can't keep their legs together.'

Dilkhush wondered whether Madam kept her own legs together. 'I have no one you need to worry about.'

'Then, because I am who I am, I will give you a chance. But if I am not happy at any point, you will go without any fuss, understood? Don't sit outside crying. Too many times you women do that and put your tension on my head.'

'I won't. I will just cook for the girls and—'

'Girls? Already your lateness has spoiled my mood, and now this over-familiarity. I call them girls, not you.' Madam shook her head. 'There is something about you I don't trust.' She paused for a few moments. 'I think you should leave.'

Dilkhush pleaded and begged. She had to convince Madam to let her stay. She hadn't even seen Jiyaa yet, let alone spoken to her. Her daughter would understand everything. After that, there would be no need to please that arrogant Madam, or maybe to even see her again. 'Please just give me one more chance today.'

'I have made up my mind.'

'Please, you said everyone is hungry. At least let me show you my cooking. You don't even have to give me the job. I will try and make up for being late and making you angry.' Dilkhush listed a host of tasks she would do for Madam that day, if only she could stay and show that she was a good worker.

Madam took another sip of her drink.

Dilkhush took that as a good sign. 'Many people eat my food and say it is so good, they get a high from it.'

'Think a lot of yourself, don't you?'

'Give her a chance.' It was an older woman's voice, from a room at the back. The door was slightly ajar.

Madam walked to it and went inside. 'Ma, please. Let me handle this. You know very well we can't have just anyone from the street in the house. You rest, and let the girls finish their meditation.'

Dilkhush heard some murmurs of other voices as well. Naseema Bi had said there were four generations of them in the bilayati family. Before she could go and peek, Madam returned.

'Now look. I am not promising anything,' she said. 'We'll see after you have cooked.' She pointed to a door. 'Whatever's in the fridge, use it to make something. I will see how fast you cook, whether you can use minimum ingredients, and how tidy you are. After that, we will see about the bathroom and WC. I want someone who is a complete all-rounder.'

Just like that, Dilkhush was standing in a white-tiled kitchen, unlike any she had seen before. She put her bag on the side and looked through the cupboards and baskets. She picked up three potatoes, three red onions, a bag of wheat flour, and yoghurt.

Madam walked across the kitchen and returned with a plate of minced meat. 'See what you can do with that. Not too spicy or hot.' She stood watching.

Dilkhush wanted to impress Madam with the rough recipe Dalya had shared. She put the flour in a bowl, and added oil, salt, and water to bind the dough. Then she kneaded it. 'I'll just leave this for a while to—'

'You don't have to explain everything. I don't care how you make it.'

Dilkhush nodded. She found a sharp knife in a drawer and chopped the onions quickly. Her eyes watered. She used to make vegetable petis for Jiyaa and decided to make the keema burger-shurger the same way. She chopped the chips-bips potatoes into sticks and looked through the cupboards for spices. Dilkhush saw a masala tin and pulled it out for coriander seeds, saunf, asafoetida, turmeric, cumin, cinnamon, and cloves. She was aware Madam was still watching. She put a little of each spice in a bowl and dry heated the mix to grind it.

Then she ground some ginger, garlic, and green chillies. When the oil had heated up, she added mustard seeds. They soon crackled. Madam stood back away from the cooker. Dilkhush added the onions and then the spices, chilli mix, and a bit of tomato sauce, like Dalya had said. She hoped Madam noticed her using such modern ingredients.

'Well, it seems like you are finding your way round easily.' Madam left the kitchen.

Dilkhush smelled the spices every once in a while. When the oil rose to the top of the masala mix, she tossed in the keema. It felt strange to handle meat, but she was going to do whatever it took to see Jiyaa. This was not the time for questioning or fussing. She made the dough and in less than twenty minutes fried several wheat *bafla*. The patties would sit nicely in them, she thought. She did exactly what Dalya had explained.

The oil was hot, so Dilkhush put the potato sticks in for frying and turned to the keema mixture, which was now cooked. She coated her hands with oil before rolling the mixture into balls, flattening them, and coating them with flour before shallow-frying each. She was becoming nervous. A cough rose to her chest, and she tried to suppress it like Naseema Bi had told her to, but one escaped. From the other room, she heard Madam's voice. 'You don't have coughing problems do you?'

'No, no, it's just the chilli.'

Dilkhush remembered the sensation of burning chilli the night of the gas leak. She heard Madam say something and forced her attention back to the keema petis. She could put some of the opium in, but she should have done that before cooking the patties. Now they were done, and it was a bit late. But she needed that advantage more than ever, with Madam being so hot-blooded. This could be her one chance. She reached into the front of her blouse and took out one black opium pellet from her handkerchief. As she crumbled it onto the cooked patties, Madam's voice came from behind her.

'What the hell do you think you are doing?'

Dilkhush froze. Madam walked in with long strides.

'Do you want to kill us all, you stupid woman? Can't you smell the chips burning? There will be an oil fire soon if you are not careful.'

Dilkhush saw the potato sticks had become dark brown in the oil. Smoke was coming out of the pan. She didn't understand how she had not smelled the oil burning. 'I'm so sorry, Madam. I was trying to hurry up and—'

'Hurry up and kill us?' She looked at Dilkhush suspiciously. 'Is that why—or have you put poison in the food?'

'Dilkhush shook her head. 'No, Madam, I—'

'Eat a bit of the burger.'

'Madam, I don't eat meat.'

'Then we have to throw the food out and you have to leave. How can I trust what you have cooked if you won't eat it yourself?'

There was no choice. Dilkhush needed to stay to see Jiyaa. 'Madam, please.'

'Do you want to leave?'

Dilkhush took a bit of the burger and asked God for forgiveness silently.

Madam was still staring at her when voices came from the front room. They both looked in the direction of the door. Dilkhush realised she would be seeing her darling Jiyaa soon.

'We're finished,' the voices sang. One was of an adult, one of a child - one husky, one girly and perky. 'Time for lunch? We're hungry now.'

16

Hexakosioihexekontahexaphobia & Four Words Ending with '-dous'

'STAY THERE,' MADAM shouted out towards the front room. 'The kitchen stinks. And I don't want either of you to get hot oil all over yourselves.' She turned back to Dilkhush. 'The girls are ready for lunch, and my granddaughter will need a nap soon. Hurry up and make more chips with new oil.'

She walked towards the door, and without turning back, gave Dilkhush more instructions. 'Stay here and make sure that oil is safe. Get the food ready on plates. Then clean up. There is no need for you to come out. Better safe than sorry. Afterwards, the girls will rest and you can clean the WC and bathroom. Then we'll talk about the job, understand?'

Dilkhush was glad she could stay. She tried to listen in to Madam talking in the other room, and meanwhile quickly changed the oil, made more chips and got the plates ready. She could take them in herself, and pretend she had not understood the instructions to stay in the kitchen. How else was she to see Jiyaa? But before she could do anything, Madam came back and took the four filled plates out on a large tray.

'My mother doesn't eat meat,' Madam said. 'But maybe the chips. And listen, close the door behind me.'

Dilkhush watched her go. She tried to peer behind Madam, before closing the door, but she couldn't see anyone. The voices were now elsewhere in the flat. Madam looked back. 'Stay there and make sure you clean up the spilled oil. And shut the door behind me. Are you deaf?'

Dilkhush closed the door and began cleaning everything. She heard voices in the front room again and put an ear to the door.

Madam was talking about her. 'What a thing to do, leaving the oil. She'll burn us all down. How does she think she'll get the job? First, she's an hour late, and then she does something so stupid and dangerous.'

Dilkhush mimicked her silently and carried on with her work. She wasn't an hour late.

'I'll go and feed great-nan,' a girl said. Dilkhush wondered whether the girl was Jiyaa's daughter. She sounded so caring and loving, feeding Madam's mother, or getting fed a mouthful at a time herself. The girl could do that with her real great grandmother, soon. Dilkhush would tell her that Naseema Bi could be her great-nan. The old owl would love that.

Some of the oil was on the marble floor, so she looked around for a bucket and brush to wash it off. She found both in a small room attached to the kitchen.

Dilkhush began scrubbing the floor before realising the marble was getting scratched. She hid the brush back where she had found it and wiped the floor with a cloth.

A husky woman's voice came from the front room. 'Wow, tasty Indian-style burgers.'

Dilkhush smiled. That had to be Jiyaa. She had always liked her food. Of course, her own daughter would have recognised her taste.

'In fact, these are sensational. Good enough for a restaurant. What is she doing here for a servant's job with us?'

Dilkhush stayed in the kitchen because of Madam's orders. But when the praises continued, she felt braver. She cleared her throat before lining up words in her head. Stupid her, she thought.

That was one thing she should have practiced during the night. Jiyaa had only spoken in English so far and would be more used to that now, with a bilayati family. Dilkhush had heard that even in their own cities all over the country, everyone spoke English rather than their mother tongue. She needed to use whatever English she knew to convince them she was the one for the job. She remembered Naseema Bi's words to show how her cooking was the best.

'Thank you, Madam.' Dilkhush was nervous. 'I am so glad you like the food. Actually, I was an expert in cooking even compared to hundreds of restaurants.'

'Oh really? Well, we seem to have picked a winner. But you don't need to call me Madam. I am just a regular woman.'

'Watch yourself, Indira,' Madam said.

'Well Mother, you're the one who insists on being called *Madam*.'

'There are different types of Madam, you know. Not just who you are implying.'

'I didn't say that.'

Dilkhush heard Madam whisper. 'These people here need a hierarchy to separate us from them.'

'Sure. They need to know how low down you think they are, right?' The husky voice then seemed directed towards the kitchen. 'Not Madam, but you can call me Indira.'

Dilkhush twirled the corner of her sari and smiled into it. She was glad her daughter was standing up for her without even knowing it. But she was surprised Jiyaa was talking to Madam like that. It was not respectful to speak that way towards a mother, adopted or not. She suddenly felt jealous of all the time Madam had spent with Jiyaa. And they had renamed her Indira. The name held difficult memories for Dilkhush.

She would explain that to her daughter. Just before the big gas leak in Jantapur, there had been terrible riots in Delhi. She had heard it was because the government leader had ordered attacks Sikhs in the Golden Temple. Bloodshed and chaos were everywhere. Kashif had gone to rescue his wife's family. He didn't find them and couldn't even get back easily from Delhi to Jantapur. It was the reason Simran and the family were alone that gas night. Why had the leader ordered the attack? And not only that. Before then, Suresh had secretly written to that leader's government for help with leaks and illnesses in their town. But no help had come.

Dilkhush would tell Jiyaa all that. She was sure her daughter would give up the name then, and be happier to go by her own name again.

'So you speak English?' Indira asked. 'Why don't you come outside?'

'No,' Madam said. 'No need for that.'

'Mother, you can't expect—'

'Yes.' Dilkhush interrupted their fight. 'I am speaking good English.'

'Yes, yes. I am speaking good English. Most excellent English,' Madam whispered.

'Yes, Mother,' Indira said. 'It suits you to taunt others like that. You're so classy.'

'Stop it, Indira,' Madam said. 'Not in front of them.'

The tension between them pleased Dilkhush.

'Right, since this is an interview, let's check your English, shall we?' Indira said. 'Even if you are forced to speak from behind the closed door. That way, I can tell whether you will be helpful to me for homework as well, which is the main problem with this naughty little one. It would give you a big advantage over others for this job.'

Dilkhush nodded, but didn't say a word. She didn't want to get anything wrong.

'Ready?'

Dilkhush cleared her throat. 'Yes, please.'

'What is the longest English word you know?'

Dilkhush couldn't believe her luck. She used to do

puzzles like that with the street orphans. She thought hard about the one they liked to use the most. She had repeated it so many times for them and she hoped that after so long she could remember it properly. If she did, it couldn't fail her. 'Madam, I hope I say it correctly.'

'Not Madam, Indira, remember?'

'Ma... I mean Indira, the longest word I know is hexakosioihexekontahexaphobia.'

'What the...? I have never even heard that word. What the hell does it mean? It's not a made-up word, is it?'

'No, no, it means being afraid of the number 666.' Dilkhush remembered her street orphans laughing about that word. There were so many things to be afraid of, why something so silly as a number? One orphan had the idea that someone who was scared of the number could simply turn it around, so it read 999.

'That is just crazy!' Indira laughed.

Dilkhush was about to explain it was real, that she used to spend hours in the Jantapur library looking for things to teach the street orphans, and that she had a good memory. But she stopped. Maybe she had said it wrong, and that was why no one recognised the word. Madam already didn't like her. She didn't want to do or say anything to sow doubts in their mind. 'Maybe I am saying it wrong. But you can check or ask me anything else.'

'Hmm, okay,' Indira paused. 'The classic one then. Which are the only four words in the English dictionary to end with -dous?'

Dilkhush thought hard. The word 'hazardous' popped into her head; hazardous chemicals that Suresh had talked about all the time. But this bilayati family wouldn't like that if there was some gas connection. She had to make sure she didn't offend them and they didn't find out she had lived in the town. After all, the gangly recruiter had stressed they wanted an outsider. She wondered how the other servants who were interviewed had answered that question.

After a few moments, she felt more relaxed. She realised what Indira must have meant, although it wasn't clear from her question. But it made much more sense now she understood. Dilkhush pressed her cheek to the kitchen wall between them. It was cool to her skin. 'Forgive me for asking,' she said. 'But you mean four things in English that end with *dus*-t on them, which I have to clean in my job? Like table, cooker, window and floor? They all end with dus-t on them. I can think of many more words with dust to clean.'

Laughter erupted from the front room.

Dilkhush hoped she hadn't made a fool out of herself.

'Ingenious. I want my young daughter to be around someone who thinks like this on her feet. And definitely someone who can be flexible enough to understand a child's way of thinking. The girl doesn't speak Hindi, and say if—if there is a fire, and a servant doesn't speak English then—'

'She can just point to the fire,' Dilkhush said.

More laughter. Dilkhush was so happy about that.

'I like you superstar. You get the job.'

'Wait, Indira,' Madam said. 'We haven't finished all the interview tests.'

'Oh come on, Mother. Not only is she a cook and cleaner, she speaks English and is a bright spark.' Indira lowered her voice. 'Most importantly, she has a sense of humour. We need a bit of that.'

'You think this is a big joke,' Madam said. 'But I'm not going to give a job just like that. These people have to prove they are not—'

'Oh, for God's sake, they hardly cost anything. What is it, a couple of dollars each day? I didn't want someone from India in the first place, and now that I'm saying yes, you're arguing, because this one hasn't scoured the bathroom yet? Are you going to keep going like this, interviewing and testing out new servants with cooking and cleaning every day until our six weeks are up, so you don't have to pay anyone? Jesus, you and Dad! Great-nan and I need help and you are not making it easy.'

'INDIRA, stop! It was me who grew up in this country, not you. I am protecting us. I know you and your great-nan need help, but your father and I understand the ways here.'

'Yes, you do. Here and the rest of the world. Is that why we are back specifically now? What story is he telling everyone? That he is here to pay respects? Or that he is a family man and visiting our great-nan, so people see him in a good light?'

'You are on your high horse, living this life of luxury because of him. What would we all have without him? What would you have?'

'Screw you, Mother. We're quitting this little charade.

183

I'm going to tell people why we are really here. And you can forget these sham job interviews for servants. I was trying to keep you happy, but I don't want to use these people any more. Every day, you pin someone's hopes on a job. Finally, when I pick someone, you don't want her.'

'Who do you think you are? You don't understand a thing. Different people every day is safer for us. If someone comes back, we can't know whether they...' Madam stopped. 'This servant came late. She almost burned the flat down by leaving oil on the fire. How do we know that was accidental? I even had to ask her to eat some of the food she made, to be sure. She makes up words, misunderstands your questions, hasn't cleaned the bathroom yet, and you want to hire her to come again? How can we trust her?'

'It's just as well they trust us, isn't it? These naïve people. We're finished here, Mother.'

Dilkhush realised she wouldn't even have to convince her daughter to leave the bilayati family. The voices came nearer.

'I'll go and tell her, save her the bathroom job. She can leave with some dignity.'

Dilkhush panicked. She would have to convince Jiyaa about who she was as soon as she saw her. She looked around at the cooker and the clean surfaces. The door opened. Dilkhush cleared her throat and smiled. Surely, Jiyaa would remember her.

Through the door came a woman in a wheelchair. It was a real wheelchair, not a makeshift one like Jaadu's.

'Sorry, I didn't catch your name,' Indira said. 'You've been great, but we have to let you go. I'll give you some money for your trouble today.'

'Don't you dare, Indira.' Madam crossed the floor to stand in front of her.

Dilkhush stared at where Indira's legs should have been—a dark blanket hung limply across her lap. How had that happened to her daughter? A pain stabbed her in the heart. She looked closer.

The woman didn't look like Jiyaa at all. She didn't have Jiyaa's blue-green jewel eyes either. She was simply some bilayati woman angry at her mother. Dilkhush felt sorry for the woman losing her legs, but was annoyed as well. Naseema Bi said Jiyaa was there. This woman was not Jiyaa. Where was she? Had the old owl lied?

'Seen enough?' Indira said.

Dilkhush realised she was staring.

'No need to feel sorry for me. Feel sorry for yourself. I have everything I need, apart from peace.'

Madam looked at Dilkhush. 'You'd better go.'

'But...' Dilkhush needed to find out where her Jiyaa was. 'I was told...the bathroom also has to be—'

'There's no need,' Indira said.

'Didn't I say go?' Madam's voice was louder.

Dilkhush picked up her bag.

'Oh, give her a chance, Mother.'

While mother and daughter argued in the kitchen, Dilkhush walked through the living room. She bumped straight into the villain who was rushing in through the main door.

'You? What are you doing here?' he snarled. 'Did Madam...she better not have hired you.' He pushed past her into the kitchen. 'Madam, you shouldn't have interviewed that no-good bastard bitch. Yesterday she even accused me and shamed me in front of everyone.'

Dilkhush heard them shouting all at once. Why was that villain following her every move? At least Indira was defending her. The arguments got louder. Through all the noise, Dilkhush heard a sweet voice.

'Are you our new servant?' a little girl asked. She was by the door of the back room, where Dilkhush assumed Madam's mother was. The girl was wearing a yellow frock, and holding a pink princess puppet.

Dilkhush's heart beat faster. She kneeled down and looked deep into the blue-green jewel eyes.

It was Jiyaa.

Dilkhush was mesmerized. She realised this was who the old owl was talking about. Her daughter had reincarnated. There was no mistake about it. The eyes were the windows to the soul. God had sent Dilkhush there. No need to wait for death to be reunited with Jiyaa's soul. It was happening in this lifetime.

And that made more sense than the bilayati family finding her daughter alive even after she was buried. Dilkhush felt she had finally been blessed. She put her arms out and hugged Jiyaa tight. A warming jolt shot through her body.

Even within those few seconds, her ragpatched hands and body felt like they were healing. Fear surfaced in her mind. This was not real. But what if it was? She looked into her daughter's blue-green eyes. The girl started to fade. Dilkhush stared and then pushed all her doubts aside forcefully. What purpose did these doubts serve? Her heart was already ripped to pieces. Her daughter had come to heal her after all these years.

'My darling Jiyaa.' She hugged the girl again. She didn't want to let go.

The girl giggled and squirmed away gently. 'You made my mummy laugh just now. My great-nan is sick, but even she wants you to stay and make my mummy laugh like that every day. Will you stay? You can help her look after me. She will be happy then. She is so alone now.'

'I'll stay,' Dilkhush said. 'And I promise I will look after you, my darling, darling Jiyaa.' She breathed in her daughter's smells; they felt immediately familiar to her.

'Who's Jiyaa?' the girl asked.

'That's you, my baby.'

'No, I am Abha.' The little girl looked around. 'Please don't say anything to Mummy or Grandma about seeing me here. I am supposed to be doing my homework with Great-nan, but I don't want to.'

'Of course.' Dilkhush felt tears roll down her face. 'I won't say anything. We can just play together. But you know you have to do homework as well. That is how you get clever.'

'But I hate it.' The girl's face started to fall, as if she was about to cry.

'Don't get upset. Look, let me show you something that you'll like.' Dilkhush took out the peacock feather hair clip from her bag. 'Do you remember this?'

The girl took the hair clip. 'I do.'

'You do?'

'Yes, but mine doesn't have the feather. This one is prettier.'

'Pretty like you.' Dilkhush couldn't take her eyes off Jiyaa. 'It's yours. You keep it.'

The girl shook her head. 'Naaawwwww. You wear it.'

Dilkhush lowered her head. 'You want to put it on for me?'

Jiyaa's little fingers had difficulty putting the hair clip on, and she pulled on some loose strands of hair.

'Ouch,' Dilkhush teased. When she got up, she caught sight of her reflection on a glass picture frame on the wall. The clip was wonky in her hair, which made her smile. She felt her fingers tingle again. Inside herself, more ragpatches and threads disappeared. Even her heart of puspatches started to heal. She checked the door of the kitchen. Dilkhush wanted to make the most of the time they had together. 'My pretty doll, do you want to play a game?'

Jiyaa giggled. 'My pretty doll. You're funny. Come and meet my great-nan. She doesn't fight like my grandma and Mummy.' She held out her small hand.

Dilkhush hesitated, but held the girl's hand. 'My darling daughter, Jiyaa. All these lost years mean nothing now that I have you back. I wish we could go home, my baby.'

'You have a baby at home? Let's go and play with her.'

Dilkhush nodded. 'Of course.' She, too, wanted to take Jiyaa home.

The phone rang and Jiyaa ran to pick it up. 'Hi Granddad. We have a new, funny servant. She made Mummy laugh.' She paused. 'No, they're in the kitchen. Fighting.' She listened for a moment and then raised both eyebrows. 'Why are you in hospital, Granddad?'

Dilkhush realised that even if the man on the phone was a gas person, she didn't care. She had her Jiyaa now. What Naseema Bi said was true.

She looked around the room. A pile of large embroidered pieces of cloth was on one sofa. A golden and white piece hung on the wall in a frame. How delicate it was, Dilkhush thought, showing the beautiful lakes of Jantapur, as they were before, with the mosque towers and temple domes glinting in the sun. There was no gas factory. It would have changed the beautiful scene.

She looked at the girl. Jiyaa was cheerfully talking into the phone with her Granddad. How well they seemed to know each other. Dilkhush felt a stab of jealousy. A small penknife was on a side table. For some reason, she slipped it into her bag and waited patiently for a few moments. She tried to listen in to Jiyaa's call, but remained silent. If she spoke, someone might hear.

'Okay,' Jiyaa said into the phone. 'I will tell them you will be late from the hospital. Bye.' The girl put the phone down.

Dilkhush hugged her again and stroked her pink princess puppet. 'Do you remember the puppet shows I did for you?'

'For me?' The girl shook her head. 'Will you do one for me? A princess puppet show? I love them.'

'I am always ready to do a puppet show for my baby.'

'Your baby is so lucky,' Jiyaa said. 'Let's go and play with her, and you can do a puppet show for both of us.' The girl turned towards the kitchen door and shouted. 'Mummy! I'm going with this nice, new servant to her house. See you later.' The girl walked out the front door and beckoned Dilkhush to follow her.

'Shhhhh,' Dilkhush said, hurrying after her. The door of the flat shut behind them with a gust of wind. Dilkhush turned towards the gates, worried. They would never be able to leave with a guard there. 'Look Jiyaa, see that guard? He makes sure you are safe. We must stay here, my dearest, darling Jiyaa. Your mummy would be so upset if we left. Already she is sad, and it would break her heart. Your mummy would miss you too much, like I did.' Her breath caught. 'I can come here every day, maybe even stay here. We can play together after I finish work.' Dilkhush held Jiyaa close and kissed her cheeks.

'What about now? Will you stay now?'

'I can help you with your homework and it won't be hard then.' All the ragpatches inside started to throb. Many slowly disappeared. Dilkhush knew she had to find a way to leave with Jiyaa, but not when there were dangers around them.

'Will you come and do puppet shows for me every day?'

Dilkhush nodded. 'Of course.' She picked Jiyaa up

in her arms and swung her round and round. 'I love you so much, I will do anything.' Tears fell down her cheeks. 'But first, we will always do your homework. Then a puppet show.'

'No. I will only do homework if you do a puppet show first.'

Dilkhush hugged her tight again. 'I love you so much. I miss you. It hurts so much every day.'

Just then, someone opened the flat door with force. Dilkhush turned to look.

'What are you doing?' Madam shouted. 'Hey you... hey, stop. Abha, get away from that woman. You stupid girl. Get down.'

Dilkhush looked at Jiyaa. The girl's eyes filled with tears. 'Don't listen to her baby. She is angry with me, not you.' She hugged Jiyaa. Just then, someone shoved her hard.

Dilkhush fell to the ground, and Jiyaa rolled out of her arms. 'No,' she cried. She grappled to get hold of her again. 'I won't let you go this time.' It was the villain who had pushed her. Dilkhush reached for Jiyaa, but she only managed to grab the princess puppet.

The villain picked Jiyaa up and passed her to Madam. The girl cried loudly. Dilkhush shook her head at the villain. 'You don't understand. She is my daughter. I wouldn't do anything that would hurt her.' She looked at the door. Indira sat in her wheelchair, with a look of disbelief.

Madam called out to the guard. 'Call the police.' She shouted to Indira and the villain. 'I told you we can't trust anyone. That's why I get a new servant every day. See?' She turned to the villain. 'Go! Get the police. What are you waiting for, you idiot?' Madam stared at Dilkhush. 'That's where I have seen you. You were fighting with my old recruiter at the job junction. That was you, wasn't it.' She looked at the guard. 'For God's sake, call the police.'

'Not the police,' Dilkhush pleaded. 'I can't go to jail. Please, I will come here every day and work hard. I will keep away anyone who is a danger. You won't even have to pay me. I will just—'

'You're not coming anywhere near here.' Madam looked at the villain. 'Get hold of her. We need the police to lock her away.'

The villain moved towards Dilkhush, but she dodged him and ran, holding the princess puppet tight.

'Shut the gate completely, you *bewakuf*,' the villain shouted at the security guard.

The guard hurried to lock the gate and Dilkhush's body filled with bile. She didn't want the police to jail her. This couldn't be the end for her and Jiyaa. She couldn't let it be that way. She goaded herself to get in control of her mind and body. Dilkhush felt a rush in her body. She stuffed the princess puppet into the bag and ran past the villain, pushing the guard aside to get through the gates.

The villain ran after her. 'Dial the bridge phone,' he shouted to the gate guard. 'Tell them to stop her there.'

Dilkhush raced even faster towards the bridge. She glanced back to see whether the villain would notice if she veered away and hid somewhere on that side of the bridge. Then she could go and see Jiyaa after the commotion had died down. But the villain was right behind her and gaining ground. Her breath was strained as she approached the bridge. She coughed hard. It was not the time for such weakness.

Dilkhush saw the bridge guard waving, as if to stop her. She had to see her daughter again, but she knew she wouldn't be able to reason with the villain or the guard. They were following orders. She had to convince Madam, but the woman was not even willing to reason. Dilkhush decided she only had one option. She would find the girl's granddad at the hospital. If he was connected even a little to the gas, he would realise. He had to be able to convince his family.

She would explain to him how that leak had taken her Jiyaa away from her. She was left with nothing, and now she had the chance to be with her daughter's soul once more. The Almighty was giving her that opportunity, not in death but in life. Surely the grandad would understand her need to reclaim her child, even if it was at his expense. She had already paid enough. She had to be with Jiyaa, in whatever way he allowed. Maybe God was giving the man a chance to redeem as well.

The thought gave Dilkhush such vigour, she raced past the bridge guard and he almost fell over trying to grab hold of her. She ran towards the gas hospital. Her hand brushed against the pocketknife in her bag. Dilkhush flicked the blade open. It was small and wouldn't hurt much. But once inside, if she needed to, she could twist it and force the man to give back her daughter.

Yet she knew she may not be able to do such a thing. She was a coward. That was why she needed Kashif. Dilkhush struggled with her breathing. She had lost Jiyaa once. She couldn't lose her again. The night of the gas leak swarmed her mind.

17

White Cloud Hovering Like a Ghostly Presence

DILKHUSH WOKE UP *in her room coughing. Tears were streaming down her face. Her throat was burning. She wiped her eyes and sniffed. It was madness that the neighbours were burning chillies at that hour. Someone had to stop their lunacy. In the darkness, she fumbled to do up the buttons on her blouse.*

Her daughter, Jiyaa, was cuddled up on the cot. She hoped the girl slept through the night. Suddenly Dilkhush doubled over coughing, and clutched at her large rounded belly. The baby. How was she to stop that stinging getting to the baby inside her? When she looked up, she saw a white cloud hovering like a ghostly presence in the room.

'Oh Ram,' she whispered. It had to be Yama Raj, the Lord of Death. She pleaded for her life, crying that she wasn't ready to go. She still had a whole life to lead with a husband she had grown to love, a beautiful daughter, and a new baby inside her...hopefully a son this time.

Her mother-in-law, who had come to help deliver the

second baby, was sleeping by the wall. 'Hai Hai,' she complained, hacking and coughing. 'What cursed thing are you doing, Dilkhush? Are you trying to kill me?'

Shouts came from outside. 'Run for your lives!'

'Run! Run! Pakistan has dropped a bomb.'

'The revolters have killed the leader.'

'The riots have come here now.'

'God help us. Who is after us?'

'Poison gas is coming!'

Dilkhush swung open the door out into the courtyard. She saw Suresh jump up. He hurried to the main door and unbolted it with brute force. A metallic noise rang loud. He rushed out, but returned straight back. His eyeballs were red and bulging. 'Get everyone up. We have to leave. Something has happened at the factory.'

Dilkhush wiped her eyes and wanted to ask what was happening, but couldn't speak easily. Her throat hurt. There had been other gas leaks at the factory, but they had only caused irritation for a while. She hurried back into the room to her daughter's cot to check if Jiyaa was all right. 'Wake up. Wake up, Jiyaa.' The girl didn't move. Dilkhush slapped her cheeks lightly, but when Jiyaa's eyes opened they rolled backward. Dilkhush wiped her daughter's face using the end of her sari, and picked her up.

'Help me.' Suresh's mother gasped. 'I am dying.' She grabbed her throat.

Suresh goaded his father off his sleeping mat and turned to Dilkhush. 'Quick. Get wet towels or pieces of cloth for us. Hold one to your face and Jiyaa's.' He turned to Naseema Bi and Ashraf Mia. 'You two as well. Hurry and follow us.'

Dilkhush swung Jiyaa onto her hip. With her free hand, she opened a drawer and took out her wedding jewellery to pack into a small bag. She still wore them wherever she went during her pregnancy. As she moved around the room, her gaze fell on the mirror. Through the blur of her streaming eyes, she saw that the red tilak on her forehead was smeared. It was a bad omen. She reached for the tin of red vermillion powder, dipped her finger in it and quickly tried to redo the mark.

'Forget that nonsense, you foolish woman,' Suresh shouted at her from the door. 'Get the wet cloth and get out.' His father collapsed on the floor next to him. 'Come on, Baba, please.' Suresh bent down and pulled his father up. The old man put one arm around his son's shoulder and leaned heavily on him.

Dilkhush dunked small pieces of cloth in a pot of water. She handed a piece to each of them before they staggered out of the courtyard.

Outside, some women were in petticoats without their saris, their hair untied, gasping and stumbling. A few carried children. The white cloud Dilkhush had seen in their room was hanging heavy around them everywhere. Much of it was lower down, around those who had fallen and children who were closest to the ground. The streetlights seemed hazy.

Men and women yelled out names, looking around, searching. Some shouted out instructions.

'Run to the temple.'

'Give me the children.'

'Faster.'

'Don't stop for anyone.'

Dilkhush's ears filled with screams and the sounds of running feet against the ground. One man carried several children, two on each arm and one clinging to his chest with arms around his neck. He tripped and the children fell on top of him. Dilkhush tried to bend down to help him, but she was heavily pregnant and already too loaded trying to carry Jiyaa. She stretched her arm out, but realised helping them could pull her down too.

She moved to the side. 'Someone help them.' Her throat was stinging. 'The father is underneath these children. He won't be able to carry them away.' She coughed. Crowds of people ran around the children and father. Some stumbled and sidestepped them. One person ran over them. Two men stopped and helped. They carried the children between them.

Dilkhush looked at Suresh.

'Hurry,' he shouted. 'There is no time.'

She followed him, passing some older people she recognised. They had collapsed and stayed down. A few had crawled to the sides of the streets to let people pass by. Some people helped to drag or carry the elders and children. Dilkhush spotted two of her street orphans vomit on themselves. She was glad they were at least still able to walk.

Suresh shouted at people around them. 'Cover your faces with wet cloths.' Dilkhush did the same, straining her voice. She tore her own cloth into four and gave one piece each to three old women who were squinting and walking slowly, holding each other's hands. The sound of vehicles came from behind.

About fifty metres away, several lorries trundled down the road. Men, women, and children tried to jump onto them. Many missed and fell hard onto the road. A few managed to jump on. Children hung onto ropes down the sides of the lorries - ropes positioned to secure the loads carried daily. One girl fell off. 'Get up, get up,' Dilkhush shouted to her. A lorry was coming up from behind.

The girl jumped up and tried to grab hold of a rope. She missed several times before catching one. But she got pulled by the lorry and slammed into the side. A man at the back reached around to pull her in, with the ground rushing under her.

Dilkhush turned to look for Suresh. He was dragging his father forward, one step at a time. He looked back. 'Can you give Ma a hand?'

Dilkhush was still carrying Jiyaa, but helped her witch of a mother-in-law.

They struggled and passed children curled up next to their unmoving parents.

'We can't leave these children.'

Suresh turned around. 'Let us get ourselves to safety, and I will come back for the others.'

Screams came from a distance. 'God, where are you? Help us, please.'

The farther they walked, the bigger the crowds got. They passed more and more people on the road, many who had fallen on the ground.

'Temple,' Suresh gasped. 'Let's go to the Ram Ram temple.' His mother slumped to the ground. Dilkhush looked at Suresh, who was loaded down by his father. She bent to help the old woman. The witch had lost her wet cloth. Dilkhush held her own piece over her mother-in-law's face. 'Breathe,' she said.

The wind rushed from behind. As Dilkhush inhaled the air without her cloth, she almost felt faint. She took the cloth back to breathe through it herself. When she passed the cloth back to her mother-in-law, the old woman held it tight and fought to keep it. Dilkhush saw stains of faeces on the old woman's clothes. Right at that moment, Jiyaa vomited slimy water on her. 'No Jiyaa, please.' Dilkhush turned to Suresh.

He came back, dragging his father and tried to pick his mother up as well. But they kept collapsing. He looked at Dilkhush with uncertainty.

Her breath was short. 'You go,' she whispered. 'Get help. I'll stay with your mother. But come back quickly.' A man pushed past her, and she almost fell.

Suresh nodded. 'I'll take Baba, Jiyaa, Naseema Bi, and Ashraf Mia. You come with Ma. And remember to cover your face. Here.' He held out his cloth piece. 'Keep this one for Ma. I will be alright.' He reached for his daughter, but the girl whined and clung to Dilkhush. Suresh scolded her. When he tried to force her, she cried and struggled. Suresh persevered, but couldn't hold her and manage his father too. 'Go to Ashraf Mia or Naseema Bi then.' But Jiyaa reached back for Dilkhush.

Naseema Bi held her arms out for the girl, but fell

back herself. Ashraf Mia helped her up.

'Mummy.' Jiyaa vomited again.

'I can't see,' Suresh's father said. His voice was breaking. 'I can't see anything.'

'Close your eyes, Baba.' Suresh tried to carry his daughter with one arm, and support his father with the other. But the girl kept slipping down from his grip.

'Give Jiyaa here,' Dilkhush said. 'You can't manage everyone. I'll keep walking slowly.'

Suresh's eyes wavered. 'I'll come back for you. I won't be long. After that we'll all stay together.'

Dilkhush looked at his retreating back. Soon there were people between them. She just caught a glimpse of Suresh bending down again to pick his father up. They all shuffled towards the temple, with Suresh putting his hand out to Ashraf Mia who walked slowly behind them, holding on to Naseema Bi. They steered around slower people and those on the ground. Dilkhush looked at other people fleeing around them.

They were screaming, coughing, vomiting. Many ran towards New Jantapur across the bridge, away from the cloud. She had asked Suresh to find a room in the richer, cleaner areas before. But he didn't want to abandon Naseema Bi and Ashraf Mia. At what price had that come? They should all have moved.

As the white cloud enveloped the area, dogs, goats, pigs and cows also stumbled. Cowbells rang with awkward sounds. Many of the animals fell and remained on the ground. Jiyaa vomited again. Dilkhush put her hand across her daughter's forehead and then on her chest.

The girl's breath was shallow. Dilkhush looked to where Suresh had been, but could no longer see him. It was a bad decision for them to separate. Their daughter needed a hospital. The gas was too much for her. And now Dilkhush was alone with Jiyaa and their baby. 'Suresh.' Her voice was strained. He was too far to hear her.

She was sure Suresh would find her at the hospital. She had to make sure Jiyaa was safe. Her mother-in-law clutched at her and pulled her down. Dilkhush twisted and broke free. She told her mother-in-law to wait there. 'Keep Suresh's cloth around your face. I'll be back soon. Or Suresh will.' She held Jiyaa tighter and walked with one hand on her swollen belly.

'Don't leave me here to die,' her mother-in-law said.

Dilkhush started to turn, to reassure her, but heard the old woman curse her.

'God will punish you if I die. A husband's parents are your gods, and you are a wretched whore that you are leaving me with this poison gas.'

Dilkhush closed her eyes and continued walking. She shut out her mother-in-law's voice. Memories of the witch's beatings returned. And the evil woman had almost suffocated Jiyaa. Surely God would punish no one if that old witch died.

And yet, after walking for a while, Dilkhush became upset. She should have helped the witch, not left her. She was simply slowing them down. Jiyaa was still alive. The witch hadn't succeeded in killing her at birth. As soon as she saw Suresh, she would tell him to hurry and get his mother. There was love between son and mother at least.

Dilkhush remembered her dearest friend then. She had been so grateful to Simran and Omera for saving Jiyaa as a baby. In spite of the chaos, she turned towards their house because it was nearby. Kashif was away for a few days and Simran was alone with her in-laws and daughter, with no other help. Would they even know about breathing through a wet cloth? Omera might be suffering, like Jiyaa was.

The white cloud obscured her view. When she reached Simran's house, no one was there. Just then, Dilkhush lost control of her bowels. Faeces ran down her legs too. Her eyes watered. This was nothing like the other times. She had heard Suresh and Kashif talk about occasional leaks at their work, and the stinging and burning. One worker had died. This was even bigger. Something was very wrong. The doctors at Ahmed Hospital would help them. They would know what to do.

She had to get Jiyaa there, and hoped Simran forgave her for not finding her. But on the way, she saw Simran collapsed on the ground outside Jantapur Talkies. She was holding a piece of wet cloth in her hand. Dilkhush couldn't see Omera or even Kashif's parents. She tried to reach for Simran, but found it difficult to bend down. She didn't want to squat or sit, in case she was not able to get up again. Her breath caught in her throat and her eyes welled up. Blood and faeces had stained the bottom half of her dear friend's clothes too.

Simran's eyes opened slightly. 'Dilkhush, my dear sister. You...you came for us... Omera is with her grandparents, but they sent her ahead because they were too slow. They are going to the hospital. Please find her.'

'Come on Simran.' Jiyaa dangled from Dilkhush's arm as she bent down a little.

'No, don't waste time on me. Save Jiyaa and Omera.' Simran's face softened. 'We didn't save your little one so the gas could kill her.'

Dilkhush tried to bend again, but collapsed. She was feeling weaker now and wanted to cry but she had to save her daughter. After struggling for a long time, she managed to get up.

Simran put her hand in her bag and got the gold-encased mirror out. 'Give it to...Omera. Tell her I said... you would be...her mother. Find her. You give this to her on her wedding day.'

'You keep it,' Dilkhush said. 'Nothing will happen to you. You will give it to Omera yourself when she is older. Come. We'll find her together.' Dilkhush tried to help Simran again, but Jiyaa heaved as if to vomit. Nothing came out. Then she coughed up frothy blood. It shocked Dilkhush.

'You have to go.' Simran was trembling now. 'Go.'

Dilkhush felt herself nodding. She couldn't think straight. Everything around her seemed so confusing. She had to get Jiyaa to the hospital. 'I'm sorry.' She had to tell Suresh to get Simran as well. Her face felt wet from the tears streaming down. But she wasn't crying. It was the gas. She stumbled, looking back a couple of times. Jiyaa had scared her. She had to hurry. She would find Omera later. Not far from Simran, Dilkhush's legs gave way.

Jiyaa vomited more blood. Dilkhush felt a sharp pain

in her belly and clenched it with one hand. She tried to push against the pavement to get up, but couldn't move. 'Please God, don't do this.' Her eyes burned. An old woman lay nearby. The woman's wrinkled mouth moved slightly. Dilkhush straightened her hand out to pass her wet cloth to the woman. 'Breathe through this.' She knew she couldn't stay long.

The old woman reached out, but the cloth fell to the ground. Dilkhush's chest felt like it was on fire. 'Hold on to it.' But the old woman's hand didn't move. Dilkhush reached for the cloth and tried to put it across the old woman's nose. There was barely any breath. Dilkhush struggled along. More people fell, a few convulsed. The gas was all around. For a moment, she felt like she had lost her mind. She was imagining a mad person using a giant spray can on them - as if they were small pests or parasites.

It was like something she had seen on Kashif and Simran's television. It seemed like a nightmare, but even if it was, she had to save her children. Almost instantly, her mind seemed less foggy. It was all real. There was no time. She got up and pulled Jiyaa up. They would leave the town as soon as this was all over.

Her daughter had become a dead weight. Dilkhush's heart raced. 'Get up please, my child.' She held the wet cloth to her nose and took a deep breath to push herself. She felt a strange sensation in her head. 'Come on.' She was now almost dragging herself and Jiyaa towards the hospital. The night seemed so long. Where was Suresh?

A bullock cart stopped nearby. 'Climb on.' A man

jumped out and helped her. During the journey, the owner whipped the bullock harder and harder. The animal was staggering and slowing down. It snorted and stumbled before crashing to the ground. Everyone clambered off and made their own way. Finally, Dilkhush was at the gates of Ahmed Hospital.

All around her were moans, and chants, and wails. The bells in the hospital temple rang. She dragged herself and Jiyaa through the grounds. Dead bodies were strewn around the compound. The orderlies were putting tents up, hurrying each other. The cloth from the shelters flapped in the slight breeze from the lake, before falling limp. She looked around for Omera and Simran's in-laws, but couldn't see them. Dilkhush was glad that at least Omera had run ahead, but felt a stab of jealousy. Why wasn't her own daughter well enough to run?

When she reached the glass doors of the hospital, the mounds of bodies inside stopped her in her tracks. Hundreds of dead lay on the floor, stacked on top of each other. Others seemed dead, with their eyes wide open, staring into space, with froth coming out of their mouths. A few were grabbing at their throats, holding wet cotton pads to their eyes as they tried to swallow halted gulps of air. Several women were splayed out on the floor, still holding their children. The doctors were moving amongst the patients, changing wet pads and giving injections.

Dilkhush saw orderlies separating dead bodies out and lining them on the floor next to each other, covering them from head to toe with white cloth. Some of the dead were still in sitting positions. It took several of the orderlies to stretch the bodies and lay them down with other corpses. Women lay on the floor crying, with blood clots stuck to their clothes. Small sections of patterned straw mats were visible from under the bodies. The air stank of faeces, vomit, and blood. Dilkhush didn't understand what was happening. People were dying or were already dead.

It wasn't like this any time before, otherwise they would have left Jantapur. She saw a doctor with a large mole on his cheek. He was giving injections in the reception area to people around him. He had a kind face and was sure to save them. A group of people was behind him, each person rubbing an arm. Dilkhush realised they had already received their injections. A few of them got up and walked about. They had got better. Dilkhush felt relieved. Once they got the injection, they would get well too. She didn't want to think about the dead people around them.

'When will I feel better?' an old man asked.

'It takes fifteen, twenty minutes,' the kind doctor with the mole said. 'You will need to urinate the poison out.'

Dilkhush was thankful. She had found their saviour. He knew what was wrong and what injection to give. She would ask him to go to Simran and save her. Everyone would understand she herself had to stay with Jiyaa. The doctor injected the next person. Dilkhush held Jiyaa tight and climbed over several people and pushed through others to try and reach him. A woman grabbed hold of her arm, and Dilkhush tried to move away. She couldn't help anyone else. Not yet.

'We were here first,' the woman said. 'We have been

trying to get ahead as well in this crowd.'

Dilkhush explained to her and each person in front of her that she had to save her daughter and the child growing inside her. An adult was stronger. Children couldn't wait. She looked up to find the doctor even further away, surrounded by a heaving crowd. He picked the last vial of liquid from the tray that a nurse was holding, flicked the plastic tube and injected an old man. Dilkhush thanked God for the doctors. Otherwise, how would they have survived? Those who were dead must have reached too late. She simply had to keep pushing ahead and they would finally be safe.

'Can you bring another batch and—?' Before the doctor had even finished his instruction the nurse had picked her way through the people and rushed off, carrying the empty tray.

'My children,' Dilkhush shouted towards the doctor. She tripped, but didn't let go of Jiyaa. They both landed on a cushion of bodies. She struggled and got up to move closer to the doctor, again persuading others who were waiting for their own injections to let her go ahead. 'Please.'

A few people didn't let her go past.

'My daughter's so young,' she cried out towards the doctor. 'I am carrying a child as well. Eight months. Please give us the injection first.'

The doctor looked up and acknowledged her. 'Let that pregnant woman come through.' Dilkhush was grateful. When she managed to get closer, she realised she had no money. She must have dropped her bag of jewellery along the way. Suresh would be so angry. 'My husband will come and pay,' she told the doctor. 'He is with his parents. They will need injections as well.'

The doctor waved away her words. 'Nurse.' He looked around and frowned, and then turned to another nurse and orderly further away. 'We need more vials fast. Where are they?' He looked at Dilkhush's distended stomach. 'The injection might be too strong for your unborn child. We'll have to think about what to do.'

'But you have to save my baby.'

Just then, a tall orderly hurried over and whispered into the doctor's ear.

'Have you checked the bigger medicine room?' the doctor asked.

The orderly handed over a piece of paper.

'No one has any more?' The doctor looked down a corridor.

The nurse from before hurried back. 'Doctor, I can't find...' her voice trailed off. They stared at each other.

'Round up the others,' the doctor said to the orderly. 'I'll go and make a few phone calls straight away. Send everyone to the big medicine room fast.' He hurried down a corridor. 'And keep looking for any remaining vials.'

'Doctor,' Dilkhush called out. She didn't understand what was happening. They still needed their injections. She hurried after him.

The orderly touched her arm. 'I'm sorry, but you have to stay here.'

She turned to other doctors nearby. 'Help my daughter, please.'

The orderly directed more doctors down the corridor. Dilkhush started to follow, but he stood in front of her. 'You can't go there.'

'Please help us.'

'The doctors will come back soon. Stay here so you don't lose your place.'

Dilkhush nodded. 'Please ask them to hurry.' She looked around.

'I will,' the orderly said. 'You stay here and I will find out what to prepare for the doctors' return.'

A woman lying nearby looked up. 'The nausea will pass, sister. Our colony is just outside the factory. This happens often. Only this time, it is worse. But it will pass. Don't worry.'

After a while, Dilkhush went down the corridor herself, searching room by room. Finally, she reached a large room. Several doctors were there.

The doctor with the mole raised his voice. 'Come on, we have to hurry. Those people outside need something.'

Another doctor shook his head. 'We didn't think this antidote would be needed for such a gas leak. How could we have planned for this? We only have the vials here by chance, for poisoning and suicide attempts with cyanide, so the stocks are limited. We didn't foresee we would also need them for... this is a disaster. We don't have any left. We wouldn't have kept thousands for suicides and poisoning... unless... we just didn't know they would be needed in such a situation.'

Dilkhush pushed through the group and looked at the moled doctor. 'Please give my daughter the injection.

Don't let her die.'

'You shouldn't be here.'

'That injection you were giving. It made those people better. I need that for my daughter.'

The doctor with the mole looked at the others around him and hesitated. 'We are calling all dispensaries and clinics if they have more. Ours...ours have finished here.'

'Can you give her anything else?'

The doctor nodded. 'We are calling the factory again. They told us about this antidote in the first place. They will know what else can work.'

Another doctor nearby cleared his throat and spoke to the group. 'They might even keep stocks of this antidote.'

Dilkhush turned so they could see Jiyaa's face. 'Please find something.'

The doctor with the mole nodded again. 'We are trying our best to get more information. We want to save your daughter as well.'

Another doctor spoke from the back. 'Sir, if we can find out what is in the gas, we can try different antidotes.'

'I have asked. I have sent a message as well.'

'Just give my daughter one injection, that's all.' Dilkhush said. 'Please. You don't even have to help me. Only my daughter. You are all doctors. You must have something that will save her.'

'If we give her something without knowing what is in the gas, there could be a reaction. She could end up worse.'

'What is worse than her dying? Please try anything.'

'We are just waiting to hear back. I will phone again.'

'But, how long...' Dilkhush looked inside the glass cabinets standing against the wall. 'There have to be more injections here.' She tried to yank the locked doors open.

'Please stop that.' The orderly held Dilkhush's fists gently for a moment, before releasing them. 'The wrong injection could harm your daughter.'

'But look at the dying people outside,' Dilkhush said. 'What if that happens to Jiyaa?' She didn't understand why the doctors were waiting. 'Those people you helped, they look well now. Please doctor, maybe a similar medicine even.' She was shaking. 'I won't ask for anything else. Just make my child better.'

The orderly guided Dilkhush away as the moled doctor picked up the phone on a nearby desk.

When the doctors returned to the main reception area, Dilkhush hurried to them but fell. She landed on someone's arm and struggled to balance as she got up. She picked Jiyaa up with a grunt. 'Did they tell you what to do? Can you help us now, Doctor?'

The doctor with the mole knelt down and spoke softly. He was so close to her and his face seemed so kind. 'It has been confirmed that the gas is only a mild irritant. It will last for a short time, like tear gas.'

The orderly came from behind with tablets, cotton wool, and plastic glasses. They handed out the tablets. 'We can give this antibiotic and wipe your eyes with water. And I can give you a drug for breathlessness.'

'They told you which medicine to use before,' Dilkhush said. 'And it made people better. How will cotton wool and water help instead of that?'

The doctor didn't say anything.

Dilkhush stared at him. 'Why aren't you doing something? My daughter—'

'We're dying, Doctor,' a woman near them said. 'The nurses wiped my eyes with water, but it is not helping.'

Dilkhush's throat felt thick. 'My Jiyaa is going to die unless you do something.' She looked into the doctor's eyes, but they wavered. 'Please tell these people who are saying it's tear gas to come. They will see with their own eyes that it is that it is killing people.'

'I have explained to them everything that is happening,' the doctor said. 'I have also asked around for more injections so please stay within the hospital grounds.'

Dilkhush's eyes filled with tears. 'I will worship you forever, doctor. We will fast in your name. Please, just save my daughter.'

The doctor crushed the antibiotics in an empty glass, and the orderly filled the glass with water. Dilkhush looked at both of them. She didn't say a word, and supported her daughter's head to help her swallow. The orderly wiped Jiyaa's eyes and made a space for them to sit. But Dilkhush held her daughter to her chest, and went from one doctor to another, asking each for help. They all said the same thing. They had no injections left. She couldn't understand it. This was the medicine they needed, so why didn't someone send enough for them all?

People were struggling towards the hospital and filling up more of the courtyard. The noise of coughing, heaving, vomiting and crying increased. The doctors became busier with the pads and water. Dilkhush didn't know why they were left to suffer like that. She had to help herself with whatever she could. She would pray hard that the poison didn't affect Jiyaa. And that the injections from other places arrived fast. Where was Suresh? Was he all right?

For a fleeting moment, she thought about Omera and looked for the girl. But there was such chaos, she couldn't see her anywhere. Dilkhush didn't know what to do. She hoped Omera saw her and came. She had let Simran down already. No one had medicines to take back to her friend. Dilkhush walked slowly towards the temple in the hospital courtyard and sat on the wall, resting her back against a pillar. It seemed only the God that had allowed this to happen could save them all. She couldn't move any more. Her swollen belly was starting to hurt. And she had to make sure Jiyaa made it through.

The shiny red curtains that normally shielded the idols in the night were open. Did God see anything? Dilkhush held Jiyaa close. 'How are you, my jewel?' Jiyaa didn't open her eyes, but her cheeks were rosy. Maybe that was a good sign - that her blood was healthy and running through her body. Dilkhush felt a little better about that. If the doctors wouldn't help her, at least God would.

She held her daughter through the rest of the night in front of the temple idols. 'You will be fine, my baby. I am your mother after all. And you know mother knows best.' Around her, people died. Men, women and children cried. Two babies lay still next to a sobbing mother.

All night, more people arrived and died. Dilkhush

prayed throughout for her daughter to get better fast. They should have left the town as soon as the leaks started. She simply hadn't wanted to go back to her witch of a mother-in-law. Why hadn't they gone elsewhere? Her punishment was so severe.

She prayed harder. Surely Jiyaa would wake soon. Her sweet innocent child had done nothing wrong.

In the early hours of the morning, Jiyaa's body stopped moving.

With her eyes shut tight, Dilkhush kept patting her daughter's chest and kissing her head. Her thoughts jarred. Even the gentle movement of Jiyaa's slight breathing had stopped. Dilkhush stayed like that for a long time, hugging her daughter and stroking her hair. Her heart felt so heavy that she struggled to breathe. She pleaded with God. He had the power to save her.

Soon Jiyaa woke up and giggled. She had been teasing her mother. Dilkhush felt such joy in her heart and held her daughter tight. She let herself breathe more easily. They were through to the other side. Everything would be fine. They would leave Jantapur as soon as she saw Suresh. She hummed and sang to Jiyaa.

'...Kyu na phir ham dono, taaron mein ghar basaayein...'

It came out stilted. Jiyaa sang along and tickled her mother's swollen belly, as if playing with both mother and the baby inside. Dilkhush wanted to laugh. They had escaped. Somehow, with God's grace, she had managed to pull life back into her child. Her heart swelled and she felt at peace. She tickled Jiyaa too and played with her. Thank God they were through the worst.

When she finally opened her eyes, her daughter lay still in her arms, not moving. Dilkhush's insides tightened. She held Jiyaa close. 'Everything will be fine, my baby. Your Ma is here, nahn? I will take care of you.' She didn't believe her own words any more. 'You hear me, don't you?' She stroked her daughter's cheek. 'I will always be here. We are together forever, you and I. Don't be scared. I love you so much, my baby. I will always be with you. I am not going anywhere without you.'

The night had almost passed when Dilkhush got up. The orderly from before walked towards her with his arms held out, but she turned away from him. Her body ached. Her tears had dried up. She nuzzled Jiyaa's neck and kissed her forehead. All Dilkhush wanted was to lay on her bed with her daughter. Maybe everything would be fine then. Back to how it was. 'Let's go home.'

She struggled with her thoughts. At the back of her mind, she knew she had to make sure the gods looked after her daughter until she could be with her again. She mumbled the funeral mantra. 'Ram, Ram. Ram, Ram. Ram, Ram.' As she walked, Dilkhush stumbled several times, but steadied herself and resumed the chanting. She held her daughter tight. 'It's okay. God will look after us.' She stopped to cough and rest. Then she pushed herself to carry on. She had to find Suresh.

Dilkhush saw a pregnant woman on the ground. Her legs were wide apart and bent at the knees. She was struggling to scream and pushed her fists against the ground, frothing at the mouth. Dilkhush held Jiyaa close and lowered herself to the ground. She held the woman's hand tightly for a long time. Finally, the woman gave birth to a stillborn, whose skin seemed blackened and burned. Dilkhush looked at them and moved slowly. The baby must have died in such pain. She held the dead child and put his tiny body onto the woman's chest.

'Don't leave me, please,' the woman whispered. 'I have no one.'

Dilkhush felt numb. There was nothing more she could do. But she remained. The woman simply stared at the sky in the morning twilight. Soon she stopped breathing. Dilkhush reached out and closed the woman's eyelids.

She had no strength left to go and find the others. What would she say to Suresh? She felt nothing.

Soon after, Dilkhush saw groups of young men picking up dead bodies. They worked fast and seemed so strong, as if not affected by the gas. Where were they from? A policeman was standing nearby. She got up and walked to him. 'What is happening to us, Police Sahib?'

'Be on your way.' He tapped her shoulder with his baton, hard enough for it to sting. 'Everything is only getting cleared up. Nothing to worry about.'

She didn't say anything more to him, and headed home. Maybe Suresh had returned there too. Why hadn't he come to find them?

The sun began to rise. The grass and plants had withered. Streets and drains were strewn with bodies of cows, dogs, goats, bullocks, pigs, men, women, babies, and children. Nothing seemed cleared up. Everything was silent. Dilkhush accidentally stepped on broken red and green bangles. The glass pierced her soles.

She reached their house and stepped through the door into the courtyard. The peacock mural she had painted on the wall became blurred. Dilkhush kneeled on the ground and her daughter fell out of her hands. She reached for her and pulled Jiyaa to her chest. Blood had encrusted around the corners of the girl's lips. Her hair was still in pigtails and a peacock feather hair clip pinned her fringe back. It had belonged to Dilkhush's mother. They had attached a new feather only a few days ago.

The muezzin gave the call to prayer. He roused the men and women of Jantapur to help bury the thousands of dead. The temple bells rang.

Dilkhush felt suffocated. When she passed out, she had only one thought. Jiyaa was dead.

18

When a Child is Scared it is All our Duty

DILKHUSH'S INSIDES FELT as if they were alight. She had to be with Jiyaa again. She ran from Volog colony and raced past the bridge guard. Soon, she reached Ahmed Hospital, and walked through the gates, looking around at the empty courtyard. It looked so different from the night of the gas leak. The temple curtains had changed colour. They were closed, allowing God's idols to rest. A few people walked towards the doors. Inside, the nurse at the reception desk didn't know anything about an important gas person being there, but she went to check.

Dilkhush folded the blade back into the pocketknife's sheath and waited. She didn't know how she would be when she saw the man face-to-face. What would she say? He would know very well what had happened that night, and was sure to help. No one would want to keep such a heavy karmic load.

Outside, a temple bell tinkled. A rickshaw

put-putted. Dilkhush took out her handkerchief and wiped her nose. Several minutes went by. The hospital clock ticked louder.

After half an hour had passed, she walked down the corridors to find the nurse or the man she was there for. There were several patients waiting in line to see a doctor or nurse. Dilkhush couldn't find the nurse who she had spoken to and tried asking a doctor instead.

He shook his head. 'We don't know about any big, important gas person coming to our hospital.'

Dilkhush explained that she had heard the plan on the phone herself.

'Is it possible you misheard?' the doctor asked. 'There is also a Gas Hospital. Maybe—'

'There is another hospital?'

'Across the town. Not many people go there, but maybe that's the one you want?'

Dilkhush hurried there. The bilayati man wasn't at the Gas Hospital either, and they didn't know anything about a visit. She asked about other hospitals.

'There are a few private clinics,' a nurse said. 'Or maybe he went to a hospital in another town?'

'But he said he would be late for dinner.'

'There you are,' a patient said. He had been listening. 'If it will take someone till dinner to travel from the hospital, it can't be in this town. Even with our traffic, you can get across in two hours.'

As she left, Dilkhush saw a board outside of the Gas Hospital.

SICK SIKH'S MEMORIALS
MOST RESPECTFUL MEMORIALS 4 MOST
RESPECTED DEAD ADULT PEOPLE
& MOST BEST MEMORIALS 4 LITTLE BUDS
WHO DIDN'T BLOOM TRAGIDILY.

(Best price + design = lifewalla result for every budget
suited, even 4 your good selves)
((1 0 1 % guarantee to connect to gone souls))
((((No low-class memorial with low-class result)))
(((((Get finest memorial to live with yourself))))
((((((Tell friends and get cent per cent discount)))))

At the bottom of the sign was a painting of two children, a boy in khaki shorts and a pigtailed girl in a polka dot green dress. Both lay on the ground with heads limp on their shoulders at awkward angles, arms outstretched, eyes staring, purple lips turned downward. Beside them were toys frozen in motion - a striped spinning top and a hoop. Dilkhush didn't like that signboard. What kind of cunning-conning person used people's grief and guilt for profit?

She realised why Naseema Bi assumed Jiyaa's soul had returned because of a memorial. That is what Sick Sikh wanted people to believe. But Jiyaa had returned to her without any memorial. His sales were all a hoax. Still, she looked at the sign again and wondered whether her 'low-class' result was because of her low-class, absent memorial. She was being taunted with Jiyaa being so close, yet just out of reach. What if a high-class memorial got her within reach?

Maybe the bilayati family had built a fine memorial for the dead and were given her daughter. But Jiyaa was hers, not theirs. She had to explain that. If she built a memorial, would they understand and be less hostile?

She walked back towards the bridge gates, steeling herself to get across the bridge. Her heart softened when she saw there was a different guard on duty, not the one she had run past earlier. There was a glimmer of hope.

'My daughter is stuck on the other side. Please brother, let me go and get her.'

The guard looked concerned. 'When did you lose her?'

'Just now. Not even an hour ago.'

He checked to see whether she had a permit or pass. 'And your daughter was there with you today, you say?'

Dilkhush nodded.

'Ah, these rascal children,' he said. 'You turn away for a minute and they hide.' He looked across to the other side of the bridge, but hesitated. 'You don't have a permit to cross again. Someone will have to go and find her. Where did you see her last?'

Dilkhush realised the guard thought she had gone across with her daughter and left her there. 'I don't know exactly. I passed so many houses. She could be anywhere. But she will be alone and scared without me. Please brother, if you let me go through, I will find her. We will both say prayers in your name forever.'

'Don't worry about that. When a child is scared, it is all our duty. Give me your daughter's description.

I will call for a second guard. It will take a few hours for someone to look for her. But if they see her, they will pick her up.'

Dilkhush tried to persuade him to let her go across herself, explaining that her daughter wouldn't go with strangers and would hide instead.

'I'm sorry,' the guard said. 'I can lose my job like that. Anyway, she won't be able to stay there, so she will have to come out of hiding soon.'

Finally, with no other choice, Dilkhush gave Jiyaa's details. 'She was wearing a yellow frock and has beautiful blue-green jewel eyes. They will recognise her straight away and can bring her to me.'

The guard started to walk to his cabin, and then turned back. 'Keep calm. Your daughter may surprise you and find you herself. I will take down your address in a moment, just in case.'

While his back was turned, Dilkhush ran past behind him and headed to the other side of the bridge.

'Hey,' he called out. 'Stop, or you'll get us both in trouble.' He blew his whistle several times. Dilkhush saw two other guards run towards the bridge, but they were still a long way from reaching her. She looked back at the bridge guard. He headed into his cabin. Dilkhush went straight towards Volog Colony.

She would explain everything to Madam and Indira in a calm manner. They had to be made to see that they should give her work and even take her back with them. Then both sides would be happy. Naseema Bi would understand. Omera would be happy she was out of their home. Dilkhush would tell both of them that Kashif was alive. They could find him with Dalya's help. Even that bit of information could help restore some peace for everyone. And she could finally be happy again.

By the time she got to Volog Colony, the bilayati family was getting into their car. Madam saw Dilkhush and barked at the driver. 'Hurry.' They sped off through the gates. Jiyaa was sitting in the middle of Madam and her great-nan. Indira was in the front.

'Jiyaa,' Dilkhush shouted. 'Please, just listen for a moment.'

When the bridge guard caught up with her, he had a stern look. 'You didn't say you went for an interview with that bilayati family today and tried to steal their child of the same description you gave me.'

'I didn't do anything like that. They misunderstood.'

'You tried to trick me. You have made matters worse for yourself.' He marched her back to the bridge. The two other guards had taken over in his absence. He assured them he would handle the matter. After they left, he rebuked her. 'You took advantage of my good nature. And for that they will give me a good firing or kick me out too.' He paused. 'They want to put you in jail.'

Dilkhush's heart beat harder. She would have to run.

'Lucky for you I said it was my fault. That I made a mistake and let you through without checking. I don't know why I did that. I am so careful normally.' He shook his head.

Dilkhush looked at him, confused. Neither said

anything for a moment. She didn't know how to respond. He had shown her kindness. She should take advantage of that and share her predicament. 'Brother, these people have my daughter. What would you do if you were me? I just wanted to work for them. I was not going to do anything wrong.'

He scolded her again for trying to deceive him. 'I can see you are in pain. Why else would you risk something like this? But you are playing with fire. They don't think she is your daughter, so you have to get hold of yourself. You know very well that when you give up a child to another family, she becomes theirs. They are bilayati. They must have given good money for the baby. And if they bring her here to visit you, that is more than you should expect.'

'You don't understand.'

'It is you who doesn't understand. Another recruiter has been fired. No MBBS can arrange interviews and get commission. How many people's livelihoods have you harmed? You made your choices. Come to terms with them. Pray for another child and don't give that one away. These people have their rights too.'

Dilkhush stood with her head bowed while the guard kept up his rebukes. So, Madam had fired another recruiter. That would mean it was not the villain or the gangly one. Maybe the new one would give her a chance. She just needed to see the bilayati family once again, to first apologise, and then explain everything. She would work so hard for them. They would understand why and accept it. Whatever they wanted, she would agree to do, free of charge. How else had she been living till now? If that was her fate, so be it.

She decided this time she would remain mute with the recruiter, and not risk any outbursts. She had learned as a child from her father that silence was a tool not to be taken lightly. The first time she had used that tool was when someone asked if she wanted more sweets. The tool of silence hadn't worked then. Her father had explained why it was not the right time to use it. Now, if she didn't open her mouth, that snake of hers, or any of its cousins couldn't come out. She wouldn't ruin anything.

'I am sorry for causing all this bother,' Dilkhush said to the guard. 'Please forgive me. I will be no bother from now on.' He waved her away. It was lucky the guard hadn't called the police. She would need to keep him on her side. She had to go across the bridge at some point, unless she managed to entice her daughter to cross over towards her.

As Dilkhush hurried to the job junction, she remembered something Omera had said the night before. Could that be why she had lost out on the bilayati work? Hadn't the girl said she hoped Dilkhush didn't get the job? And now she had been banned from crossing the bridge altogether. Omera's cursed words could have ruined everything. If she found Kashif, then Omera would have her father back, which could stop her spite. But what if she never found him?

Maybe she should have asked Dalya to set up another interview time and chased Kashif on his motorbike instead. If that was him, she could have contained any revenge plans he had and reunited him with Omera. Even her own meeting with Jiyaa might be ruined because she had relegated Kashif and Omera's reunion to being less important. She had to get Dalya's help.

At the bus station, the line for the bilayati's outsider job was there again, in the same place as before. But there was no recruiter in sight. Then someone started to speak. Dilkhush recognised the voice. It was the man she had seen on her way to Volog Colony earlier that morning; the backward jogger who said she had beguiling eyes. She sighed with relief. That had to be God's work too. Surely this man would recognise her and give her the bilayati job.

19

We All Have to Help Ourselves

DILKHUSH THANKED GOD as she walked towards the jogger-recruiter, yet part of her questioned whether such a lucky chance could really have come into her life. As she passed other groups, she was grateful it was such a busy place. No one would remember her. But to her surprise, many of the job seekers recognised her. She overheard whispers about her unashamed returning. That was the power of work. People had such strong memories when it was in their own interest.

'That delusional thief is back.'

'Block her from taking our jobs.'

'We all work hard to find day-by-day work, two hours, four hours, whatever we can get. Then we come back to find her here again, trying to ruin our chances for evening work as well.'

A few of them went to the jogger-recruiter and pointed in Dilkhush's direction. Her skin felt clammy. Why did the local job seekers have to put their noses into her business? The jogger-recruiter looked up.

He squinted, as if straining to see. She was about to go and explain the misunderstanding the day before when a car started hooting. Beep, beep, beep. It was the same as the day before.

Dilkhush hid behind a tree. She gathered her courage to speak to Madam. But as she walked to the car, she realised Madam wasn't in it. Only the villain was sitting inside the car. He was everywhere. The bridge guard said he had been fired. She couldn't even rely on such hearsay any more. The jogger-recruiter went to the car and bent down at the door to listen.

He soon returned to the line of job seekers. 'Sorry, my brothers and sisters. I know you have been waiting patiently. As I was saying, actually there is an issue now. I am sent to tell you that the job is cancelled. I am sorry to ruin your hopes. Getting a job for locals is not easy, so I know it is even harder for outsiders. I understand you are frustrated, but I wish you luck in finding work.'

'But why is there no work all of a sudden?' some job seekers asked. 'We have been waiting here patiently.'

The jogger-recruiter nodded. 'I am sorry. An incident happened today. That's all I know.'

Dilkhush felt a stab in her heart. She had to find a way to explain to the bilayati family, even if that meant begging the villain for help. She hesitated about what to say and then hurried towards the car. The crowd obscured her view for a moment and before she reached it, the car sped away with all the tinted windows rolled up. She couldn't see the jogger-recruiter anywhere either. One of the job seekers pointed at her.

'That widow had a big fight with the bilayati's recruiter yesterday. That must be why none of you outsiders have that chance for work now.'

Dilkhush walked away to hide from the accusations. She looked around at the job junction. There had to be other work, to get her across the bridge. She remembered the large embroidery pieces in the bilayati home. If she could convince someone to give her some samples, she could use them as an excuse to show Madam. She milled amongst the crowd of job seekers. Dilkhush remembered her father's tip about pulling her shoulders back to seem confident. Inside her mind, she would pretend she had her own embroidery business. She would speak quietly, but with certainty. She practiced some words under her breath.

But now there was no embroidery queue. When she asked, someone laughed. 'For sewing and such, you can't come so late and ask about the work. It is given out immediately. Otherwise, how can people finish work fast in a day?'

Dilkhush tried other job queues, but they were longer now with outsiders also crowding around and joining them. A few job seekers, vying for work, reminded each other and recruiters about bad workers, including Dilkhush.

'Kick the widow out. She is a thief and has even lost the chance for all those outsiders to get a job.'

The same happened at the soap-making line, the shoe-repair lines, and even the cleaners' and leatherworkers' queues. Dilkhush was sure all those people had not seen her the day before. Were they passing on rumours to guard their own chances? She pleaded. 'I just need any small job across the bridge.'

'Eh, look at that. Job across the bridge. Branded a thief and wants only prestigious jobs in the most secure area. Look, once you are an outcast, that is it. No recruiter will risk his reputation for you, especially with those across the bridge. There are enough people here for them to pick from.'

Dilkhush tried to explain what happened before, why she had behaved that way. But no one listened. There had to be some other way to be with Jiyaa. God had got her this far, and she must have to do the rest. She only needed help to get to the other side of the bridge. Afterwards, she would manage, and convince Madam, her mother, daughter, and granddaughter, all four generations.

She begged silently for God to send a sign. Her eyes fell on one of Sick Sikh's memorial notice boards at the job junction. Of all the signs, why did she have to look there? The sign looked almost exactly like the one in the Gas Hospital, but some parts were painted over. The children foamed at the mouth in this one and their eyes were blood red. There was an additional warning at the bottom.

'NO REGRETS 4 BUILDING A MEMORIAL.
BUT REGRETS 4 NOT BUILDING. DON'T
LEAVE TO CHANCE!!! LOWEST PRICE THAN
OTHERS 4 LAST CHANCE FROM ORIGINAL

MEMORIAL MAKER! TRUST US. LIFEWALLA
MEMORIAL IS OUR ANSWER. WHAT IS
YOUR REAL QUESTION?'

Dilkhush had no money for whatever low price Sick Sikh would give. But her eyes had fallen there and the sign had to mean something for her. Naseema Bi thought her capable of pulling Jiyaa back. She didn't have money, but maybe her love was enough to build a memorial without any help.

Dilkhush went to the lakeshore and stood at the spot they used to go to for picnics, by the large rock that looked like Lord Ganesh. What better place could there be for a memorial? Volog Colony was across the water. Her reincarnated daughter might even somehow see her.

She remembered how they used to go boating there. Suresh collected water chestnuts with Jiyaa after swimming. Dilkhush had made Jiyaa laugh there with her shows, using different voices and puppets she had made. How sweet the water used to be at the lake, how she loved walking into the shallow parts, wearing her sari, to feel refreshed. But when Dilkhush got to the edge, she saw a very different reality.

Her reflection was barely visible. Under the water were heaps of filth and rubbish bags, as if it had become a dumping ground. Her memories came to an abrupt halt, fighting with the stale rubbish in front of her. Dilkhush sat on the shore and hugged her knees. Far out, the water shimmered. She imagined her daughter emerging from the lake giggling, as if they had never been separated.

Jiyaa ran over and asked for a puppet story. She wanted a new one this time. Dilkhush remembered the one Makodi used to tell her. But she didn't have any puppets with her. She pretended her fingers and hands were a snake and a frog. As she told the story, she loved the feeling Jiyaa's laughter triggered inside.

After she finished, she wanted to feed her daughter. She wished she had some of the special Jantapuri kachoris. Some shouting close by dragged her mind back.

A few teenage boys stood some distance away from the lake. They were yelling and whistling. Dilkhush ignored them. She had to start working on her memorial. She got up, scoured the shore and found a few large stones, which she moved to the Lord Ganesh rock. Then, she lined up several stones into a big square, about two feet by two feet. She filled this with pebbles and made a mound in the middle, like a pointed temple dome. She wanted water from the lake for her prayers, but it was too dirty. What answers to prayers would she get with that filth? She had to clean up. Cleanliness was next to godliness.

Dilkhush waded into the water and pulled out several rubbish bags and piled them onto one side on the shore. She knew the dirtied water would make her sari smell, but still she carried on. Further down, a few women washed their clothes in the lake. A dog appeared and took her by surprise. She looked to check whether it was the one from the job junction. But this one didn't have mottled skin or a red lump in either eye. Dilkhush picked up a stick and waved it around. The dog did not move back. Instead, it used its teeth to pick up a rubbish bag from the pile she had created on the shore and ran with it into the lake, dropping it back into the water.

'Eh, get out,' she shouted. 'Before I give you a beating.' The dog cocked its head for a moment, but went for more bags. It stopped to look at Dilkhush now and again. They both competed back and forth, taking bags in opposite directions. Sometimes the dog dropped a bag and paused to lap water from the lake. Dilkhush had started with four or five bags at a time. Now she carried six, seven, eight, depending on how heavy they were.

At one point she was carrying nine bags, barely able to walk back with the weight of her drenched sari. All the time she laboured, her cheeks burned. She saw the teenage boys looking at her and the dog. They shouted out to her, but she looked away.

'Eh, Sridevi,' one of the boys shouted. 'Have you gone crazy?'

'Leave the rubbish there, Hema Malini. Come with me and clean my house.'

'Yes, if you really want to clean, come clean our streets.'

'No, no, clean up the ghost gas factory.'

'Wait, let me say one. Come and clean me. Why waste yourself here?'

The boys laughed and slapped each other's palms.

'Yes, yes, make fun of me,' Dilkhush mumbled. 'It's not me who has been living like a sewer rat in all this rubbish for years.'

She carried on with her work, but soon realised that the boys were sidling towards her. Her face flushed. She'd had enough run-ins with others. Dilkhush made sudden vigorous dance movements. Hands up, sweeping around and down. Her eyes widened as if she was about to pop them outward. One leg up, foot against her knee, then down as she bent her waist, and swung from side to side. She held her nails out as if they were claws and lunged forward and back, twirling and jumping once, twice, three times. She showed them her teeth, pulling her lips back. Her breath was fast.

The boys backed off. 'She's a lunatic.'

'A good wife for you then.'

'Not me, you. You're not going to get anyone else.'

They laughed as they watched her from a distance. The dog also stopped and looked. Dilkhush finally fell to the ground and the sharp stones prodded her. She was breathing hard and her coughing hurt. Her chest was the stiffest and heaviest part of her, with ragpatches stuck haphazardly on top of each other, layer upon layer. They had become coarser and darker over the years. Some had disappeared after seeing Jiyaa earlier, but others had returned after their temporary absence. In the village, even when Dilkhush struggled to breathe, she continued to work, sometimes even harder. She could do the same now.

The whistling from the boys changed, and she turned to look. The jogger-recruiter from the job junction was walking towards her. Had the bilayati family seen her across from Volog Colony and sent him over? Maybe they wanted to hire her after all. Or was he there to keep her away from them?

When he looked at her, for some reason she felt a familiarity. He had a lot of grey hairs and his eyes were the colour of light honey, behind gold-rimmed glasses. When he smiled, his face softened. Dilkhush's eyes wavered with a sense of recognition again. Her heart fluttered with hope, yet something felt uneasy. But she didn't know where she could have seen him. Maybe at the bus station or from before the gas leak when she lived in Jantapur. The uneasy feeling lodged inside her, with a niggling wire sticking out from her brain to her chestful of patches.

The boys laughed.

'Eh, get your tickets. Love Story 2015 is starting.'

'Arey, Loony Laila Majnu.'

'Craaazy Heer-Ranjha.'

'Eh Brother, be careful with your heart there.'

Dilkhush's cheeks burned. Her wet sari clung to her body.

'Are you okay?' the jogger-recruiter asked, bending down. 'Maybe I can help you with those bags?'

His clean white clothes looked like someone had washed and ironed them. He shouldn't sit down on the dirty ground. A noise from the pile of bags distracted Dilkhush. A pig had trotted over to the pile of rubbish she had pulled out. It pushed its snout here and there. The dog hurried over and chased the pig away. Then it pulled a bag from the heap and dropped it into the lake.

On its way back, the dog wagged its tail.

'Eh, Brother Dog,' the jogger-recruiter said. 'Can't you see this kind lady has worked hard taking the bags out? You are undoing away all of her hard work.'

The dog stopped for a moment, then turned its back to them and carried on.

Dilkhush felt the jogger's eyes on her, but she stared straight ahead at the lake and didn't say anything.

'I remember the lake differently too,' he said.

The wire from Dilkhush's brain twanged. How did he know she remembered it differently? That meant he knew she wasn't an outsider and shouldn't have gone for that bilayati job. He was there to warn her away. She looked at him for any sign of what he was doing there.

He cleared his throat. 'I am Salman.'

A few moments passed.

'I'm Dilkhush.'

'Dilkhush? Joy of the heart indeed,' he said.

She heard the smile in his voice, but didn't like it. She was a widow. It was not appropriate of him.

'I saw you from afar and—'

'You saw me dancing just now?'

'I did.'

She turned away. What would he think of her?

'I thought I would come and help with the bags.'

Dilkhush stiffened. The man was spying on her.

They didn't speak for a while. The dog stuck its mouth into the water and thrashed around for a while. It returned with a water chestnut in between its teeth and dropped it in front of them.

'Well done,' Salman said. 'Proper treasure hunter, aren't you? Go and find some silver coins now.' He talked to the dog at length, as if the animal understood.

Dilkhush's mind drifted away. Maybe there was a way Salman could help her.

'I work in the library there sometimes.' He pointed to the brown building. 'I was just sitting down to do some work when I saw you.'

'I thought you worked for the bilayati family. I saw you at the station.'

'Ah.' He paused for a few moments and wiped his forehead with a handkerchief. It had the initials, I.F.

Dilkhush wondered whether he had someone else's handkerchief or had given her a false name.

'I do some administration work for the bilayati family. But just now, I was at the library and saw you, so I thought I'd check on—'

'Are you checking something here for the bilayati family?' She remembered seeing him that morning when she was walking to Volog Colony.

'I was checking if you were okay.'

'You are helping the family find a worker?'

'No. There is no work with them. Not any more.'

'But if you found the right person they needed, then?'

Salman shook his head. 'They are leaving soon now.'

'Leaving?' Dilkhush felt hot. 'When?'

'A few days. A week. Maybe tonight. They are not telling anyone.'

'Tonight?' Dilkhush's mind buzzed. No clear thoughts or words formed. Instead, they collided with

238

each other. She stared at the lake. The shimmering now seemed threatening. When the dog looked at her, she thought it was getting ready to pounce on her, like the one at the bus station. The jeering of the teenage boys seemed louder. When Salman got up, her words came out jumbled, about needing to speak to the bilayatis.

He was quiet for a moment. 'Don't worry. I'm sure they won't go tonight. I was probably being over-dramatic.'

But Dilkhush persisted. Salman knew them. He could help. She talked about all her skills. Her niggling wire stopped her from telling him the truth about Jiyaa.

'I'm sorry, but there is no work there,' he said. 'I have no influence or power over them.' He explained patiently that many people asked him for help with work, but he couldn't do anything. 'Also, I don't actually know you, so I can't vouch for you personally. If something happened...' He took a step back.

The snake inside Dilkhush stirred. Even with its head half cut off, it was spitting and spluttering. If Salman's child were there with that family, he would do anything. But she didn't say that. She walked away towards the water before he even finished speaking.

After a few moments, he turned towards the library. 'I'll ... I'll go.'

'No, please,' she said quickly. She had moved away for fear of lashing out and offending him.

'It's okay,' Salman said. 'I can see you have work here. You can visit me at the library any time. Or maybe I'll see you here again.'

Dilkhush blurted out whatever words came to her

mind. 'My daughter loved puppet shows. I cooked and cleaned for her, loved her, taught her to read and write. She did more reading practice if I promised puppet shows. I can do that again. Please help me with that.'

Salman looked at her with surprise. 'Oh, you mean you can do the same with their young one.' He scratched his chin. 'It's true that Abha is a nightmare with homework. No one has the patience.'

'She would love to see puppet shows,' Dilkhush said. 'I am sure of it. Ask her. I can help with her homework and do the puppet shows afterwards.'

Salman shook his head. 'It wouldn't make sense. They are leaving, so they don't need anyone here any more.'

'I can go with them,' she said quickly. 'I have nothing here. I will do all the work in their house, and help with the homework, and do puppet shows and even play other games. They don't even have to pay me anything. Just enough to eat. I can sleep in any small space.' It wouldn't be like her servant role in the village. There would be a heart-warming purpose this time. She tried to use some charm, but it felt sickly and sticky.

Salman didn't promise anything. 'If they already needed someone, that would be different.'

Dilkhush wanted to say something to compel him, but was afraid if she pushed him the wrong way he might not help at all. 'If a chance comes up today, you will ask, won't you? In case they are going. I can make their life so much easier, even in bilayat.'

'If the chance comes up, I will say something.' He

looked towards the stones and rocks she had gathered. 'I see you are making some type of memorial. You know, if you want a really good one - an effective one - you should go to Sick Sikh. He is the master. Then your memorial will deliver exactly the right result. Sometimes we simply don't know what we need, only what we want. Sick Sikh's memorials are truly brilliant. There is no hiding with them. His stall is across from the defunct gas factory.'

Dilkhush didn't tell him that her daughter's soul had found her even without some scammer's moneymaking memorial. Yet, where was her daughter now? What if Salman was right? If she didn't try it, she could end up regretting it, like Sick Sikh's signs stated.

'Can I ask...why do you want to work only with the bilayati family?' Salman asked. 'They were going to pay good money, but you don't even want that.'

Dilkhush didn't say anything.

'The other work at the job junction might be easier to get. If you need money, I can help you find some other work maybe? Like I said, sometimes we think only one thing will make us happy. Perhaps because we only know about that. Inkling tells us when a similar thing comes along. But it can be misleading. We all experience that. Other work may also give you the same feeling. You have to try without any ego.'

Dilkhush wondered why he had really come. He had seen her widow's garb and knew people could make the wrong assumption about them sitting together, just like the teenage boys did. Yet he had come and sat down, with no hesitance, explaining life as if she had asked him. Before she could say any more, he started to walk away. 'We all have to help ourselves.'

Dilkhush turned to the lake. She scooped up some water. When she saw it was dirty, she walked further down to try and get clean water. She let it dribble from her hands over the mound of her memorial. Dilkhush wanted to feel a jolt like before, as if Jiyaa was answering. She wanted her ragpatches to feel softer. But nothing changed. 'Bless me, God. You have already brought my child's soul here. Bless my fate to connect to her straightaway. Please God, be merciful and give me a chance.'

She chanted Lord Ganesh's name 108 times to remove all obstacles in her way, using the segments of her fingers to count. Dilkhush grappled with her heart when she finished. What if all she had done was not enough? She shouldn't be stubborn. That would be stupid of her. She had to try everything. The family was leaving soon. If she couldn't even cross the bridge, how would she persuade them?

Even if Salman spoke to them, there was no guarantee he would succeed. She couldn't leave it to him. He didn't understand. The family could leave without her ever seeing Jiyaa again. She couldn't go back to that. Salman was right. She had to help herself. She would convince Sick Sikh to build a memorial that would deliver her daughter to her.

20

Sick Sikh's Lifewalla Chaiwalla

DILKHUSH WAS AFRAID the bilayati family could cross over the bridge while she was away at Sick Sikh's. If they left that very day, she might miss them altogether. Would God be so cruel? There would be no point in ordering a memorial then. It was more important to go to the family straight away. She walked to the guard who had been kind. Maybe he could let her through or delay them leaving.

'Look sister, I don't have that authority. What job do you think I am doing? Keeping you out or keeping them in? Anyway, my shift is over. And as it is, the family never comes over to this side. Now with all the anniversary preparations, and commotion-emotion being so high, you think they will be rushing over? Too much mess and noise.'

Dilkhush was going to try with the guard coming to take over the shift when she saw the villain in the distance. He was walking towards the bridge. She had to leave, but felt better for hearing the family was unlikely to cross over while she was away. But the guard's reasoning meant she would have to go to the other side herself. On her way to Sick Sikh's memorial stall, she passed several groups of people busy with tasks. Three men were slumped on the ground. A boy sprayed white paint around them to draw the outline of their bodies on the dust. Every time one of them moved a little, the outline rubbed out. In front of them was a pile of brown rocks with a sign.

'PURE POISON. THIRTY YEARS OF SLOW KILLER
AROUND GAS FACTORY.'

One of the men on the ground cleared his throat and spoke into a megaphone. 'Thirty years of rains drove these poisons straight into Mother Earth. No magic removes them. For all generations up to now and the future, here it is poisoned but...' He stopped and cleared his throat again. He mumbled something to the other men and boy with the spray paint.

They continued doing more outlines of their bodies. 'For generations now and the future,' he said again into the megaphone. 'Now where could the poisons and gas disappear? There is no wind in space. Even the gas from that night had to go somewhere - inside people and animals, in the ground, in the water. It all stays here with us on Mother Earth.' He coughed, cleared his throat and practiced the words again.

Nearby, a boy was holding a paintbrush. Red colour dripped down a white sign. 'Eh Pyaara,' the man said through a megaphone. 'Your spelling. You are missing "NT".'

Dilkhush looked at the boy's sign. It read, '30 *Year Legal Negligee or—*' Several other placards rested against poles and pots of paint, freshly painted.

GAS PEOPLE: QUIT LYING! QUIT PLYING!
OR QUIT INDIA!

CUP OF TEA COMPENSATION FOR
GENERATIONS DEAD AND DYING

One placard was cut in the shape of a fish:

100% DEATH WHEN FISH DRINK OUR
POISONUS WATER!

All of a sudden, a police car drove up and screeched to a halt. One policeman in a khaki uniform hopped out. Dilkhush hid behind a tree. What if the bilayati family had sent them to arrest her?

'You people keep your preparations quiet, okay?' the policeman said to the groups. 'No need for everyone across the bridge to hear.'

'But that is the exact reason we are doing this.' The man with the megaphone stopped speaking when he saw the policeman walk towards him.

'I think you agreed to keep the noise down. If you don't keep it down after I leave, whose fault is that?'

'Mine.'

'Yes. Yours. Not mine. Make sure you don't get me into trouble. Make sure you say I warned you.'

The megaphone man doled his head side-to-side. 'Yes Sir.'

The policeman walked ahead and hit his baton against a tent labelled 'Hospital.' Two men at the entrance were making sounds of ghosts and laughing. They had black bodysuits, which had crooked skeleton bones painted on them. 'Eh, keep your noise down. Disturbance that I can hear means I have to shut you down. So, when I am here, quiet! Understand?'

The policeman went from group to group to warn everyone. Dilkhush didn't want to be seen by them, because of the incident with the bilayati family. She stayed hidden behind the tree. A cow ambled over. It stood in the shade and pushed against her. She squinted up at the sun, which strangely didn't seem to have moved much. The heat and glare were as fierce and punishing as before.

A boy came over and tapped his stick on two goats, egging them towards the shade. One of the goats, a black-and-brown one, nibbled the bottom of Dilkhush's sari. The boy nudged the cow to move it a little so his goats got space. He nodded at Dilkhush. 'Hot. They need shade and water.'

Dilkhush signalled towards the water pump nearby.

'No, no,' the boy said. 'We will go to the lake. This is all poison water here. I can't sell the milk then.'

The policeman left. Dilkhush hurried towards the factory to find Sick Sikh's stall. She couldn't waste any time and walked the remaining distance in the heat without stopping. She was thirsty, but didn't want to drink the pump water after the boy's warning. She had a reason for living now. The road got wider and soon she saw the factory looming. All of a sudden, something changed. She couldn't face getting any closer.

She wanted to sit down, right there on the broken pavement. Dilkhush told herself she needed time to think about the memorial design. She was about to sit when her snake turned on her. It was ailing and sickly now, but still taunted her for being a coward. Why was she dawdling? The memorial would need to be finished fast if there was to be any chance of getting to her daughter. The bilayati family could leave soon. She had to move whether she felt ready or not. Dilkhush kept walking.

Above the tea stall was a sign:

SICK SIKH'S LIFEWALLA CHAIWALLA

Underneath was a smaller sign.

SPECIAL TEA FOR RELAX AWAY FROM BOSS AND WIFE

Dilkhush was annoyed with Sick Sikh even before she had met him. The man deliberately pitted husband against wife. A group of men sat on plastic chairs around tables in front of the stall. They talked, drank tea, played cards. Many others sat on a heap of broken benches nearby. The small kitchen area had an earthen oven. Dilkhush saw a boy hurrying from table to table. She realised it was Dalya. She had to ask him to look for Kashif, and he would also know how she could get a memorial without any money. He would help her. That's what he had said. He was Dalya MBBS.

Dalya delivered glasses of hot tea and steaming snacks on metal plates. On his return journey to the cooking area, he picked up empty glasses and continued doing that loop. When he saw Dilkhush, he ran over. 'Heroine! You're here? Did you finish your work already? Vah, the bilayati family is generous, letting you go home earlier rather than finding extra work to keep you late.'

He ran to the back of the stall and brought out two folding chairs. He didn't sit for long, but explained he was there for the daily gas demonstration, and very busy organising everything. After they spoke, he ran to the back and returned with a large book.

'All the memorials are here,' he said. 'Just tell Sick Sikh after you have chosen one.'

'Wait Dalya. That man on the motorbike outside Volog Colony. You saw him as well, didn't you? Have you seen him before? Do you know who he is, where he went?'

Dalya had never seen the man. 'When I was racing away from that recruiter I saw the motorbike smoke. It looked like he was heading to the gas hospital. I don't know him. But if you want me to, I can find out. I know everyone in this town.'

Dilkhush asked him not to tell anyone else. 'I'll pay

you good money later.' She wanted to convince the boy to be silent. He assured her he would go to find everything out about the man after the gas demonstration was finished at the stall.

She flicked through the book he had given her. There were hundreds of photos of memorial statues and sceptres, with words of praise from Sick Sikh next to each. Some memorials were colourful. Some were a sombre holy orange or green colour. Underneath each photo was the name of the person the memorial was dedicated to, and the price. There were also a few words about the purpose: For blessing widower's new marriage; For liberating from all wrongs; For Godly luck.

Dilkhush scanned several pages and finally saw the one Naseema Bi had mentioned: 'Lifewalla Memorial - Reuniting lost souls with lifewalla happiness.' The memorial was a sculpture of a large white flower sheltering a small bud, both with curved stalks on a lotus leaf. This was supposed to be the secret to all her joys? She didn't know why, but Dilkhush would promise to pay Sick Sikh as soon as she could. When she asked for him, Dalya explained he was busy.

'You are also here to see the gas demonstration, aren't you?' he asked. 'Of course, that is why you have come at this very time. Sick Sikh will be able to speak afterwards.'

Suddenly a loud voice shouted. 'Get everyone ready!' A man with a megaphone urged everyone to get into their positions. Several children with various disabilities appeared. Dilkhush realised they had been sitting in the shade of the tea stall's walls. She had seen a few of them on the previous day, on her way to Naseema Bi's house.

She remembered the boy with the bulging eye and oversized head. There were many children with weak legs, unable to support their bodies. Some had malformed hands and feet. A white van came to a slow stop, and a guide jumped out. He led a group of loud-talking, wide-stepping foreigners to the stall. Many in the group were young. Dilkhush stood in one corner of the stall, watching. She jumped when a man's booming voice sounded. It vibrated right through her body.

'Feed everyone first. That will get them ready good and proper.'

21

A Fascinating but
Questionable Venture

'Hello tourists,' Dalya said, as he ushered away two tables of people in front of the tea stall to create space for the tourist newcomers. Instead of finding other places to sit, the displaced people stood with their cups of tea right next to the visitors, talking over their heads. A few tourists were in colourful clothes: T-shirts with pictures of Shiva, Ganesh, or the Aum symbol. Many had beige or green trousers and beige T-shirts. Dilkhush thought they laughed and chatted so easily.

Two girls jabbered away at each other and looked at a man sitting with them. One took her camera out. She took pictures of the stall, and when she pointed it towards Dilkhush, Dalya hurried over.

'Widow.' He doled his head side-to-side. 'No photo. Please, be respectful.'

Dilkhush was glad at first, but then she saw the

woman taking photos of the children, asking them to stand in groups or separately. She gave each of them coins. Dilkhush realised she too could get coins that way. She hesitated at first, but waved discreetly to the woman. The guide called all of them to order food just then. The woman put her camera on the table and turned to her group. Dilkhush wanted to interrupt her to ask whether she wanted a photo. She could look even more of a miserable widow if that would attract money for a picture.

Maybe then others would also want her photo, and give her money. But Dalya appeared again. Within moments, he was busy making trips to the kitchen and back with plates of snacks. The tourists ate, drank and talked. Some said they did not like the food, but the plates still emptied fast. The booming voice from before sounded again from the back of the tea stall.

'Who the hell is here?' A tall, stocky man with an oversized multi-coloured turban appeared. He stood watching everyone. His beard was tightly packed in a black net against his chin, and his eyes were bloodshot. He seemed a terrifying, vulgar man. That was Sick Sikh, of the memorials? How could such an elephant be in a business dealing with delicate lost souls? With giant steps, he soon reached the tourists' table. 'Benchaud new people here and everywhere. Come to see the gas spectacle have you?' He stood in front of them. 'Bastards, every one of you tourists.'

Some of the younger tourists giggled. Dilkhush was glad he did not shout as loudly as before.

'Got your cameras, have you?' Sick Sikh leaned over their table, almost covering it with his big frame. He put his hands on the edges, and scanned the used plates and leftovers in bowls. 'Get your dollars ready to hand over.' He collected notes from each of the tourists. 'Good. I will go and prepare everything.' He counted the money as he walked away.

Sick Sikh seemed to make money fast. Some of the tourists opened their books and talked amongst themselves.

'Yes, look. Here is a photo,' one of them said. 'That is definitely him. Who else could be so rude to his customers? The food isn't even that good.'

'Eh Dalya,' Sick Sikh shouted from the back. 'You forgot the drinks coasters.'

Dalya rushed around putting coasters under each of the glasses and cups on the tourists' table. 'Gifts,' he said. 'You can buy new packs for the home or hotels in your country. Mementos, presents. There is a photo of the same people before and after the gas leak.'

Sick Sikh's voice came again. 'Get some new packs out, Dalya. Tell them we have used good-looking faces. These foreigners can't bear the truth otherwise.'

The tourists looked at each other's coasters and passed them around. Dilkhush wanted to see the pictures as well. She caught a glimpse. They were pictures of people. Happy pictures in colour, others in black and white.

'Colour pictures are before the gas leak,' Dalya explained.

Dilkhush didn't understand why tourists would want

photos of strangers. But Dalya sold new packs and went to give the money to Sick Sikh. If she had some with her own face, she could sell them too. But she would have to get visitors to bypass Sick Sikh's packs.

A woman wearing a pink dress pushed back her chair and came towards Dilkhush. She was holding a camera. 'Hello. You are a widow, aren't you? I read about the dull, white sari widows have to wear. What a bore. But I saw your colourful peacock hair clip from over there.' She gestured at her seat. 'It's so pretty. Shall I straighten it for you?'

Dilkhush had forgotten about her crooked hair clip. She saw Dalya from the corner of her eye. He was coming over. She waved him away and slid the clip from her hair.

'Gorgeous,' the woman said.

'I made it.' Dilkhush was glad she could still remember some English. She had rarely spoken it over the last thirty years, and now twice in one day she had used it. The only other times were when she had tried to teach Makodi how to read, but the orphan was not interested. She preferred to hear stories. Dilkhush used to bribe her with puppet stories in return for learning to read. She told Makodi stories without using puppets, so that she didn't betray Jiyaa.

'You made this hair clip?' The woman sounded surprised.

Dilkhush nodded. She had attached the feather herself but it had become old now. She should have put a new one in for Jiyaa before going that morning. That might have helped. It would have shown she cared.

Sick Sikh's voice reached out to the front. 'Come on then.'

The woman handed back Dilkhush's hair clip. 'It's really lovely. And you are really beautiful.' Before she walked back to her chair, she quickly took a photo as Dilkhush put her hair clip back on. It was the only colourful thing she was wearing. She wished she could wear better clothes for pictures. She might be more popular then. Dilkhush saw the woman take the photo and so, straightened up, but the woman had finished.

Dalya came over. 'Madam,' he said to the woman in pink. 'These coasters give you perfect before-and-after photos. Better that you buy these.'

Dilkhush pursed her lips. If the woman wanted to pay her for a photo, it was not anyone else's business. But the woman didn't give her any money.

Sick Sikh returned to the table. 'So, are you ready to see what you greedy fucking people did to us?'

The woman in pink scowled. 'Excuse me, we're not all the same. And even if we were, we didn't have anything to do with all this personally. Besides, foreigners didn't come here and poison you. Your own people were also in charge. Do you treat your Indian tourists like this as well? Or your ministers who should have helped you? Just because we are not from here, you are—'

'And just because we are from here, and poor, you people can stand by and watch us die?'

The woman frowned. 'You take our money for the demonstration and all this no-good food and then are so rude—'

'You are a foreigner, so you have read the guidebook, yes?' Sick Sikh smiled. 'So play the game. Otherwise, why are you here?'

A few in the group laughed. 'He's right.'

The woman shook her head.

'If you are not happy, you can have your money back,' Sick Sikh said. 'You don't want to come and see, I don't care this way or that. If not you, then your brother, father, mother, aunty will come. If not them, your neighbour, doctor, teacher, friend. Trauma tourism.'

The woman argued back, but Sick Sikh walked away. The rest of the group followed him. Dalya hurried to her.

'He was not an angry man before the gas leak,' Dalya explained. 'But he smashed up all this place when his family died.' He pointed to the broken benches by the side. 'You came to see that, no? We have kept it all same-to-same like before. All these reporters who used to write about him, and all the guidebooks - that's why you all come here to see him, isn't it? So don't miss it Madam.'

'I haven't come to be treated badly.'

'Madam, I can understand. But in the travelling book, he is *"The Rudest Sickest Sikh with the best food along the poison stretch. A fascinating but morally questionable venture."* Now to keep business, he can't be different to one and different to the others. Please understand.'

After a few moments of talking, the woman followed Dalya. They snaked between the tables to a small, brick building behind the tea stall. It had a corrugated metal roof. Sick Sikh opened the door into a dark room and urged all of the tourists to enter. He told them he would return in a moment and locked the door from the outside.

Sick Sikh stood with Dalya by the front of the tea stall and drank his tea. Dilkhush decided to ask him about the memorial for Jiyaa. He didn't seem busy then.

'That's fine,' he said. 'You can just put a deposit.'

When Dilkhush explained she had no deposit, he frowned. 'That is a problem. It will not help you then. If I pay for it, the memorial becomes for me. I hope you understand?'

He looked at his watch and carried on drinking his tea.

'Hello?' someone said from inside the shed.

Sick Sikh didn't answer them.

'Hello?'

Then Sick Sikh went back into the shed. Dilkhush had to find a way of convincing him. She could ask the woman with the camera to take more pictures for money, so she could collect enough for a deposit. But it would take too many photos to save that amount. She looked around for other ideas.

Across the way, two bare-chested boys were gluing large photo posters to lorries. One picture showed white chemical sacks full of skulls and bones. The factory's label was on the sacks. One of the boys came over and spoke to Dalya.

'Tell Sick Sikh the glue has finished. We have many more lorries driving around the town without any posters stuck on them.'

'He's just got some money from the coasters and tickets,' Dalya said. 'When he comes out he will give you some.'

Dilkhush heard coughing from the dark room. She called Dalya over. 'What's happening inside?'

'The gas demonstration.'

'The tourists are paying to breathe that poison gas?' Dilkhush was shocked.

Dalya laughed. 'Heroine, no! Sick Sikh has to keep the brick room dark like that gas night, so he covers the windows. Then he boils cabbage inside for the smell, and burns chillies for the stinging. He locks the door so that even if someone wants to get out, they can't. All there is to breathe is chilli air. Sick Sikh says we couldn't get away that night, so they have to get some of that experience. He keeps it going long enough for them to get sick.'

'No one complains?'

'Everyone, but they choose to come. And one of the policemen takes a percentage. You'll see. He'll be here soon. He will take every complaint and do nothing.'

'Then what? They know from that what it's like dying from the gas?'

Dalya smiled. 'True. It's nothing. But if they want to try something real, we give them some pump water from the *jhuggis* by the factory. It still comes out poisoned. Most of the tourists who drink it immediately get a rash down their necks, legs, or arms. They say they feel their mouths burning. But we only give it to them if they ask.'

'So Sick Sikh behaves badly and uses our bad luck to

make money?'

'He has to. These people come for that. Business goes down when he is nice. He has two daughters from his second marriage and weddings cost a lot. We know that. Still, he wants to stop being angry, so I help him. Peak season, like now, there are many visitors and we have to do this demonstration many times. It's not easy. If he is calm, there are tourists who come and ask, 'Didn't it make you angry they killed your family? Did you really smash up those benches after that night?' They want to see him mad like this.'

'So he does make money out of everyone's misery to pay for his family luxuries? The memorials. The gas demonstrations. The photos on the coasters. He simply pays for some poster glue? So what? He should do something in return for everyone. He won't even help with my memorial.'

Sick Sikh's voice became louder in the shed and the door slammed open, hitting against the wall. All the tourists came out, coughing and spluttering, wiping their eyes. Many hurried to the back of the shed.

Dalya ran there. 'I forgot to give them vomiting bags.' He rushed to them and after a while returned to the front with a tray of bottled water. The tourists gulped the water down.

'God, my throat is burning like fucking fire.'
'I thought my ears were going to blow up.'
'I feel sick just from the smell.'
'Look at your eyes. They are like snooker balls.'
'I think I have a rash inside my eyes. I can feel it.'

Sick Sikh laughed. 'So you weaklings, how are you managing?'

'That was cruel,' the woman in the pink dress said.

'Think about going through that for hours and hours, throughout the night. But with poisonous gas, you lose control of your bowels, froth at the mouth, your lungs fill up, and then you die by drowning in your own body's fluids.'

He looked at the woman in pink. 'Or if you are a pregnant woman, you abort your baby there and then. Maybe, a blackened, burned baby comes out because of the gas. If you haven't died, you give birth to defected children, who might pass gas defects on to their children. And you can get cancer too. Highest rate here. Cancer of the tongue, lungs, stomach. You can feel depressed for years. Many times higher rate here than anywhere in the country. Your body can't process the poison, so you carry it inside. Living dead.'

'How do you know these are actually related to the gas?' the woman asked.

'What you believe is your business,' Sick Sikh said. 'When someone doesn't want to believe, they find any excuse. When someone wants to believe, they find any excuse. You are old enough to know what is being said here.'

'Madam,' Dalya said to the woman. 'Don't mind Sick Sikh. We don't want him getting angrier so let me explain.'

'You are trying to excuse his behaviour?'

'Madam, please listen, even for a few more moments,'

Dalya pleaded. 'In this town, there are six times higher spontaneous abortions. Twenty times higher cancers. Two hundred times more defects at birth. They said the poison gas is like tear gas only, and only prickling the skin or eyes or lungs and then leaving. What made people die that night then? What makes all these things still happen? Later, you will watch the film of the gas night at the information centre. At the clinic you will learn about long-term and short-term effects of the "tear gas" from the factory. The tears actually still come from the deaths the gas caused. Then you can understand fully.'

'Look, you all know nothing and speak rubbish,' Sick Sikh shouted. 'Everyone knew then. Everyone knows now. But who does anything? Which country? Our own country didn't. Everyone is afraid of losing business.' He pointed to himself and Dalya and the other men sitting on the tables or standing around. 'We helped each other. That is all. But how can we fight the poison when we don't even know what is in it, or how to get rid of it from our bodies and the ground? Nobody will even clean it. It seems enough for everyone to say it isn't their fault. That is all we deserve as humans?'

He lit a bidi. 'We will keep surviving, however defective our children are born. Maybe one day, when everyone needs us, someone will do something. Until then, it is up to us to live and do what we can to help ourselves. We never did anything to anyone. This is not bad karma for us. It is bad karma on those who did it, and for those who stand by and watch our suffering.

They will pay. It is the way of the universe. Balance is paramount. Action. Reaction.'

The woman in pink still argued. The rest of the tourists took photos with Sick Sikh, even though they looked terrible with red eyes and noses. Some still looked sickly.

Dilkhush cornered the woman in pink and asked her about taking photos for some money.

'No, thank you,' the woman said. 'I am not in the mood any more.'

Dilkhush bit her lip. She saw Sick Sikh looking over.

His voice was loud. 'You will be telling this story of survival to your friends at a dinner table or with drinks. That is why everyone comes. But I ask, if you need photos of people here, please buy the coasters. You can share a little of what we go through and pay towards some awareness activities to help the affected people in the town.'

Many in the group thanked Sick Sikh. A few more bought the coasters. They finished their bottles of water and picked up their belongings. Most put extra tips into a box Dalya held. The woman in pink avoided eye contact with Sick Sikh, but he went over to her. 'It was clever of you to ask such questions, so everyone could learn more. Thank you.'

In spite of how terrible they looked, the group chattered amongst themselves and seemed excited. When they were all in the minibus, the driver slid the door shut and started the engine.

Dilkhush was glad they had gone. The tourists had

paid to listen to Sick Sikh's lecturing, but she didn't need reminding of what had happened.

'So.' Sick Sikh turned to her. 'Which memorial do you want to put a deposit down for? I will give you the best price. A little more discount for being Naseema Bi's daughter. She said you have already built a super memorial and it brought your daughter back. This is correct, yes? Or is the old owl trying to fool me for more discount?'

Dilkhush tried to convince him to build a memorial in exchange for her own design. As far as he knew it had brought Jiyaa's soul back.

'But you are here because your memorial did not do the full job, yes? So I cannot do an exchange. Let's do this. You tell me where your memorial is and I will come and take a photo tonight. It is full moon, so it will be a special light. When someone puts a deposit down for your design, I will use that as deposit for your memorial. Fair?'

That could mean a long wait. But Dilkhush couldn't convince him to start sooner. What if the bilayati family left that evening? She told Sick Sikh where her makeshift memorial was and didn't say she had only just made it, but asked whether he could come earlier. She was wary of pushing him, but wanted the lifewalla memorial for a chance of catching Jiyaa that evening.

Sick Sikh looked at her intently. 'You are desperately sad. Not like a mother who has just got her dead daughter back. Are you sure your memorial is for the right thing? Whatever your focus is on, it should complete you.'

Dilkhush looked through him. What could be more right than wanting to be with Jiyaa again?

'What is truly aching you deep in your core?' he asked. 'That is the pain to do a memorial for. But this is not straightforward to know.' Sick Sikh took a puff on his bidi. 'You said you wanted a reunion with your daughter. You think that is your answer. It may not be correct or complete. What is your real question? What is that deep pain, that hole inside you, that you are trying to fix? Ask this in silence, and the answer will come.' He didn't keep quiet to give her any silence. 'This reunion you want is a symbol. What do you want to get from it?'

Peace, Dilkhush thought. I get peace with my daughter, you idiot. Because the pain will be soothed.

Sick Sikh carried on. 'When you touch that hole inside you, that darkness that needs lighting up, you will understand the feeling you desperately seek. Then look around. Ask what can help you fill the hole, light the darkness? Maybe it is one thing. Maybe it's a little thing here and a little thing there, and soon you could see the hole filling up.'

Dilkhush didn't want to fill the hole with anything other than her daughter. This man didn't know a thing.

'The flower design of the lifewalla memorial shelters a bud. The flower is you now, and the bud is you when the pain first happened.'

Dilkhush looked away. He had started lecturing her as if he knew. Even if he had lost his family, he had got himself a new one. How could he know?

Sick Sikh cleared his throat. 'That bud is the hole

in you and it doesn't bloom. Until it can, you will reincarnate. Perhaps your daughter helped the bud bloom a little, so you have become sure she is the answer. If you die with the bud, then again in your next life you will seek things to help fill that hole. Why not seek those same things in this life? It may not be your daughter. Maybe you will still gain liberation. No more suffering and struggling.'

Sick Sikh smiled. 'When you buy a memorial, we dig like this for the true question and answer. It is different for different people. But the cycle is the same. Birth, death, birth, death, until liberation, when every feeling is resolved and you have gained complete balance, and everything has bloomed. It is not the memorial that costs, but my obligation to help you find these truths. The memorial symbolises getting your real answers.'

Dilkhush swiped aside his justifications for charging. She already knew her answer was being with Jiyaa. What nonsense fears was he sowing in others who didn't suspect his greed? Yet, a doubt niggled at her. Just then, she saw Chandni through a gap in the wooden walls.

22

Who Else Trusted their Lies?

Dilkhush didn't want Chandni to see her. She was convinced the girl was Omera and didn't want any more curses put on her memorial efforts as well. She excused herself and hurried away to the factory. Maybe she could make her own gas tour there. It would be more realistic in the actual surroundings.

She could ask Dalya to bring tourists and she would get money fast like Sick Sikh. She imagined having notes like that in her hands. Now that she had seen the design of the lifewalla memorial, she would do an even better one. If Jiyaa stayed with her in Jantapur, they could do gas tours like Sick Sikh's to earn a living. She could even earn enough to bribe tour guides to bring people to her as well.

Even from outside, as people entered her gas tour in the factory, they would see the pipes and towers and tanks. Inside would be another tour. Suresh had explained the various functions to her and she would try and remember them. That would be more than Sick

Sikh knew. It could be a much better tour than his. Or they could both even help each other. The newspapers at the clinic said the factory still had poison chemicals, so that was a bonus for her tours.

But when she got closer, Dilkhush realised the factory was completely closed off behind walls and barriers. There had to be access. Otherwise, there couldn't be any tours. Through the small cracks in the wall, she could see the factory grounds were overgrown with grass, trees, and weeds.

Stray dogs wandered around. A group of children played cricket inside. She walked along the white wall that surrounded the factory and stopped now and again to look at drawings of the gas leak. She still couldn't find a big enough crack in the wall to enter the grounds. The children inside were a bit too far for her to call over, but someone could tell her how they got in. The slums around the factory were still there.

A few homes were made from brick. Most were built with corrugated metal sheets, or cardboard, with doors made of plastic sheets. More people had moved into the area. Suresh had said it was free land. Maybe she could live there with Jiyaa. A water pump nearby was marked with a red cross. It looked freshly painted.

She remembered the government doing that with spray cans soon after the leak, to mark the pumps affected by the poison gas. Were they still being marked for avoiding? No wonder the goatherd had preferred the dirty lake water instead. She walked around the slums and soon saw a baby, gurgling and playing naked on a mound of gravel. Dilkhush felt an urge to pick up the baby and look after him, as if he were her own. She too would have had a son.

For a few moments, she pretended in her mind that she was the mother. A man in a red turban was working a few feet away, mixing cement to build a wall. He kept looking back at the baby and making noises. 'Are you doing better?' he asked the baby. 'Hehn? Is baby doing better? Kukuuuu.'

He put a few bricks on the wall, slapped cement across them, and then turned again to the baby. 'If you stay still, you will get a big surprise later. Nice warm milk. And tickle, tickle for you.' He turned back to the bricks before looking at the baby again. Then working again with the bricks and looking back to the baby.

He wiped his arms and forehead with the trailing end of his turban that lay on his shoulder and made funny faces at the child. 'I'll tell your aunt you have been so good. Then she will have to put extra jaggery in your milk. No teeth to worry about, hehn?'

Dilkhush wanted to pick the baby up, away from the gravel. She wondered who put the black kohl mark on the baby's face so neatly to keep away all evil. Just then, a girl came over wearing only her underwear. She had a little oil in one cupped hand and giggled as she rubbed it into the baby's hair. The child started to cry. The father looked up. There was yellow diarrhoea on the gravel.

Dilkhush hurried over and picked up the baby.

'Leave him,' a woman nearby said. 'The mother is a jealous hag. Can't look after her own, but won't let anyone else touch them. If she sees you pick up her son, she will go crazy.'

The father shook his head. 'She only gets that way when she is gambling. Everyone loses their head sometimes, don't they?'

Dilkhush paid no attention to them. 'Aléy, aléy,' she said, holding the baby close. 'What is wrong, my little baby? Too hot for you out here? Too much oil on your head?'

The father smiled. 'A bit of sun is good for him.' He resumed his rhythm of working and speaking to the baby. 'Hush now, good boys don't cry, hush, hush. I will be finished in a few hours.'

The baby let out more yellow, watery faeces onto Dilkhush's sari. The girl in the underwear burst out laughing. 'At least it's almost the same colour as your sari.'

The father hurried over. 'Oho,' he said. 'You should put him down.' He wiped the baby's bottom with the end of his turban. 'Sorry about your sari.'

'He is only a child.' Dilkhush had held her son to her bosom before, but he wasn't like that.

The father took the boy and handed him to the little girl in her underwear. 'Tell Aunty the sun is too much for him. Find money in the tobacco tin and tell her to buy proper cow's milk for a few days. Not poisoned cheapness.' He went back to his work.

Dilkhush rinsed her sari at the nearest water pump. Before the man became too busy with his task, she asked whether he made memorials that needed bricks.

'Anything for money, nothing for free.'

When she asked about getting into the factory grounds, he warned her to be careful. But he also said there was a big enough gap not far from the entrance.

Dilkhush thanked him and walked to the main gates of the factory. They were locked. The metal was hot, but she didn't flinch. She could see beyond the gates. The gigantic, rusted corpse of the factory, with tall pipes and tanks sounded like it was moaning in the breeze. The flare tower had fallen. Some of the drums and sacks of chemicals were still supposed to be there. Weeds wound around the metal remnants of the factory. She kept walking along and finally spotted a big enough gap in the wall. Dilkhush squeezed through.

The grounds looked like a graveyard, but at least she would be able to show visitors what it was like inside. She could share what Suresh told her about some of the buildings. He had been so impressed when he first saw the factory.

She came across a store area, which had sacks of chemicals that looked like hardened white powder. She used her handkerchief to pick some pieces up and tied them into a ball. She would give that to Dalya to attract the tourists, showing everything on her tour was real. Tourists could even pay to take away some of the white powder to show at their dinner parties. It would be better than only coasters and stories from Sick Sikh.

She was sure Suresh had told her that the workers often picked such chemicals without aprons, gloves, or masks. So, she would explain that as well. In the way the tourists tried the cabbage smell and painful burning of the chillies, with her tour they could try seeing how it was working at the factory. She could even direct the tourists to try repairs of high-up pipes and imagine faulty valves or a chemical drip on their skin. She would need to pour chilli water down on them, so it stung their eyes and any broken skin.

If she could get permission to go to the Palace Hotel on the other side of the bridge afterwards, she could show where there were parties for inspectors, journalists, ministers after any small leaks were reported. Suresh told her he had heard there was a lot of drinking and laughter at these parties.

But her plans for a tour felt so far-fetched now. Nothing could be done for that day. There was barely any time. Dilkhush was thirsty and drowsy but there was no tap nearby. She sat by the storage area and saw hearts drawn onto the walls with different names inside them.

Ali & Punam. Janam and Janu. Krish and Tulsi. Some of the chemical sacks were positioned like sofas. Some lay side by side, with plastic sheets on top. Young lovers must hide and meet there, she thought. As she scanned the factory grounds from where she was sitting, she saw something glint and move in the distance. Immediately Dilkhush hid in the shadows.

A figure walked around, checking inside the buildings. At first, she thought it was someone from the slums. Maybe there was a guard around. When the figure came closer, she slid further back into the shadows. It was the villain in the black leather jacket. He was still haunting her. She should have kept her mouth shut on the bus and let him get away with his pinching and rubbing.

She didn't dare move. There was no one else there. Had he followed her from the bridge? The bilayati family could have sent him to make sure she stayed away, or to find her and jail her for the trouble she had caused. A sick feeling grew in her stomach. The villain kept one hand on the inside of his jacket. When he approached the storage building where she was hiding, he took his hand out, revealing a long dagger.

Panic set in. Dilkhush had to get out, but the villain was standing in the way of the nearest large opening in the wall. She glanced around for another gap. But the cracks were too small. She decided to try the same trick as outside Volog Colony. She picked up a stone and lobbed it at a small building behind the villain. He spun around and ran in that direction. Quickly and silently, she slid past behind him with her back against the wall.

Dilkhush kept her eyes on him as she climbed through the gap. It opened up directly into the slum neighbourhood. She heard a noise behind her. The villain was heading in her direction. She moved fast, but was worried that if she tried to hide in any of the slum homes, the dwellers may think she was a thief like before and raise an alarm. The villain would catch her and maybe get her jailed.

She walked through the maze of alleyways. Even if her tour plan was possible it would have to wait until she got Jiyaa. She had to make a successful lifewalla memorial without any money. She noticed many of the slum homes had cardboard signs stuck to their doors. 'Most delicious tea, coffee, cheaper than Sick Sikh's.' They all had the same idea as her. Were they also offering factory tours?

They would accuse her of stealing their business. Dilkhush turned left and right and followed the paths. At one point, she was moving so fast without knowing where she was going, that she ended up only feet away from the villain who ran past. He probably knew the alleyways better than she did. As he stopped and turned, Dilkhush quickly sat down by a woman sewing something.

The town had many widows. Surely she couldn't be the only one in a white sari. She hoped the villain didn't see her.

She leaned into the woman as if they were working together. 'Hmm, hmm.'

The woman stared at her. Moments later, Dilkhush heard the villain approach. She hunched towards the woman and didn't dare look up. The villain's trousers brushed against her back. She heard his shoes turn on the ground as he ran towards the factory again. Even when the sound of his footsteps receded, she didn't dare move. When she finally turned to check, the villain was heading into the factory again. He looked around. Dilkhush turned away. She realised a few people in the neighbourhood were looking at her and talking amongst themselves.

The woman sitting across from her gathered a globule of spittle and ejected it through a gap in her teeth. Without looking up, she cleared her throat. 'Hiding?'

Dilkhush saw the woman sewing, so she lied fast about working for a bilayati madam across the bridge. Her first few words were garbled, so she took a breath. 'It looks like you have good sewing skills. If you can show me some embroidery, I can take your work to her. Maybe she will order some.' Dilkhush hoped the woman didn't know the villain. If she did, she might call him back.

The woman turned to the side and blew out mucous from her nose. It landed on the dusty ground beside them. 'So recruiters are coming directly to offer jobs now?' She moved around, extending a leg, transferring her entire body from place to place, and squatting the whole time. Many people around them were waiting in line for water from a truck. The ones in front were busy filling buckets and pots. One man swept the dirt path in front of his home. Dilkhush looked again for the villain. She decided if nothing else worked, she really could try and take embroidery pieces across the bridge. A few boys leaned against a wall and stared at her.

The woman looked at them. 'Eh, get away. Stop harassing respectable women.'

They smiled lazily and ignored her.

'Don't worry,' the woman said. 'They are mostly harmless. You should come around evening time and see the heroes dancing like Shah Rukh Khan. Big, big dreams they all have. They say Shah Rukh Khan himself was only an ordinary man once. And that one of them might get there like him.' She laughed. 'They haven't learned about life yet. Now, tell me. What kind of work do you have?'

Before Dilkhush could answer, someone interrupted them.

'Arey, you?' It was the embroidery woman from the job junction and the woman who had accused her of being a thief.

'Oh, Shanta, you know her?' The first woman asked.

'Yes, she is a thief.'

'Is she? I didn't know whether to trust her, but she says she has a direct connection with a bilayati madam across the bridge. We will have a better chance for work then.'

'Lies. All lies. You should have seen her shouting at the bilayati recruiter. They stopped giving out work because of her. And now, she is saying she has a direct connection to the bilayati family?'

'If you just give me some samples, I promise to try and get work for you.'

'No, no. If you want samples, give me some money. Then you can take samples.'

'I tell you, don't trust her. She is an outsider creating problems for us.'

Dilkhush saw people coming out of their homes to look. She tried to explain again and apologised.

One woman shook her head. 'What do we have that anyone should steal from us?'

Dilkhush looked towards the factory and saw the

villain turn around and head towards them. Had he heard the commotion? She hurried away from the group. They continued talking about her behind her back.

'Let it go. Desperate widow that she is. She tried scamming us, and we didn't fall for it.'

'But seemed like she needed the money.'

'Like all of us, but we don't scam each other. We have nothing, so we believe such lies about getting work. Can't get a job herself and makes promises to us. We believe everything, fools that we are.'

Someone laughed. 'It's just in poor people's blood.'

23

Heart in a Thousand Pieces

DILKHUSH'S PLANS WERE unravelling. If the villain caught her, that would be it. She would be locked up in jail and, in the meantime, the bilayati family would leave. Nothing was working. She didn't have any other clever plans. Fate was forcing its own course. She heard a noise nearby and cowered under a bush. If it was the villain, she had to wait for him to pass.

Her thoughts were hazy. Why was God punishing her for things she could not have known about? She had stayed in the town and the gas had blown. She and her family should have left. Why had she thought the problems with the small leaks would be fixed? Why had she told Kashif about seeing Omera on the funeral pyre? If she had kept quiet, those two would be together now and Omera would not be putting curses on her attempts to mend her life.

Her karma would have been clear. She could have reunited with Jiyaa immediately. Yet, what if there were more reasons behind her fate? Dilkhush's throat was dry, but she didn't dare move from under the bush in case the villain was around and heard the noise. She stayed still and let her mind dig up sins from her past.

Dilkhush refused to leave the house after they buried Jiyaa. She had seen enough mass graves and pyres.

'Kashif looks haggard,' Suresh said. 'Don't tell Naseema Bi he is back. Otherwise, she will tell him to stay with us and he wants to stay in his own house, even during dinnertime. He thinks Simran and Omera, or his parents, will go there to find him. He doesn't believe the girl you saw on a funeral pyre was his daughter. He doesn't want to believe they are all gone. He can't.'

They heard Kashif shout often, even outside their courtyard. 'Omerrraaaaa. Siiimmmrrrraaaaan. Ma, Baba.'

'Kashif will hate me for leaving Simran by the talkies,' Dilkhush told Suresh. 'But what was I to do? She was so sick, she herself told me to save Jiyaa and find Omera. I promised I would get the doctors, but they had nothing left for anyone. Kashif won't understand that.'

'It's better you don't see him then,' Suresh snapped, as he did often, after the gas leak. 'If you stay away, you won't have to lie about anything.'

Suresh's mother had not been on the road with others who fell. Someone had found her by the river. She was sick, but still alive when they brought her to the house.

Dilkhush knew Suresh blamed her for leaving his mother, but she had done it to get their child to the hospital faster. The witch had been holding them back. Yet Jiyaa was gone, and he blamed her for that too, asking why she

278

simply hadn't just grabbed an injection.

She thought Kashif would sympathise with her. He knew about Suresh's mother trying to kill Jiyaa. She wanted to tell him she had also tried to look for Omera at the hospital, and had been heartbroken seeing his daughter on the mass pyre. She had wanted to help Simran as well, but hadn't been able to. The next day, Dilkhush told the old owl she was visiting the temple. Instead, she went to Kashif's house.

She had to tell him there was nothing she could have done. On her way, she hid when she saw Suresh helping tailors. They had been sewing kafans all night and day for the cemeteries. She loved Suresh. But in his own pain, he didn't understand her anguish and kept lashing out.

She hoped for some understanding from Kashif. He, too, had lost his child. But he wasn't at home. She hurried back, ashamed of herself for going there. Her life darkened even more the following day. She had such pain in her belly. Suresh was out helping in the town. Naseema Bi was at the mosque. So Dilkhush took a rickshaw alone to the hospital. The baby that was growing inside her came out blackened and burned. He had been her last hope.

Suresh saw her in the night. When he found out what had happened at the hospital, he spoke without looking at her. 'Are you capable of holding onto any life apart from your own?'

Dilkhush's days passed in a blur.

Then one day, Suresh came back angry from the makeshift clinic he helped at. 'The police came and closed us down. All of the antidotes these doctors bought by themselves were taken away, and the patient files as well. The doctors were threatened not to restart the medicines unless they wanted to be responsible for those people who stayed alive. Because they could end up suffering for longer. Imagine! Kashif fought with the police, and ended up in jail.'

Suresh went to see him the next day. 'They have beaten him badly.'

Dilkhush wanted to visit him too, but was too afraid to ask. When the police let him out, she gathered her courage. She had a bit more strength then.

'He doesn't want to see anyone,' Suresh said. 'Refuses to even wash or change his clothes.'

Dilkhush told Simran's soul she would help Kashif in whatever way she could. After Suresh left for the evening shift at the cremation grounds and Naseema Bi fell asleep, Dilkhush sneaked out with some of Suresh's washed clothes, and some rice and yoghurt.

Kashif's house was in semi-darkness with only moonlight flooding through the windows. When she saw his black and purple body, bruised and beaten, with dried blood still clinging on, she burst into tears and rushed to him. They hugged each other and sobbed.

She felt as if each knew the other's torment. After a few moments, Kashif fell to his knees. His body shuddered as he wept. She lowered herself and held him. When he quietened a little, she went and filled a bucket of water. In the hazy moonlight, she helped him take his clothes off and wiped off his blood, dirt, and tears.

Each time she dipped the cloth into the bucket, she

280

wrung out the old dirt as fiercely as she could. Kashif flinched as she wiped a bruise or cut. She dabbed his skin with care and helped him get dressed. He had lost so much weight that Suresh's clothes looked big on him. When he got up again, he lost his balance and she steadied him against the nearest wall. It was now almost dark outside. She was worried that Suresh and Naseema Bi would wonder where she was. But when she looked into Kashif's eyes and he held her face, her tears rolled down. 'I...Simran...please forgive me for...I tried...You and I...how can we...this pain...my child...she's gone. Your daughter...How will we...' she sobbed.

Kashif pressed his lips against hers for a moment. His tears fell and his hands moved down her back. Then he kissed her again, more softly this time and she yielded without thinking. His lips grazed her neck. She buried her face in his chest, which made him wince with pain. But he leaned back on the wall and pulled her so close she almost lost her breath.

His lips touched her lightly on her forehead and eyes. Then he kissed her hungrily and they slid to the floor. Their breathing mingled as his body moved slowly against hers. She lifted herself to him. His stubble scratched her neck as he pushed himself inside her. He was devouring her, breathing hard, pressing against her body. Nothing else mattered. He gasped out Simran's name and Dilkhush came to her senses. She pulled away.

'Kashif...I'm...Simran is...Simran is no more...I'm...It is me, Dilkhush.'

His eyes searched hers in the darkness. 'No!' He pulled

back. His voice was a whisper.

A sound came from behind them. Dilkhush turned to look, but the door creaked shut. She hurried home, and was relieved that Suresh wasn't there. She closed the door to her room. Her tears fell slowly. When Suresh came home, she pretended to be asleep. In the days that followed, he became more cruel. She knew he needed comforting himself. They had both lost everything, and she needed to be a better wife to him. But she couldn't bring herself to do anything. He should have helped her to save Jiyaa and their unborn child. Why had he left them?

The next day, the remaining stored poisons in the factory were to be mixed safely to make them harmless. The storage tanks of poison chemicals had been overfilled and they could still blow. No one believed that the operation would be safe. People left town. Hundreds of thousands found shelter in a stadium on the outskirts. A minister gave commentary on the radio. Helicopters flew above the operation to report each stage. Kashif was nowhere to be seen in the stadium, but it was so big. They went home after the radio confirmed it was safe to restart their lives. Suresh went to look for Kashif. When he returned, he flung a note at Dilkhush.

My Friend Suresh,

My heart is in a thousand pieces without Omera and Simran. My parents are also gone. I am a disgrace, unable to face you. Those responsible for the evil that has befallen us are at large. My work is there now. But how will I ever allay what I feel inside? If I avenge my family, *can that ever bring any justice?*

Save Naseema Bi some heartache. Tell her I am dead,
so she doesn't wait for me. May God keep you sane in all
this madness. Live in peace and take care of your family.
You still have that chance. My sorrow is that I couldn't
take care of mine. I should have been here to help you
save them all. I cannot ever forgive myself for that.

Your wretched friend,
Kashif

Dilkhush knew she should have never gone to him.
That ultimate betrayal they had committed had driven
him away. He would have stayed otherwise. She should
have managed her own misery. After everything Simran
and Omera had done for her, she had betrayed them like
that? She would pay for it.

Dilkhush looked around. The factory and slums were in
darkness. She thought about the memories that haunted
her. She was so scared she would never get Jiyaa because
of what she had done. Kashif might have stayed. Maybe
then he would have been living with Naseema Bi and
Omera now. Their separation would not have stained
her karma.

What if there was no way out for her? Even if she got
Jiyaa, she could lose her in a more tragic way. Dilkhush
wished she could swim across the lake to her daughter,
or take a boat there. Her whole life would change if she
got Jiyaa. But there weren't any boats in the lake. The
other side had large barbwire fences. Maybe that was
how they made sure no one got through.

A few streets around her were lit with yellow bulbs. Dilkhush got up and brushed off her sari. She walked towards a water pump near another slum. Everything was quiet. She pushed down the pump lever and cupped her hand. When she slurped the water, it seemed to scratch at her throat. She heard someone shout.

'Eh, who is taking the water this time of night outside the morning rota?'

'Leave it alone. Must be a thirsty person, otherwise who would cross you?'

'It's not like that, but the tanks for the water haven't come either.'

Dilkhush walked away. She hoped no one saw her. Behind her, the voices faded. At the bridge, the gates were locked. No one was being allowed through. There were now four guards. She couldn't see the kind one from before and wondered what had happened to him. She went to speak to one of the other guards. Maybe he would help her.

He stared at her, and then went to his small cabin, and spoke into his radio. He returned with a piece of paper. His face became harsh. 'Were you here this morning?' Just then, Dilkhush thought she heard the villain's voice from the guard's radio. 'Keep her there.'

'Was it you here this morning?' the guard asked. 'Say the truth and I won't let you get into any trouble.'

24

What Kind of Man Preyed on their Losses?

Dilkhush shook her head. The guard looked at her and then down again at the piece of paper from the cabin. 'Are you sure you weren't here? I'm giving you one last chance.'

'I took a wrong turn just now. I was trying to find my memorial place by the lake.' She moved deliberately, trying not to seem like she was hurrying away. 'Oh, there. I think I see it.' She walked away. There was just hurdle after hurdle. This day had stretched out as if there could be no end, and both her body and mind were drained. Her torture of separation seemed like it would never end. Maybe when she added the lifewalla design of the flower and bud to her own memorial, Jiyaa's soul would fly across to her. Whether she believed Sick Sikh's claims or not, she had to try everything.

Without money to pay for a proper brick and cement one, a makeshift addition could still be made to her memorial. Surely, it was the design and intention that mattered. Even Sick Sikh said that when he asked what her real question was.

How far would she go to get Jiyaa? That had to be her question. She had rejected life itself so that she didn't betray her dead daughter by living. Whatever the gas had done, her one selfish act to stay in the town, even after the small leaks had cost them everything.

She had no power to change anything that had happened. She had suffered, sacrificed and begged God. And she wanted to believe that this led to her daughter's soul truly breathing through this bilayati girl. She would have a chance to make up then. When Dilkhush reached her lakeside memorial, the stones and pebbles she had arranged had been demolished. She felt as if someone had kicked her insides, reminding her about the real truth.

The mound in the middle had been flattened and rubbish bags were strewn all around. It had to be Sick Sikh or Chandni...Omera, whatever the girl called herself. The memorial was the only hope she had left. Her heart fluttered and her knees buckled. Even when she had been ready to take her own life, she had stopped herself. The only reason was for a miracle like this reunion. But it was being ruined. She couldn't face being a living corpse again, knowing her daughter was on the other side of the world.

Did God have no pity? Her snake agitated inside. Dilkhush smashed a stone into the remnants of the memorial. It was all worthless. She couldn't go any further with the charade that had taken over her mind.

But what else was there?

She hit more stones into the memorial, one after the other. Stone after stone. Soon, grunts escaped her body and she smashed big rocks down with force. She was heaving and panting. Dilkhush carried on until no sign of the memorial remained. But she continued beating one stone against another, catching her skin. Her hands were bleeding. She didn't know how to escape the nightmare.

Her chest heaved as if she was sobbing, but no tears fell. She beat herself and that released some of the pain wrecking her insides. Just then, Salman's voice came from behind.

'Dilkhush, stop that! You'll get hurt.' He kneeled beside her.

She remained still. How had he found her? No library was open at night. 'Did you ruin this?' she asked. 'Only you had seen me build my memorial.' Her breath was fast. 'You want me to fail.'

'At what? And why would I want you to fail? I have nothing against you. I only came because the gua—I was passing and saw you. I realised something had gone wrong. What happened?'

She ignored him and smashed more stones.

'Stop. You will really hurt yourself.' He reached out.

Dilkhush got up and pushed him away. 'Who am I to you that you are so worried about me? Pretending. Everywhere I look, you are there. My saviour. Yet you won't do what I really need help with. Did you get me that job with the bilayati family?'

He shook his head. 'They were late for a puja and in a bad mood already. It wasn't the right time. I will speak to them. They are still here. I didn't realise it was so important to you. If you just explain to me why...'

Dilkhush walked away. Maybe Sick Sikh had come to take photos of her memorial and destroyed it. If everyone found out they too could get what they wanted, with their own memorials, they wouldn't need him. Hadn't she been blessed so far without his help? But she didn't know how to reach the end. Maybe he had some secret after all. She had to ask him. He could stay secure in that knowledge and not ruin anything more for her. What kind of man preyed on others' losses? But she had to try. It was getting late, so she hurried towards his tea stall, past several groups still working on signs and placards. The words all passed in a blur.

Salman called after her. 'Dilkhush, please, I promise I will speak to the bilayati family. Just don't do anything you will regret.'

She didn't reply.

'Sick Sikh isn't there.' Salman tried to keep up with her. 'You are walking towards his stall, but he is at some meeting for the anniversary.'

They passed lorries with posters stuck to them. One had large photos glued all around. Dilkhush rushed away from Salman. But soon after, she turned too fast to take a second look at a face in a picture and almost tripped. Her breath was unsteady. She looked again at the pictures pasted on the lorries. Black-and-white bodies of children lined up on the dirt ground, with labels tied around their toes or stickers pasted on their foreheads. Sacks of chemicals. Bodies stacked on top of each other in the hospitals. She stood in front of one poster and stared.

Salman caught up with her. 'It's alright.' He put his hands on her shoulders.

She reached up to pull the poster down.

'What are you doing?' One of the men by the lorries ran over. 'We just finished sticking those up yesterday.'

Dilkhush didn't listen and kept pulling. The poster started to tear.

'You're ruining it. Stop it!'

'Ruining your photo?' She felt wetness above her lips. She didn't look at the man or stop what she was doing. 'My whole life is ruined.'

The other men also made a commotion.

Salman went to pull her away.

'Let go!' Her voice was hoarse.

He tried to lead her away. 'You have to listen to me.'

For a moment, she didn't move. Then she looked into his eyes. 'You don't understand. That's my daughter.' Her throat hurt. 'They have stuck my daughter's photo up. She...she might be across the bridge, but the guard won't let me cross to see her. You won't arrange anything with her. Now these people won't let me take her photo. What else do I have?'

Salman let go of her.

She turned towards the poster again and looked at the child's face, exposed from a grave. The small body was barely buried. Stones and dust strayed over her cheeks. Her eyes stared into nothing.

'My Jiyaa.' She stroked the face with her fingers. 'See how she had rosy cheeks till the end.'

Salman didn't say anything.

'Only I can tell she had rosy cheeks. You wouldn't know. No one else could tell.'

Salman went to talk to the other men in a low voice.

Dilkhush moved closer to hear.

'Salman brother,' one of the men complained. 'You know this photo hits everyone hard, and it's our only copy. We can't lose it.'

'I'll get another one done,' Salman said. 'Take it down for now, without letting it tear any more.'

'No,' Dilkhush said. 'You won't make another copy. Promise me. Jiyaa is my daughter. This is not the way to remember her.'

'They didn't know,' Salman said.

Two policemen sauntered towards them, each holding a glass of tea. Dilkhush backed away. What if they were there to put her in jail? Salman led the policemen to the nearby tea stall. From there, he signalled to the man by the lorry who peeled off the remainder of the poster and gave it to Dilkhush. She held it to her body, wrapping her hands around it. As she walked away, her heart felt a little soothed.

She could almost feel Jiyaa in her arms. And until they were really together, she could take solace in holding her picture close. It was like she had done on the way to the hospital, and at the hospital temple, and on the way back to their home that night. She kept stopping and looking at her child through teary eyes.

A streetlight near Naseema Bi's house was buzzing and flickering. Dilkhush stopped under it and held the poster out again. Jiyaa's favourite song played somewhere nearby and they both danced. Round and round. The rhythm got faster. Soon, Dilkhush's whole body was filled with joy that only true laughter could bring. How lucky she was that God was helping her. Not everyone got that. She held Jiyaa out and looked deep into her eyes. In an instant everything changed.

She stared. In her desperation, she had allowed herself to be tricked. But she could see clearly now. The face on the poster was not Jiyaa's. The semi-darkness by the lorries had misled her. Even the streetlights hadn't helped. She had been so sure. The child looked just like her daughter. What was happening? Wherever she looked, she saw what she wanted to, even if it wasn't there. People would think her mad. The men by the lorry did. She heard footsteps behind her.

Dilkhush held the poster out without looking. 'Give it back to them, Salman. It's not Jiyaa. This is someone else's child.' She heard a snort and turned around. Dilkhush broke into a run up the incline to Naseema Bi's house, still holding the poster in one hand.

The villain had found her.

25

All Dreams Can Come True

DILKHUSH'S BACK WAS to the villain, but she could hear him. A cough started to rise inside her chest. She turned to check how far away he was and saw his hand go into his pocket. She had seen what he had in there before and ran faster, swallowing her coughs. The poster fell from her hands. She picked it up. The girl in the poster was still someone's daughter. Dilkhush looked ahead and saw that the door to Naseema Bi's house was shut.

The poster crushed as she held it under her arm and searched her bag for the key. She needed to be ready to open the door fast. Even the old owl had struggled with the padlock when Dilkhush first saw her. She couldn't afford for that to happen. What if Naseema Bi had given her the wrong key in the hurry that morning?

When she reached the house and pushed the door, it wasn't locked. No one was in the courtyard. Newspapers and pieces of rags were strewn all around. It was as she had seen through the gap in the wall when she first came, straight after going to the clinic. She quickly slammed the door behind her. The metal stopper was rusty and the two sides seemed misaligned. It was difficult to lock the door, so she pushed hard. But the bolt remained stubborn.

'All alone?' the villain's voice came from outside. 'You don't have to be by yourself, you know. There are other ways.' He pushed against the door.

Dilkhush heaved and leaned with her whole body weight to push the stopper. Finally, she managed to lock the door. She was trembling, not wanting to think about what could have happened if the villain had got in. She held her breath for a while, and then let her coughs out without restraint.

He pounded on the wood. 'Open the damn door, you bastard bitch. Lying about me, creating all that trouble with Madam and trying to take that girl. Taking what isn't yours. I knew I would find you, one way or another. And now the police are after you as well. You have crossed the wrong people.'

Dilkhush rubbed her head to clear her thinking. She had to focus on what she needed. The metal bolt rattled against her back.

'You think you are winning, hiding inside there? How stupid! Look around you. Think. How can you be winning? Everything is against you. You are a cursed, no-good widow. Nothing you think is real is even here.'

She didn't want his words to be true. She was just about to restart her life. Things had aligned in an unexpected way. That was all. She had been taken aback herself. She simply needed to finish the last task of getting in front of her daughter. Jiyaa would recognise her if she gave her some clues.

'No lies to scream out now?' The villain asked.

She looked around the courtyard. It was empty and felt eerie, as if time had turned back. It felt like she was there again on the gas night, coming back alone, holding a lifeless Jiyaa. The poster fell out of her hands, onto the ground. She closed her eyes and took several deep breaths. She had to stay in the moment. Otherwise, her entire world would crumble around her, as it had time and time again. She didn't have to believe she was utterly alone there.

'Think you are the only one who is so wronged that you have a right to bite and bark at others.' The villain laughed. 'Look around and realise what life is for you and everyone else.'

Dilkhush pleaded with God. She had finally found a possibility to be with her daughter, and she was ready to accept anything. But she was not oblivious to what the villain was sniping about. There was no Naseema Bi, no girls. Was Jiyaa across the lake?

He banged on the door. 'Open up.'

Dilkhush moved away. She didn't know how long the rusty stopper would hold and went to the other side of the courtyard. Her insides were shaking. She wiped her sweaty palms on her sari. There had to be something to hit the villain with if he broke the door down. Dilkhush crept along the side of the back wall until she got to the larger room where all the girls slept.

All the time, the villain kept shouting. 'Eh, bastard bitch. Talking about my mother letting me dangle on her breasts? Let us see how you like it when I dangle on yours. You don't want to shout your vulgar words at me now, do you?'

Someone in the neighbourhood yelled. 'Shut up your pig's grunting.'

'Say that again,' the villain shouted. 'I'll cut off your dick and stuff it up your arse, you hear?' His footsteps headed away from the door.

Dilkhush hoped the neighbours had scared him away. The stopper on the door wasn't strong enough to withstand the villain. He soon returned.

'Not brave enough to come down, are you,' he shouted. 'Big mouths up there. Cowards.' He turned his attention to her again. 'Eh, widow, stupid fool that you are. Now I even know where you live. Shouldn't have come here, should you? What does that tell me? That you have nowhere else to go. How safe do you think you are now?' He laughed. 'Delusional woman. Think we can't see through you. You don't fool me. I know no one is there to protect you. Open the door now and get this over with. Otherwise, you will have to watch your back every time you go out.'

Dilkhush felt robbed of any fighting spirit. She realised she was getting further from Jiyaa, not closer as she had thought. Her mind had tried hard to keep the illusion going. But the truth was catching up with her. She became scared. Inside the room, she couldn't see her razai, or anyone else's.

Dilkhush made a makeshift razai from rags and newspapers that lay around. Then she unrolled the poster and straightened it. She rested next to it. The girl in the photo wasn't Jiyaa, but she looked enough like her to feel like balm. Dilkhush pinned her peacock feather hairpin onto the girl's hair on the poster. Soon, even though the villain kept shouting and threatening, his voice faded from her mind.

She sang a lullaby, hoping Jiyaa's soul heard and felt her love, even across the lake. She gazed at the poster and touched the girl's cheeks before tracing her eyes and nose. The lips were slightly parted, with a little dirt on them. She felt a pain in her chest as she picked up the poster and held it in her arms. She was so scared of losing Jiyaa again.

If she went to the door and spoke to the villain calmly, she could explain her predicament. Maybe he would pity her and help her to reunite with her daughter. Dilkhush slipped into the laughing, giggling memories of playing with Jiyaa. There were only a few short years of those, but she was grateful for them. She remembered how funny Jiyaa's attempts were to dance and sing when Naseema Bi was sick with a cold.

When the girl massaged the old owl's legs, she always said they were like roti dough. Jiyaa tickled her mother or Naseema Bi, and snuggled for hugs to avoid getting into trouble for something she had done. More memories flooded in and Dilkhush surrendered to them.

'Mummy,' Jiyaa squealed. 'See how I am dressed?'

Dilkhush turned to look. Her beautiful daughter had somehow unlocked her almari. *Jiyaa was wearing Dilkhush's bridal sari and gold bangles. She was so small, the gold necklace almost hung to the floor. 'You're a little rascal, aren't you?' Dilkhush teased her and hugged Jiyaa.*

They were laughing and dancing when Naseema Bi heard and came inside. They all started to sing. Naseema Bi brought sweets for Jiyaa and combed her hair into two pleats.

'How pretty our Jiyaa looks,' the owl said.

'But we don't want to lose you to your husband too soon,' Dilkhush smiled. 'First, you will wear a school uniform, then nice work clothes for teaching children, then when you are absolutely ready, we can let you dress in a bridal sari for your husband.' She smiled. 'And you have to live near us. In this town only.'

Jiyaa giggled as she sang. 'I'm getting married. I'm getting married. How pretty I look, how sad you are.'

Much later, when Dilkhush stirred, there were voices outside. She bolted upright. She was in Naseema Bi's house, but the old owl and the girls were not there. More footsteps. She gathered her thoughts and remembered the villain was outside, waiting for her. Maybe he had called more people to break the door down. If only Dalya had found Kashif and brought him, she too would have had people on her side.

'Well, well, well,' the villain said. 'What do you want?'

'What are you doing here?' It was Salman's voice.

Dilkhush's heart filled with tenderness and the

sweetness of honey. Salman had come to save her. She wasn't alone after all.

The villain laughed. 'Defender of all widows now, are you? Or have you marked this one for special attention? I can guess why, firecracker that she is, and all alone. No one to guard her, or notice when she's gone. Why fight over her when we can share her?'

A scuffle broke out with shouting and thuds against the door and walls. People in the neighbourhood appeared at the windows and balconies, even several floors up. They whistled and cheered. Dilkhush could hear them all. She put her hands over her ears.

The fight went on for a long while. When it all became quiet, she heard her name. At first, she didn't move.

A gentle knock sounded. 'It's me.' Salman's voice was soft. 'Don't be scared. I'm here.'

She hid the poster of the child under her makeshift razai before walking into the courtyard. 'Salman?'

'Yes, it's me.'

She hesitated. How could she let him in? If it was a trap, everything would be ruined. 'I can't open the door.' She kept her voice low. 'I am alone.' She didn't want him to go, but didn't have a choice. What would the neighbours or Naseema Bi and the girls think? That only in one day she had let a strange man into the house, while she was all alone.

'I understand. I can just sit here. Is that alright?'

'If you like.' She sat down against the door.

They stayed like that for a few moments, and it seemed the neighbourhood became completely quiet. No sound came from the other side of the door. But Dilkhush thought she could sense Salman there. Something about him made her think he would try not to let her down this time. After a while she whispered, 'Salman.' There was no answer. 'Salman?' Still no answer. She panicked. Had he gone? Why should he wait? There she was sitting like a fool, thinking she sensed him there, that he felt he had a sense of duty to her. Had she imagined it all? 'Salman?' she whispered louder.

'Yes?'

'I...I thought you'd gone.'

'No, I'll stay until you're safe.'

The minutes went by. She imagined that her breath was almost in rhythm with his. Soon her eyelids drooped, but she fought them. After a while, she told herself she would only close them for a moment. The relief she felt was so sweet.

'Are you alright?' Salman asked.

She sat up with a start. 'Yes. I'm fine.' She touched her hand where Jiyaa had held it. Some of the healed area was still there, without the ragpatches. 'Thank you.'

'For what?' he asked.

'Coming to look for me after I told you to stay away. I was just angry and that villain—'

'I want to tell you something,' he hesitated. 'I really tried everything.'

Her forehead touched the door. Salman had to have bad news about speaking to the bilayati family. Otherwise, he wouldn't have waited so long or been anxious about telling her.

She heard him take a deep breath.

'I will explain what happened. At least you will know how hard I tried.'

Dilkhush didn't want to hear his excuses. She blocked him out. When he didn't stop and kept asking whether she understood, what she heard was his guilt. 'What are you really saying?'

There was a long silence.

'Salman?'

'You just have to wait until it is time, and soon you can be together.'

Her heart jumped.

'The family has agreed,' he said. 'You can go to them later this evening. Those who were in charge are at Jantapur Palace Hotel to sign some agreement. It will happen at midnight, in time for the anniversary. Don't go anywhere before. There are a lot of policemen on alert. They won't think twice about jailing anyone. After midnight, meet the family at the train station.'

'Why there?'

'There are no flights for two days,' Salman explained. 'The family will take a night train to Delhi. First class, so it will be fine to sleep in. But Abha, you met her?'

Dilkhush didn't tell him that that sweet jewel-eyed Abha was simply her Jiyaa's soul reincarnated. Others may not understand.

'She is always restless when they travel,' Salman continued. 'It will be very long for them to be on the train and plane. They said maybe someone can keep Abha entertained on the train.'

'I can do a puppet show for her.'

'I suggested that. Abha was very excited, but there are several puppeteers for the anniversary, so they can take any one of them. Or maybe a storyteller, or game player. That is up to them. But I arranged for you to use the puppet stand at the station to show your skills, before the train leaves.'

'They will do another interview?'

'Another interview? I don't understand. They need someone trustworthy. They already had one bad experience. But if you do your best and if Abha likes you, I am sure they will take you, at least to Delhi.'

'What about after that?'

'Who knows? They have not said anything about taking anyone abroad, but these people have the means to do anything. You never know what they can manage when they want to.'

It seemed too good to be true. They had agreed to give her a chance. She would have a whole train journey with Jiyaa. It would be easy to take her and leave.

She couldn't give Jiyaa the life they could, but the two of them would be together. Dilkhush worried that if she failed and they caught her, the consequences would be awful. No. It would be better to gain the family's trust. That way, they might take her back with them. Living with them would provide a roof and food for them both while she worked out another plan.

She would make sure the silly girl did her homework properly. And not go so easily with any stranger. People didn't always have good intentions like her. Maybe Jiyaa would miss her bilayati family when they both finally left, but there was Naseema Bi and the girls, and Dalya, to take their place. Hadn't that bilayati family taken her place? How had Salman managed such a miracle for her?

Everything she had wanted was there. If she had come to Jantapur before, she would have left with nothing. No forgiveness, no peace, no reunion. Now was the right time. Perhaps something inside her sensed that. She had to explain everything to Naseema Bi.

She would also tell Chandni about Kashif. At least now she wouldn't be letting anyone down. Being a mother again made Dilkhush feel she could wear a little colour. She would ask the old owl for a change of clothes for the puppet show at the train station. It would look livelier and she might not be as recognisable without her widow sari. Excitement flowed through her veins. Then, something occurred to her.

The bilayati family had agreed to take her in spite of the earlier incident. What if Salman knew that she was the same person they had kicked out? Could this also be a trap? It all seemed too good to be true.

What if she went there only to be jailed? She panicked. She should ask Salman some test questions. Before she could get any reassurance from him a shriek came from afar.

'Salmaaaaan, eh my Salmaaaan, my heeeeerrrrrro.' It sounded like Chandni.

Salman greeted Chandni with some gentleness in his voice. The other girls also called out. He asked them all in turn how they were.

'Have you taken a new job of guarding our house?' Naseema Bi asked.

Dilkhush hurried into the bedroom. She heard some fiddling on the door.

'I only came because—'

'The door is locked from inside,' Naseema Bi said. 'But why?'

'Dilkhush is inside,' Salman said.

'You met her? At Volog Colony? You escorted her back because she had to work late? Good man.'

'Oh, good man,' Chandni said. 'You escorted a woman you've never met before.'

'Come, my child. Open the door from inside,' the old owl called out.

Dilkhush didn't want to. The possibility of really being with Jiyaa again had muddled her thoughts. The snake, gave a strained whisper of a hiss, warning her. She knew the true story, but wasn't ready to face it. Memories and such illusions were safer. The knocking stopped. There was no noise coming from outside.

All became quiet.

Dilkhush only wanted to do what she could manage. One step at a time. Her eyes felt like they were burning and she closed them tight.

Soon, she heard loud noises again, coming from outside. Dilkhush was relieved. She hid the poster, so it wasn't visible from under her razai, and wiped her face with the end of her sari. When she unlocked the door, Naseema Bi and the girls poured in almost all at once.

'Come, come, Salman,' Naseema Bi said. 'Dilkhush, why did you make him sit outside? Have you been here long?' She motioned Salman to the charpoy.

Dilkhush felt his eyes follow her as she moved towards the wall with the peacock mural. It seemed newly painted. 'A goonda followed me,' she explained.

'Oh, and Salman came to save you?' Chandni asked. She turned to him. 'Vah, vah, hero.' Her tone was mocking.

The other girls held their hands to their hearts. 'Hero, my hero.' Preeti looked at the stars in the sky and held out her hands in a dramatic gesture. 'Come to me, my hero. Become mine forever.'

Chandni sat down on the charpoy and put her arms around Salman. 'You should have come with us today. We went to watch *Jodha Akbar* again. Three hours of gawping. Cut price tickets so half the town was there.'

He laughed. 'Yes, I would have looked very good sitting there while you all worshipped Hrithik, that man-god of yours.'

'You can be my man-god,' Preeti said.

'And mine.' Chandni smiled.

'You can be a man-god for all of us girls,' Jaadu said. 'After all, you can have many wives, and we will be happy to share you.'

He rolled his eyes. 'I am old enough to be your father.'

'Even better,' Preeti said. 'You can pay my college fees too.'

Naseema Bi tutted. She looked at Dilkhush. 'These girls. Love-lailas. All of them saved for weeks to go and watch Jodha Akbar again. It is the same as with

Veer-Zaara. They can't get enough. A hundred times to go, sing, and sigh. Oh my Shah Rukh this, my Shah Rukh that. They see repeats so often, they know all the lines, and don't mind which hero they fall for.'

'But with our luck, naturally we have to be flexible,' Jaadu smirked and started singing. '*Hum Dil de chuke Sanam, Qayamat se Qayamat tak, Kaho naa pyaar hai*, and then *Dilwale Dulhania Lejayenge*. Whoever that Dilwale is, Aamir, Salman, Shah Rukh, Hrithik. Flexible love.'

'Yes, yes, I know. *Zindagi na milegi dobara*.' The old owl laughed along with the girls at her own joke and untied her handkerchief. She took a beetle nut shaving and popped it into her mouth. 'Today again, all dressed tip-top in their best salwar suits as if we are not going to see a filum but Hrithik Roshan himself. As if he was going to walk out from the screen and take all of them to his Jodha-Akbar palace.'

She shook her head. 'Hrithik this, Hrithik that, all the way home. To listen to them, you'd think he was walking beside each, holding their hands and smiling, hearing in his mind all the world's women cheering, Hriii-thik, Hriii-thik. God must be playing games to put only one of him on this earth. All these lailas have to share him now.'

Preeti sighed. 'I tell you, Naseema Bi, there is no God. Otherwise, how is it possible that that man can only take one wife at a time? Unless he chooses me. Then it is very fair.' She smiled. 'If I were his wife, our romance would last forever, like Jodha Akbar's. Akbar loved only one, even if he married so many women.

Every time I would see my Hrithik, I would have pomp and ceremony. I would be jubilant. My king is here.' She cocked her head and turned to Salman. 'You think that would work?'

'Yes, yes,' Salman said. 'Because that is romance for us men. Building us up like that. Instead of these plans, why not think about how he would celebrate being with you and be jubilant when you went to him. Isn't that how Akbar felt about Jodha?'

'Have you seen my face?' Preeti laughed.

'Arey, your heart is the most beautiful though. And so, to my thinking, your whole self is beautiful.' Salman looked at Dilkhush, but she looked away. 'I better go,' he said. 'I have a lot of work for the anniversary still. All you girls are helping, aren't you?'

'Wait, wait. You just said I was beautiful,' Preeti said. 'Why not marry me first and then you can go.'

'I have so much work with the anniversary.'

The girls teased him. 'Yes, but that is later. Is all this talk about romance embarrassing you?'

'Can't you see how shy I am?' Salman laughed.

Preeti threw her veil over his head. 'Shy as a bride, aren't you? But we can't let you go now that we have you here.'

They all giggled and the girls copied Preeti, with their own veils. Salman tried to shake his head away from the myriad of veils before giving up. He was covered with yellow, green, fuchsia, black, and turquoise pieces of cloth. Dilkhush smiled when his face turned red. She caught Naseema Bi looking at her.

'Are you alright?' The old owl came and sat on the floor next to her. 'You said a goonda followed you. Tell me who that was. At this time of night, decent people should be in their own homes.'

Dilkhush wanted to ask why the old owl hadn't been at home then? She had been all alone when the villain had threatened to break the door down.

'If I was here, I would have poked his eyes out,' Naseema Bi said.

'No, no, he seemed dangerous.' Dilkhush lowered her head. 'I saw him at the factory with a dagger.'

'They are no good, those leather jacket goondas. Why did you go there? To upset yourself? I should have stayed and waited for you, but the girls insisted. I wish I had laid eyes on that goonda. I would have...'

The girls had stopped fooling around and were listening to Naseema Bi.

'What would you have done?' Preeti laughed.

'Me?' the old owl asked. 'I would have...' She tied her scarf around her waist and picked up a pan, straining as she bent down for it.

'Like lightning, aren't you,' Preeti said.

Naseema Bi took a deep breath. 'I would have ...' She breathed heavily and walked with the pan to the door and pretended to swing the door open before hurling the pan at an invisible man outside. 'It would hit him straight on his head. And while he was bent over, I would thrash him with words. "Tired of doing other people's dirty work that you are harassing widows?" I would scold him solid and disturb the whole neighbourhood.

"Hai, hai, well wishers, devotees, all come out and see this spectacle. Your very own old owl is in danger of being sent to heaven right in front of your eyes, by a coward of a goonda.'"

'What a film actress you are,' Salman said.

'Not acting.' The old owl pouted.

'Yes, we were all trembling when you were threatening that invisible goonda, with your scarf tied around your waist, just like Gabbar Singh.'

Preeti and Shaila jumped up. Each puffed up her chest like a big man. They started the famous Gabbar Singh film dialogue in *Sholay*. Dilkhush had seen the film with Suresh, Simran, and Kashif at the Jantapur talkies many years before, but she still remembered the famous lines that everyone seemed to know. She was so happy they were all together again. She didn't have to be alone. It was almost like the old times.

The neighbourhood chatter and laughter that she had heard when she came to find Naseema Bi was now coming right from their own courtyard. Then she caught Chandni looking at her. There was a deep sadness in the girl's eyes. Dilkhush knew her own happiness couldn't last. She had no right to it with Chandni suffering alone. The truth would come forth soon and her time would be over.

'*Kitné aadmi thé?*' Shaila's voice was high-pitched, even when she was trying to lower it to sound like a man.

Jaadu joined in with Shaila and Preeti, saying the same Gabbar Singh dialogue. All three pretended to be the one villain. After all, he was larger than life and the most famous. Jaadu beckoned another girl to wheel her forward now and then to be in step with the other two girls. They recited the lines, word for word. The others, even those sitting and watching, joined in. 'How many men were there?' they chorused.

Chandni stood with her head lowered. Her face changed and she quickly assumed a role. She was acting the parts of all three shamefaced cowards in the film. It was as if the cowards had all shrunk down into the size of her one body, while his boss, Gabbar Singh had expanded out to fill the three bodies of Preeti, Jaadu and Shaila.

'Sardar, there were two men,' Chandni said.

Salman had a lopsided smile as he watched them. Dilkhush thought he had such a gentle face that wanted to do only good. But something about him was unsettling.

'Hmm, two men,' Jaadu, Preeti, and Shaila said, rubbing their chins, pacing up and down together. Neither stepped down from the prized Gabbar Singh role. 'You sons of pigs. They were two, and you were three. Still, you came back empty handed. What did you think? Your Sardar would be pleased with you? He would congratulate you?'

Jaadu made an action with bossy spitting when the trio of girls said again in unison, as if they had practiced the lines as one big Gabbar Singh. 'I despise you.'

The other girls laughed.

All of a sudden, Naseema Bi broke into the scene, dancing with one arm up, one down, then switching them. She turned around a full circle and wiggled her hips as much as she could. She croaked the song that the heroine, Hema Malini, danced to in the film on broken glass to save her lover. 'Yesss, as long as there is life in me, love of my life, I will daaaaaanccccccccccce.' The old owl lifted her feet here and there and made pained faces as if she were really dancing on broken glass. After a while, she stopped and looked at the girls playing the villain. 'What do you think dance is, Gabbar Singh?' Naseema Bi asked. 'You think dance is a joke?' She looked at the sky and put her palms together. 'Dance is a prayer... Dance is an art, aaarrrrrt.'

Everyone broke into laughter and chorused that she was mixing up films and dialogues. The rest of the girls jumped up and danced along with Naseema Bi, singing different songs like some dance-*antakshri*. As one song ended, someone would voice the letter it ended with, and come up with a song that started with that letter. They tried to coordinate tones and lyrics alongside as well. Preeti pulled Salman up from the charpoy.

Everyone was dancing except Dilkhush. Neighbours' voices joined in with the songs and one man whistled. Others clapped in time. The merriment continued as the girls and Naseema Bi added song after song.

Dilkhush liked the comforting feeling of having the noise around her. But her heart was with Jiyaa and she let her mind drift away. She thought about the puppet story she should do for her daughter at the train station. It would have to be so good that the bilayati family took her immediately without stopping to think. 'Now,' she would say, looking at Jiyaa. The train station would be busy with people coming to Jantapur for the anniversary events. 'This is a special performance just for you.'

Jiyaa's eyes would twinkle.

'This is the story about the princess and the pistachio.'

A whole group of children would gather in front of the stand. That would be a good sign. 'But what about the king and the snake?' a boy might say. He might think her special puppet show was for everyone, until Jiyaa squealed. Dilkhush's heart melted. Her new life was starting.

'Yes, princess story, princess story.' Jiyaa wore ponytails with red ribbons and a red-and-white dress. Madam shouted that it was almost time to go.

'Please, let's get on the train only after seeing the princess story. Please. Tell Mummy to rest inside. I promise to come afterwards.'

Dilkhush wanted to tell Jiyaa that she could go on the train with them and do the puppet show there. For some reason, no one mentioned anything about that. She hoped she had understood Salman correctly. Madam asked Jiyaa to hurry with her silliness. 'The train is going to leave soon.'

Dilkhush didn't like that at all. She had to do a show that enthralled Madam as well. Then, they would all want her with them.

Jiyaa looked at her. 'I know you said princess and the pistachio. But I don't like pistachios.'

By now, even more children had gathered and were sitting and waiting for the puppet show. They threw out suggestions to replace pistachios. Dates, chocolate, peanuts, but Dilkhush only had ears for Jiyaa.

'I like raisins,' Jiyaa said. 'The princess and the raisin.'

'Raisin?' Dilkhush knew it would make the story more difficult to believe, but changed it anyway. She didn't want to upset her daughter. She opened her bag to get out Jiyaa's princess puppet, which she had taken earlier that day at Volog Colony. The puppet wasn't in the bag. Dilkhush felt sick to her stomach. Had she forgotten it at Naseema Bi's house? She wanted to kick herself. This was her one chance. She turned to Jiyaa. 'I'm so sorry. I don't have the puppet. But we can pretend.'

'Princess...princess,' Jiyaa chanted. Some of the other children joined in.

Dilkhush checked whether Salman was there. She could ask him to run to the old owl's house and look for the puppet. But Madam seemed impatient. Dilkhush swallowed. If only she herself were enough to captivate Jiyaa, but it wasn't working. Whatever she said, Jiyaa asked for the princess puppet. Finally, Dilkhush decided to show her that it wasn't there, and emptied her bag out onto the platform. A gasp escaped from Jiyaa's mouth.

On the concrete floor was the princess puppet with its body mangled, head cut wonky and stuffing pulled out of its face and body.

Omera! Dilkhush knew it had to be her. Changing her name to Chandni didn't mean anything. The girl had vowed to ruin everything for her. The princess puppet looked defeated. Instead of making her laugh so that Madam took her on the journey, Dilkhush had made Jiyaa cry. Omera had probably wanted that to happen.

Had she found out from Salman about the puppet show test? But there was no satisfaction in blaming her. Omera had suffered all this time because of Dilkhush's mistake.

'Come on.' Madam tugged on Jiyaa's hand.

Dilkhush spoke fast. 'I will do an elephant and mouse story because the princess is sleeping.'

'Puppets don't sleep,' a boy with glasses said. 'They are not real.'

'Well, you have to believe. Then these stories become real.' Dilkhush smiled. 'They can even save you.'

The other children were happy to listen to the elephant-mouse story while the princess slept. But Jiyaa wasn't. 'My princess is dead.' She started to cry again. 'I saw her.'

'Come, baby girl,' Dilkhush said. 'The princess just sleeps more than others. She is dainty and delicate like you. So she needs her rest.' Jiyaa stopped crying. Dilkhush looked up at Madam for approval. She quickly started the elephant and mouse story, but Jiyaa got up.

'Maybe I'll listen to the story later when the princess has woken up.' The girl left with Madam, and they boarded the train. Dilkhush hurried after them and tried to explain. She climbed onto the train as well, to show them how she could be entertaining even without the princess puppet. 'I will fix up the princess so well that she will look even more beautiful than when you bought her.'

Madam called the guard.

'You don't understand,' Dilkhush said. 'I can look after this baby girl like I was her own mother.'

Madam's eyes narrowed. 'I thought it was you. Today you are in a green sari, so I thought I must be mistaken. What traditional widow would wear colour? But, of course, someone like you would.' Madam gestured to the guard. 'This is her. That princess puppet belonged to Abha.'

It was a trap.

'Please, let me explain.' Dilkhush rushed her words. Whatever she said sounded unreal, even to her. She pleaded. When Madam didn't waver, she fell to the woman's feet. 'Please, take me with you. Only that can save me. I have nothing else to live for.'

Jiyaa had a puzzled look on her face. She huddled closer to Madam and turned away.

'I'm your mother,' Dilkhush said to her.

The guard came and pulled her away. Dilkhush tried to fight him off. But a part of her knew it was no good. This could not be happening. And it wasn't.

She relented. As they stood on the platform, and watched the train move away, Dilkhush panicked. What if this really was happening and it was her last chance to be with Jiyaa? She tried to get away from the guard. When his grip got tighter, she turned to explain everything to him. His face had changed.

He had become a gas person whose photo she had seen in newspapers straight after the big leak. A loathing rose from inside her. She hit him and when he held her wrists, she tried to pummel his chest. 'You did this to me. I am reduced to begging for my own daughter now.'

He held her wrists tighter. Dilkhush struggled to

pull away and ended up scratching his face. 'Look at you. What has changed for you?' she shouted. 'Can you see what you have done to me?' She looked around for a weapon but there was nothing there. The train whistle blew. She tried to break free and run after it, but the man held her back. Dilkhush kept struggling hard, but nothing worked. Madam looked out of the window. Jiyaa also saw Dilkhush battling. 'You're my daughter, Jiyaa,' Dilkhush cried out loud. 'I'm your mother.'

When the train gained momentum, Dilkhush managed to free herself and ran. She tried to jump onto the last carriage, but didn't manage it. The train sped away from them fast.

When Dilkhush turned around, she realised it was the guard she had scratched, not any gas person. The guard warned her to behave.

'Otherwise, you will land yourself in jail.'

Dilkhush knew she should have got on that train and found the bilayati family's carriage. The princess puppet could be sewn up beautifully to do a story later. She imagined what could have happened but even that didn't please her. She saw herself jumping onto the train, and standing in front of the family, but Jiyaa was cowering away from her and hiding behind Madam. 'That puppet woman is scaring me. Make her go away.'

Dilkhush tried to cajole her, but the girl vanished in front of her eyes.

Noises around Dilkhush became louder. She realised that she was still at the old owl's house. Salman was there. The girls and Naseema Bi were still singing and dancing. That meant she had not gone to the station for the puppet show yet. That was still to happen at midnight.

Dilkhush was relieved and quickly went into the room to check the princess puppet in her bag. It was intact. She had imagined her defeat at the station. It was what she feared most. She went back into the courtyard, but didn't feel comfortable. Her stomach fluttered.

The girls were chattering away to Salman.

Naseema Bi beckoned Dilkhush over and stroked her head. 'You look exhausted. Those bilayatis are already making you work so late?'

How could she tell Naseema Bi she hadn't got the job with the bilayati family, even when being with her daughter was at stake? She was grateful Salman had set up the puppet interview at the train station. It might well be a trap, but what other choice did she have? She decided she should go to the station early to make sure she didn't miss the train.

'Oho,' Naseema Bi whispered in excited tones. 'With all this craziness going on here with goondas and Gabbar Singh, I haven't even asked you about the most special thing about your job.' She laughed. 'Our Jiyaa. Isn't she a doll? Did you see how I knew?'

'Yes, but I didn't—'

'Of course,' the old owl said. 'She is not exactly our Jiyaa. We buried her, so that would be impossible. But she has reincarnated. I told you. You must have known immediately when you looked into her eyes. I told Sick Sikh your memorial must be so good to bring Jiyaa and you back here at the same time. He is an expert in such deep matters.' Naseema Bi sniffed. 'And still, he said he wanted to see your memorial. I'm sure he will pay you money to copy your design. It got such good results. And don't be afraid of bargaining with him. I can even come with you. I know his weaknesses. I can arrange everything.' The old owl doled her head side-to-side. 'Now tell me what happened today,' she said. 'Right from the beginning. What did you do with our Jiyaa?'

Dilkhush was about to explain that some of her inside ragpatches had healed after their hands touched, but Chandni came towards them.

'Have you told Naseema Bi that you didn't even get that bilayati job? I saw you at the lake, making something with rubbish bags, and then at Sick Sikh's stall. And people from the factory slums said you stole from them.'

For a moment, there was silence. There was nothing Dilkhush could do to change the past. She had not done it knowingly, but that didn't matter. Maybe when the girl found out about her father, she might change her manner. But she would not be ready to hear the news from just anyone. Dilkhush whispered into the old owl's ear. 'Kashif is still alive, Naseema Bi. Ask Dalya for help to find him. Maybe then our Omera will appear from Chandni.'

'But how can that be?' The old owl had sadness in her eyes. 'This is all wishful thinking now.'

'Haven't you caused enough upset already?' Omera said to Dilkhush. 'Now you are whispering more lies and accusations or whatever it is you are spouting.'

Salman got up and interrupted them. 'Naseema Bi, I wonder if I may speak to Dilkhush. Can we have your permission to step out for a moment? She will be safe with me.'

The old owl blinked a few times.

'It's only to make sure that the villain doesn't harass her again.'

'Of course. Go, go.' The old owl waved away Salman's bow of thanks. 'You make sure she stays safe from the villain. We trust you.'

'Salman, we want to know too,' Omera said. 'The villain might follow us in the future.' She turned to Naseema Bi. 'Why should only your new darling get everything? She betrayed us all by going for that job in the first place! Twisting the knife the gas people plunged into us. What is the need to prostrate like that?' Her look was accusing and angry. 'And now this favouritism?'

Dilkhush wanted to tell her not to worry. Whatever Salman was going to say wouldn't change her fate. She knew what she wanted could never happen. This was all only to soothe her heart until reality confronted her once more. It would be like all the other times, again and again. Nothing would change, because nothing could. Salman opened the door and stepped outside.

He called out from there. 'Bye, my queens. Don't stay up too late. You can keep getting some beauty sleep then.' His laugh was warm. He didn't say anything else. Only his footsteps sounded. Soon, even they stopped.

Dilkhush didn't want to follow him any more. She would bear Omera's abuse instead, with all the girls still there. But the old owl looked at her as if to tell her to go.

'Not yet, please,' Dilkhush said. 'I need some time, Naseema Bi. I'm not ready.' She was afraid as soon as she stepped through the door everything would change, as it had a thousand times before. These imaginations were all that she could hold on to. Tears welled up in her eyes.

'Look at her,' Omera smirked. 'Putting on that miserable look as if she is going to get hanged, rather than be saved by Salman.'

Dilkhush didn't mind the harsh words. She stood at the door waiting for more. All the girls looked at her as if expecting her to leave. She turned to Naseema Bi, who nodded and wiped her eyes. 'It is time, my moonbeam. You don't worry. I am always here for you, nahn?'

Dilkhush didn't even want to blink, in case that changed everything. After a few long moments, she pulled the door and stepped outside. It was dark. No one was there. The sound of crickets became louder. She turned back to the courtyard. The girls and Naseema Bi had disappeared. It had happened.

26

#Gotcha

Dilkhush stayed by the door for a long time, waiting for her mind to conjure up Salman standing outside. But for some reason, it didn't work.'

She didn't do anything for a while and looked around the courtyard without really taking anything in. Then she sat outside on the step by the door, with her back against the wall. She pulled her sari over her head and let the sounds around her engulf her. The laughter around the neighbourhood sounded exactly like Naseema Bi's girls, but it was not coming from the old owl's courtyard.

Songs and arguments, and the noises of people cooking and cleaning surrounded her. She waited for the kick. The old owl should be coming soon, holding her coriander in one hand and a potato in the other, wearing the same green salwar kameez that Dilkhush had made for her on their first Eid together. But even after a long wait, Naseema Bi didn't appear.

Much later, Dilkhush looked at the newspaper cutting in her cloth bundle. It confirmed what she already knew. Yet, she didn't want to believe it. It took her a long time to get up from where she was sitting. She kept hoping to see the old owl call out to her. 'Dilkhush, my moonbeam, piece of my moon.'

Finally, she walked out into the dark alleyways, away from the house towards the busy areas where the lights were bright and groups of people mingled. Amidst the crowds, she saw glimpses of anniversary events. People on stage were singing and acting in a play. Others formed circles with flame *diyas*. Poetry was being read out, about God's compassion to those who faced their own wrongs, and made amends to balance out their karmas. And about His love for those who suffered and survived the wrongdoings of others, seeking resolution anywhere.

Spiritual music sounded from stalls and an announcement also intermittently reminded everyone that it was almost exactly thirty years since the gas leak, with only a short time to go. Many carried signs and placards towards the train station. Dilkhush followed.

There were no trains there. Instead, hundreds of people had laid down on the platforms, with bright red colouring dripping from their mouths. Placards and signs hung from the corrugated roofs of the platforms.

'In honour of the trains that stopped to save others, but died themselves.'

People with lights, cameras and microphones milled around the crowds. Men and women in pristine clothes, many of them foreigners, spoke to the cameras, pointing to the scenes behind them. Dilkhush could see what was happening. She still reminded herself that her train with the family was supposed to be at midnight. So, it wouldn't be there yet. She went to the timetable board and almost tripped over people lying down.

'Jiy... Abha. Abhaaa.' Dilkhush's throat felt thick but she forced the name out. 'ABHAAA...' If her daughter was there, she might respond to the right name. Dilkhush saw a man in a uniform. 'Where is the train that is going to Delhi at midnight?'

He looked at her blankly.

'On which platform will the midnight train to Delhi be?'

'All trains stopped at 6 pm exactly,' he said. 'Today, it is only enactment, but you can imagine a little like how it was.' He stumbled over the bodies and opened the door to the train station office. 'We had to start earlier so the cameras can go to all the different places of the full programme.'

A camera followed him and the female presenter talked very precisely, with feigned concern. 'All night, trains came and passed the hundreds of dead on the platform. The first ones that stopped and opened their doors or windows lost passengers to the gas within minutes. The stationmaster signalled every train after that to carry on, not to stop. He stayed here and risked his own health and life to save those on the trains.'

Dilkhush felt trapped. She could see she was in a very different reality now. She didn't know whether she could trust anything any more.

'The last train was two hours ago,' the stationmaster told her when she persevered. 'All the rest are cancelled until tomorrow morning at 6 am.'

She went to the bridge. There were no guards or guard cabins. No gates. There was no Volog Colony. In place of that were several grey buildings that were sprawled out. No one knew a bilayati family with four generations. They had never heard of any important gas person returning there with his family. 'Are you crazy?'

At Jantapur Palace Hotel, no one knew about any government and gas people being there. No one knew about a midnight agreement being signed.

The library was open, but no one knew about any Salman working there. Then Dilkhush saw a leaflet with his face.

'Oh, him? That is Salmanji. See his name at the bottom? He comes here to give talks, but he doesn't work at the library. The prime minister wants to clean up the country, so Salmanji wants to become the chief minister to help the PM clean up this town of poisons. Try him at the clinic. He goes there sometimes.'

Dilkhush saw Salman's election posters everywhere now. She realised she had seen her first one straight after coming off the bus at the job junction. 'Vote for our Saviour.' She looked at his photo more closely. Dilkhush recognised his eyes, but something did not seem right.

At the clinic, people were sitting in the courtyard, making a *rangoli* design with black-and-white flour. Both men and women patiently sprinkled the outlines and then filled them in. Dilkhush gently manoeuvred around them and went inside. She checked a few of the rooms, but couldn't see Salman.

She located the set of photos she had seen before. A woman's voice came from behind her. 'Oh, you are back. Good.'

Dilkhush turned to see Jaadu.

'We were worried about you,' Jaadu said. 'You left before I got a chance to come back. Are you alright?'

'Oh, Jaadu, I am so glad to see you. I thought you and the other girls—'

'What other girls, Madam?'

Dilkhush stared and then shook her head. 'My mistake.' This was not Jaadu as she knew her. She asked about the photos of the dead to find out whether they were mixed up with anyone still alive and getting treatment.

'No, no. We can't keep photos of patients on a notice board. But who are you looking for? Maybe I can help.'

'Don't worry. I think I made a mistake.' Dilkhush turned to the notice board. There were photos of Naseema Bi, Jiyaa, Simran, Ashraf Mia and Suresh. Dotted around were several photos of girls also called Omera, all of different ages, different faces, and one that looked like Chandni. The name underneath was 'Omera' but it was struck off and overwritten with 'Chandni.' Her photo was near Naseema Bi's.

Dilkhush scanned across the photos. If she was right, there might be a picture to prove it. Finally, she saw young Omera. She had not seen that picture before. It was of the girl at the time of the gas leak, with a numbered label on her. Dilkhush had not been wrong about seeing her on the funeral pyre after all. Someone had taken the photo before she was cremated.

But the old owl may have died alone then. There may be no resolution for abandoning her. She could only hope the owl forgave her. A wave of relief came. Hadn't the old couple let their old tenant go when it was time? Naseema Bi was wise and kind. There was bound to be only forgiveness from her. Dilkhush took a few steps. There was also a photo of Kashif on the notice board, older than she remembered.

She felt numb, as if she was watching herself from outside her own body. Kashif must have come back, maybe to look for her and Suresh. The label under his photo said he became chronically sick from toxic water, and died by taking his own life on the twenty-fifth anniversary.

Why had he given up? The anguish was always going to be there. Now he may not be reunited with his loved souls. Didn't she have the same torments he must have had? If she would have been there, they could have given each other strength. Dilkhush gritted her teeth.

She turned to the notice board with the newspaper pages. 'Our story in the News.' Pictures with the state of the factory were there, with its rusting flare tower and tanks, sacks of chemicals still in the storage rooms, hearts drawn on the walls, with names inside. In one photo, children played cricket in the grounds of the factory. Dilkhush also saw the copy of the page she had snatched from the policewoman.

The pictures on the page were as she remembered. One had soldiers standing over a man they had killed.

'#GOTCHA: TERRORIST SHOT BY OUR HEROES'

Below that was the Jantapur headline.

'#TRUESTORY: TOWN POISONED FOR 30 YEARS. CONTRIBUTOR @SALMANJANTAPURI'

Underneath was a captioned photo of a crowd of Jantapuri people reacting to the news.

'Will all in charge at time of Jantapur gas deaths attend 30th anniversary or reject?'

No one in the Jantapuri photo really looked like Kashif. Not even the man who had a scarf around his nose and mouth. Her need to believe it was Kashif was what had made her return to the town after so many years. Maybe something somewhere knew that she had to come back. The priest had urged her as well. She simply hadn't wanted to come and follow his advice. *'Get and give forgiveness.'* What could he know about any of that? She turned to leave.

'Did you want any more help?' Jaadu asked. 'A glass of water?'

Dilkhush wrung her hands. 'Actually...is there someone called Salman here?'

Jaadu shook her head. 'Not right now. He should be coming to drive the children's minibus later, because Chacha is sick today.'

Someone called out for Jaadu. 'Sorry, I have to go for yoga with the children. When they see me, they try even harder.' She smiled. 'Will you be alright?' Dilkhush nodded. The small boy from before came and pushed her wheelchair, grunting again with each step.

'*Shabash*,' Jaadu said. 'See how strong you have become, Manu? Who said you wouldn't ever walk, huh? You don't listen to people. Miracles happen. Why not?'

Dilkhush stood for a moment, not sure what to do. She went out and sat on the pavement. Someone was speaking into a loudspeaker. She had heard the man's words outside the clinic before. '...And if you haven't died, you give birth to a defected child, who might pass gas defects on to his or her children. And you can get cancer too. Highest rate here. Cancer of the tongue, lungs, stomach. You can feel depressed for years. Many times higher rate here than anywhere in the country. Your body can't process the poison, so you carry it inside. Living dead.' He coughed and then continued.

'In this town, there are six times higher spontaneous abortions. Twenty times higher cancers. Two hundred times more defects in birth. When they said the poison gas is like tear gas only, and only prickling the skin or eyes, or lungs and then leaving, then what made people die that night? What makes all these things still happen? Visit the information centre, see the film, go to the clinic and learn about long-term or short-term effects of the tear gas.'

Dilkhush knew she had to face Jiyaa in the cemetery across the road, in that mass grave. She didn't want to go. What was she to say? '*Sorry, I still haven't done anything to be with you?*' Someone interrupted her thoughts, asking if she was all right. She looked up. It was Salman.

Dilkhush got up quickly. 'Salman.' She wanted to hug him. He seemed shorter now. 'You look different.'

'I don't think we have met, sister. Maybe you have seen my posters. I just wanted to check whether you were all right. You seemed...' He looked at her for a moment, and then his eyes changed. 'Sorry, I didn't mean to disturb you.' He started to head towards a minibus.

'You!' Dilkhush suddenly recognised the man. How had she allowed him to get woven into her illusions? She had let him fool her again. She thought he was her saviour this time too. 'I know you.'

Salman turned back to her. His smile was unconvincing. 'Maybe you recognise me from the posters? If you want to help us we need people to give out leaflets for the anniversary.'

Dilkhush looked closer. 'Your poster doesn't show your mole, Doctor Sahib.'

The man's eyes wavered before he looked down at the ground. 'I have been honest. Before running for Office, I explained everything to everyone.' He seemed to be struggling with his words. 'You and other people, you may recognise me from the hospital on that gas night, even after all these years. Mostly because my mole is so noticeable. I wanted people to know what I was trying to do first, before they judged me. So, the photo shows a different angle, without the mole.'

Dilkhush was annoyed with herself. Why had her heart softened for him in her thoughts? She should have recognised him the moment she saw his face, even without the mole. 'You stopped the injections.'

They stared at each other.

'My daughter died that night.'

Salman didn't say anything.

'You were supposed to be our saviour.'

'I did everything I could. We didn't even have—'

'What if that had been your daughter?'

'The injections ran out that night. Later, when I could, I...we...bought injections ourselves to give to hundreds of people. Some police came and smashed up everything in our makeshift clinics. Took away our files.'

'My daughter was already dead by then.'

Salman didn't respond for a while. 'Nothing I do now can...' He faltered. 'Since that time, I have been working to help people here.'

'Out of guilt?'

He was still talking when Dilkhush walked away. He was also trying to gain resolution. But how did she ever have warm thoughts about him, even in any trances? He hadn't caused the gas leak, but he could have done something more for Jiyaa. She was not willing to believe anything else. There was no-one to lash out at otherwise. Dilkhush didn't even know who or where any gas people were. She had only seen a newspaper photo of one man straight after the gas leak. Had he given orders that ended up in Jiyaa's death? Where would she even find him?

She lay down next to the mass grave that Jiyaa was in. 'I have failed you, my daughter. Please find it in your heart to wait for me. I am only living for when our souls reunite. You are the moonlight in my dark nights and the stars in my thoughts. No day goes by without me aching for you, pining, loving you, holding you tight. You are not alone, but with your mother always fighting to be with you.' As she lay there, she felt some of her hard ragpatches soften.

Dilkhush only got up when she saw people entering the cemetery. 'I am sorry I didn't come until now, Jiyaa. But you have always been with me, and now I am here. I will go and get what I need and return.' Outside the cemetery was a sign she had seen when she had come to the clinic the first time after getting off the bus.

'FOR YOUR DEEPEST DESIRE, OUR LIFEWALLA MEMORIAL IS THE FINEST ANSWER. WHAT IS YOUR REAL QUESTION?'

At Naseema Bi's house, there were weeds under the door. Dilkhush hadn't noticed them before. Piles of rubbish had gathered around the front of the house. Flies and rotten food were mounted against the walls. Goats and pigs ate there.

She pushed open the door and stepped into the courtyard. A stench shot up her nose. She almost tripped over a root that had grown out of the ground before disappearing back into it. It was from the peepal tree she had planted. Dilkhush's heart lurched. Weeds overran the entire courtyard. She heard rats screeching. The walls had large cracks and gaps that split all the way down.

Thick, gummy spider webs spanned the length and

breadth of the courtyard, with flies trapped in them. Faded patches of rags lay around everywhere. The peacock mural wasn't there any more. In one corner, the carcass of a cow buzzed with flies. Piles of yellowed newspapers covered the floor.

Dilkhush walked through the rubbish and went into each of the two rooms. In one corner of the larger room, she saw the back of someone lying on the floor with a cream sheet over the body. She sighed with relief. Naseema Bi. Dilkhush walked up carefully to wake the old owl. She nudged the body gently, but the part she touched crumbled.

It wasn't a person, but mounds built from newspapers and rags, made to look like a person. Then something she saw startled her. She pushed away piece after piece of crumpled papers from the pretend body until there was no mound, only papers and patches strewn around. At the bottom of the mound was her makeshift razai of rags. There was even an indentation in the middle as if someone had been sleeping there for some time. The fabric looked familiar, and she stroked it. She recognised the smell and bent towards the piece of cloth. Suddenly, she pulled away. It was her own stale odour.

Among the yellowed papers and torn cloth was the image of a child's face looking up from a shallow grave. It was the poster. And with it was her faded and yellowing group photo that Jiyaa was in, which she had brought with her in the cloth bundle. The peacock feather hair clip was pinned onto the child's head on the poster. It had made holes that seemed to have grown larger with time. Dilkhush looked around.

She realised the patches and rags on the ground were hers; a red and gold silk piece from her wedding day, another from her mother's princess pink sari, the knotted rope her mother had tied around her ankles, her father's whip, some pink wool from Jiyaa's first booties, a few sequins, and silver netting from a princess puppet.

Dilkhush felt the skin on her own face. She couldn't tell how long she had lain in that place. A night? Two? Several weeks? Years? Had she ever left?

She had to be quick to rein in her thoughts. Others didn't see her confusion, but she knew something was happening in that illusion that she didn't like. She needed to escape.

When Dilkhush came round, she was exhausted. She rested for a moment, but her hands itched. There were boils on them. Her whole body was covered in boils, like Dalya's mother. And her skin was dry and wrinkled.

Her neck hurt when she tried to look around. She picked up a cracked shard of mirror and looked at her reflection. Her hair was white; her feet were old and bony. She lay still for what seemed like hours.

When she turned to her side, everything hurt. Her vision wasn't very good, but she thought she saw a baby next to her. It hurt even to reach out. After a while, she managed to edge closer to the baby. She touched its face and body, its legs and arms, all made of plastic bags. She held the child in her claw-like hands. A red shoe made of rags was on one foot. She stroked the baby's face and held it close. The eyes were two blue-green buttons, sewn on.

Dilkhush held the baby and tried to remember what had happened to her. She was so exhausted. She saw a newspaper spread out nearby. Almost sixty years had passed since the gas leak. Nothing had changed. She tried to remember some things about the time she returned to Jantapur.

All she remembered was returning to the town and finding out that everyone had died. Now she spent her time between the cemetery and the old owl's house. She had vague memories of foreign visitors on a tour coming to see her getting older, and sicker, waiting all the time to be with Jiyaa. It was strange that visitors would want to see her like that. After all, she could no longer be the beauty Naseema Bi used to call her. She closed her eyes and rested for a moment.

She awoke with hunger, but there wasn't any food. She was too tired and in pain to move. Feeling drowsy, she slept again. Some time later, someone put a spoon into her mouth and fed her, talking all the while about ticket prices going towards her upkeep. She woke up startled, and scratched the itch on her hand. It was so painful. She heard her baby cry and reached down to pick her up.

It soothed her to feel so much love for the child. When she hugged it, she heard the sound of plastic scrunching, but ignored it. A noise came from the courtyard. She would spray an intruder with pus from her boils. It was all she had to protect herself and her child. She grunted as she slowly got up. Dilkhush couldn't move without the boils on her legs rubbing against each other. It was only possible for her to limp across the room to get to the bedroom door.

The courtyard was empty. In her mind's eye, she could clearly remember appeasing thoughts and dreams about several girls living there with her and Naseema Bi. They had all made a lot of noise, laughing and joking. How colourful and full her life had become with them all cooking together, dancing, teasing each other.

Now the courtyard was different. Rotting carcasses of cows and goats lay in the corner. Rats ran around. There were spider webs everywhere. Towering blocks surrounded the outside. A fading sign hung crooked.

'BEWARE OF GHOSTS AND SUDDEN SUBSIDENCE
INTO POISON POOLS.'

It was little wonder no one else lived in the house all these years. But she was grateful for it, whatever state it was in. She shuffled slowly, avoiding the holes in the ground.

When another noise sounded, she turned around to make sure her baby was all right. But there was only a doll made of plastic bags there. A sound came from near the peepal tree. As she walked to it, the boils on her legs rubbed against each other. Some burst. It was only when she got closer that she saw what it was. A rope was hanging from one of the branches, with a noose at the end.

It swung from side to side in the breeze, making a sound. Nearby was a rusty, old metal drum. It was then that she remembered. She had been part way through her task with the rope. It had taken her years to come to her biggest realisation. It all came back to her. There was not much time left. She had to hurry.

It was as well, because she was tired of life. She didn't have the will to carry on, and now she didn't have to. She had wasted all this time. Dilkhush felt ill, which meant she needed to work faster. If she died, she could cause the opposite effect of what she needed. She was still alive and not reunited with Jiyaa. There was a reason for that. Finishing this task would seal everything.

27

Bumbling-Stumbling Around
the Truth

DILKHUSH'S INSIDES MANGLED as her mind wandered into previously closed thoughts. She retrieved the dark karma locked within her. The bud in all her makeshift lifewalla memorials was her stuck pain when it first happened. At her death, what would that bud need for resolution?

All this time, some abhorrent cruelty inside her had only remembered Jiyaa. What about that blameless blackened baby inside her when the poison leaked into her body? She had deliberately tried to forget his abandoned helpless soul. No wonder there had been no forgiveness and no reunion for her.

How could she have denied the baby's existence, almost erasing the child from her consciousness? As if not believing it meant that it hadn't happened. How naïve of her. Where else but her karma was that to be stored, waiting to be answered? He would have been sixty years old now, sixty years after the gas leak, with his own grandchildren or even great-grandchildren. Her baby son had been denied a life even in her own thoughts, because she could not bear the loss.

She had not looked into his eyes, but that did not mean he had no soul. He would have been alone, sobbing, confused somewhere, waiting to be missed. She had made a helpless child dead to his mother. She hadn't even spared him one memory because she couldn't bear it. Where else was his soul to expect all encompassing love?

Her old heart broke again at her unacknowledged son's loneliness over the years, waiting for acceptance from her. How had she passed that big burden on to him?

She had no right to reunite with him or Jiyaa, shirking her responsibilities like that. Her own loneliness in oblivion forever might help to resolve the pain she had caused her children. If she had left the town, maybe none of the pain would have come upon them. But then she went on to reject even the existence of her son's soul. For their sake, she had to let them go. A more deserving soul might be better suited to selflessly care for them.

With as much force as her old body could manage, Dilkhush ripped off the ragpatches inside her. Blood and pus oozed with her raw wounds. Her croaking sobs caught. There could be no healing. Evil had come and harmed her children and she hadn't protected or soothed them. Jiyaa might even have reunited with her. But there was no guarantee that Dilkhush would not abandon the girl as she had done with her son. She was an old crow with a selfish soul, not to be trusted.

That trait meant she hadn't even thought about releasing her children until now, and they had remained tied to her. They should not be bound to a weak, wailing soul, pining to be with them to appease her own pain, even at their expense. With her clawed old hands, she started to uncover some earth under the peepal tree.

Dilkhush had not been able to bear seeing the blackened, dead child that came out of her. She had wanted the ogress doctor to put him back inside her. He could remain safe there. He had not even taken one breath before his spirit had left his body.

The ogress doctor had shaken her head. 'Your insides are decimated. Womb, ovaries, everything.' Her eyes avoided looking at the stillborn child. 'There was no chance for the baby. No chance for you to have any more. But be grateful you are alive. Not everyone is that lucky.'

Dilkhush had looked at the stillborn child, destroyed by the poison. She broke down. It couldn't be true. She had already lost Jiyaa. She couldn't lose this baby as well. That would mean she had not kept either safe. How had the insides of her own body betrayed her like that, killing that innocent child to keep herself alive? What evil need was there for that? Why hadn't she died with the baby? Or instead of? Suresh or Naseema Bi would have taken good care of the child.

The dark thoughts swirled around in her mind and soon became too much for her. Flashes of her mother hanging from the tree in their courtyard came to her mind. She could clearly hear the branch creaking with the weight. Her breathing became uneven. Terror ran down her for a moment and suddenly she felt numb. Something inside her pushed the innocent baby away.

She was not the mother. The baby couldn't be hers. Mothers would die rather than let their children come to harm. She shut out all thoughts of the blackened, burned child. Doing that meant there was no baby, no soul, no pain. Her blouse became drenched often afterwards, and her breasts hurt, full of milk.

The milk, like the rest of her, felt full of poison. Even if her boy had survived, she would have killed the baby while nursing him. The ogress doctor's word 'decimated' rang in her ears. Decimated womb, ovaries, everything inside. On her way back from the hospital, Dilkhush sealed the baby boy in a pot like her mother-in-law had done with baby Jiyaa when the girl was born.

She hid and waited for Suresh and Naseema Bi to leave the house. Dilkhush then sneaked inside and dug a hole in the courtyard and buried the baby there. He seemed so small, so still, letting her do whatever she wanted to, uncomplaining at the treatment. She planted a peepal sapling there so the gods of that holy tree watched over him.

Old Dilkhush realised that it must have been these peepal tree gods who made sure her shadow did not fall on that baby's soul again. He was alone there for all these years, without even proper rites of burial.

The roots would have grown over and under and through his body. What kind of a restless burial would he have had? No wonder the haunting feelings had never left her. The gods had seen her as unfit for liberation to be with her children's souls again.

She dug harder with her blood and pus-ridden wrinkled hands until her fingers were raw. She found pieces of the pot in the ground. Soon after, she saw tiny bones. Were they from her baby's hand? She closed her dry palms around them. It was not like holding her baby son's hand when he had been born. Suddenly, for the first time in years, Dilkhush let tears from deep inside her fall for her baby son.

Her broken body shuddered as she sobbed. The patches that covered the pusblood inside her peeled away with the strain. Her weeping felt like it came from an ancient place deep within her. Soon, her throat and chest hurt. She couldn't even wail fully for her son. Dilkhush had wanted to call him Wahhaj— incandescent. She had to bury him with rites in that name.

She needed to release her children, not tie them to her own failed soul with its cursed karma, where they could end up suffering repeatedly, while she did only what she could manage, looking each time to soothe herself. Even if she had remained alive all these years to make a reunion possible, now she had to do the opposite and make sure they didn't reunite.

That is what a real mother would do. She would sacrifice for them, rather than burden them with her own need to be close. It was then that a thought struck her. Perhaps that's why her own mother also cut off her soul. Something inside her changed.

She felt relieved. There was no need to wait for the Lord of Death to come for her. She looked up at the noose. If she had come to that realisation before, she did not remember it. But the noose meant there had been some preparation. She struggled to get her old body to even stand up.

Dilkhush limped towards the rusty metal drum to drag it over. It was heavy. So she turned it a little at a time in the direction of the tree. It made a scraping sound on the ground as she struggled. She thought it could take her a few days. Perhaps that was the reason the noose was tied already and the drum was nearby. It might have taken her failing body time to get that far with her plans. But now she had to hurry. She was old and ailing. If she died naturally she could end up tying her soul to her children's forever.

'Heroine,' a voice called out. 'Eh, Heroine.'

Dilkhush was alarmed. Who was calling her like that? She was sure it could only be in her mind. The girls had seemed so real. But there was no one around now. Still, something about the clarity of the voice made her hurry. She strained to turn the oil drum towards the tree one more time. Then she stopped and panted.

This was something she should have done many years ago, when she had the strength. She knew that even when she got the drum under the noose, she would struggle to get on top of it to tie the noose around her neck. Then she would need to kick the drum down. But even if it took several days, she had to do that much for her children's souls. That was the depth of her love for them. As she carried on with her work, something like a memory fluttered in her mind. It was of Naseema Bi's girls dancing after one of Dilkhush's puppet shows.

They had done that so many times over the years they had lived together. Dilkhush stopped their dancing for a moment and thanked them for making her existence bearable. She explained to them why she had to end her life before the Lord of Death liberated her. 'I don't want to burden my children's souls by reuniting with them.' She wanted them to know that was how much she loved her children.

'What a show,' Chandni snorted.

The girls faded. Dilkhush wished her boil-ridden limbs were stronger and faster. She felt tightness in her chest and hurried. The door to the courtyard creaked open and an arm in a leather jacket appeared. Dilkhush didn't move. The rest of the door swung in.

Dalya stood in the doorway. He was a clean-shaven distinguished man now, no longer a boy. But she recognised him straight away. He was pushing a makeshift wheelchair, a rickety armchair tied on top of a board with wheels underneath.

'Arey, you are here again? Come on Heroine. You know this place isn't safe, especially with you bumbling-stumbling around.' He smiled gently at her.

Dilkhush stared at him as he straightened the small stone statue of Lord Ganesh hanging on the wall by the doorway, to remove obstacles for all those who entered or left the house.

Dalya sighed and rumbled the makeshift wheelchair towards her. 'Come now. Your carriage awaits. Aren't you hungry?' His eyes registered her hands on the oil drum. He swallowed. 'What is this again? And pus from the boils as well?'

Dilkhush remained silent. Dalya jumped up on the drum and undid the noose. After he was on the ground, he hung the rope around his shoulders and rolled the oil drum towards the wall. 'That's tidier.' He settled Dilkhush into the wheelchair and kneeled down in front of her. Dalya held her hands, even though they were now bloody and wet with pus from the burst boils. He looked into her eyes. Dilkhush thought he had a tired smile. He wrapped the rope around her and the chair and tied a knot.

'Now, don't fall out, okay?' Dalya avoided the holes as he pushed the wheelchair to the door. 'Makodi has made our favourite. Chis-bis-burga-shurga with extra onionskin flakes to flavour the stock. Are you listening, Heroine?'

Dilkhush awoke from a dreamy premonition of herself. She had been so much older in it, with pus and boils all over her body, like Dalya's mother. She looked at her skin now. She was not old. There were no boils on her skin. It had been a dream or a nightmare. But she could feel that tears had fallen down her face and dried. It seemed to have tired her out a little.

She tried to work through her thoughts and looked for clues. How her mind was allaying her from moment to moment. Around her, the courtyard was full of rags and yellowed newspapers. She could hear the events of the anniversary going on outside. After trying to piece everything together, she understood what she had to do while she was still young and had the strength.

She would pay heed to her premonition that had come as some dreamlike realisation. She would release her children's souls. Dilkhush kneeled under the peepal tree to dig up her forlorn son. The intensity of the pain that she had felt in her premonition returned with full force. Her chest felt tight. When she saw the first bones, tears fell fast.

Dilkhush collected the bones one by one and carefully put them into her handkerchief. She placed it in her cloth bundle. Like all Hindu children who were too young to have committed any sins, her son would also not be cremated. She would give Wahhaj a proper burial next to Jiyaa. They would be together in that mass grave in the Muslim cemetery and Ashraf Mia would be with them. He was a loved one too. Her children would not be alone.

Then, she could return with a rope to the peepal tree and find an empty metal drum to finish the task she needed to do. The gods of the peepal tree could witness her sacrifice for her children's happiness.

Dilkhush picked up her cloth bundle and left Naseema Bi's courtyard. She headed straight towards the cemetery. As she passed the bus station, she saw several crowds holding signs about the anniversary. One group was on hunger strike. They had strength that she felt she lacked. Further ahead, she was surprised to see a young woman drag a man to a policeman. Dilkhush stared. It was the same villain who had harassed her. Was this another of God's signs?

The young woman was shouting. 'You better not dare abuse anyone else like that again.' Others looked on. The villain was trying to break free, but couldn't manage it. The policeman came over and hit the villain with his baton. At least something right was happening.

Nearby a goat was tied to a tree with a rope. Dilkhush looked to see if anyone was watching. She untied it.

'Heroine, eh.' Dalya was waving from the bus station. 'Did you find the mirror you wanted? Can I help with anything else? I know you only came off the bus today. But ask anyone. I am the most trustworthy MBBS.'

Dilkhush half-smiled at him. What she needed to do was not something he could help with.

Dalya ran over to her. 'I can see you are doing something using that rope. I can help, and it will be better, surer and faster. That's my cent per cent guarantee.'

Before Dilkhush could say anything, a girl shouted from the alleyway.

'DALLLYYYYAAAA. DALLLLLYYYAAAA. YOUR MOTHER'S DEAD. HURRY.'

Dalya turned but stayed rooted to the spot. A vein in his neck bulged. Dilkhush thought she could see his soul break into pieces.

'She can't die,' Dalya said. His voice was low.

'No one will look forward to seeing me the way she does. I will be alone.'

His words hit Dilkhush hard. Her mother had severed ties with her, and curses had still befallen Dilkhush.

'Listen,' the girl said to Dalya. 'Stop mumbling and get money for the burial this evening. Because of the boils, your mother will need careful bathing. I will look for women to help with the washing ritual.' The girl ran back.

Dalya watched her disappear. After a while, he saw Dilkhush looking at him. He bounced half-heartedly towards her. 'Heroine, let me help you with your rope task. If you can just give me a little money please.'

Dilkhush's fingers loosened around the rope. She stared at the boy. Makodi came to mind. The orphan would also be struggling alone in the village. Dilkhush blinked back tears. She hadn't been able to cry for years until that day. Maybe a greater force was guiding her. If she abandoned her children, they could end up without any shelter from her soul, like Dalya and Makodi, relying on the kindness of strangers. Would someone else sacrifice for her children the way she would?

Yet, even if she remained alive, there was no guarantee of any reunion of souls. She started to make deals with God. If she looked after Dalya and Makodi, maybe their dead parents would look after Jiyaa and Wahhaj's souls until she took over.

'Heroine, any work for me?'

'I'm sorry, Dalya.'

He nodded.

'What will you do?' she asked.

'The clinic...I should let them know we won't be going today.'

Dilkhush wanted to hug him. What if the premonition about her old self with boils was also about her living with Dalya and Makodi in her old age? She had understood the message about her son and would carry out her full duty with him. But maybe, exactly like Naseema Bi in her illusions, she was to collect strays as well, so that life was more bearable for both sides. Her mind was abuzz.

Staying alive was the safer choice for now. She could maintain ties with Jiyaa and Wahhaj, and help Dalya and Makodi. And if she learned any different, and was absolutely certain, she could always sever ties with her children's souls. Was she now looking for excuses to save herself? Dilkhush took a deep breath. At least for that day, she should stay.

'I don't have money,' she said to Dalya. 'But I can help bathe your mother.' The rope felt coarse in her hand.

'Would you do that, Heroine?' Dalya looked at her. 'God will shower such blessings on you.' He looked away for a moment. 'I will go to the clinic and come right back. Will you wait here?'

Dilkhush had to bury Wahhaj. 'I have to finish some important duties. Then I will wait for you here.'

She saw Dalya's fallen face. 'I promise I will be here to help with your mother today.'

A FINAL NOTE FROM THE AUTHOR

If you have enjoyed reading Lifewalla, please do recommend it to your friends. This book is being published with the support of an independent UK publisher and we are relying on word of mouth. I would also appreciate any support, including book club choices, reviews, interviews, emails and social media shares. I thank you in advance for that.

I want to share my feelings about loss, loneliness, trauma, emotional distress, mental health and support, some of the themes explored in this book. We each have an inner life. Distress can be unseen and unacknowledged. We are all human and frailty is a natural part of our condition at different stages in life. It is often hard to share difficulties overtly, and an outer action or reaction may be overspill from inner challenges. But sometimes there can be unexpected discoveries in that too. Gaining support from others may not change the underlying difficulties, but it can help us get through challenging times and even make new bonds. Supporting each other can help strengthen our inner and outer lives, and our human community.

If you struggle with emotional support, you could consider trying the confidential, non-judgemental space provided by the Samaritans at www.samaritans. org, to talk through any issues. Samaritans have also been working with Befrienders Worldwide to support people globally. The Befrienders Worldwide centre in your country can be found at: http://www.befrienders.org. When you are strong, perhaps you may consider reaching out to support others. And when you are not, do consider accepting the hand that has reached out to you. There is humility and strength in that too.

Warm Wishes, *Nina*